Published by World International Publishing Ltd.
under the Young Wordsworth imprint. All rights reserved.
Copyright © 1992 World International Publishing Ltd.,
an Egmont Company, Egmont House, PO Box 111,
Great Ducie Street, Manchester M60 3BL.
Printed in Czechoslovakia. ISBN 0 7498 1211 7

five popular abridged stories

## Contents

# Oliver Twist

Among other public buildings in a certain town, there is one anciently common to most towns, great or small — to whit, a workhouse; and in this workhouse was born one Oliver Twist.

Soon after giving birth, his mother died.

"Where did she come from?" asked the surgeon.

"She was brought here last night," replied the old woman in attendance. "She was found lying in the street. Where she came from, or where she was going, nobody knows."

Oliver cried lustily. If he could have known that he was an orphan, left to the tender mercies of churchwardens and overseers, perhaps he would have cried the louder.

The parish authorities resolved that Oliver should be despatched to a branch workhouse, where he and other juvenile offenders against the poor-laws rolled about the floor all day, without the inconvenience of too much food or clothing, under the parental supervision of an elderly female.

Oliver Twist's ninth birthday found him a pale thin child, somewhat diminutive in stature, and decidedly small in circumference. He was keeping his birthday in the coal cellar with two other gentlemen, who, after a sound thrashing, had been locked up for presuming to be hungry, when Mrs Mann, the good lady of the house, was unexpectedly startled by Mr Bumble, the beadle.

"Lead the way in, Mrs Mann," said Mr Bumble, "for I come on business and have something to say."

Mrs Mann ushered the beadle into a small parlour with a brick floor; placed a seat for him and officiously deposited his cocked hat and cane on the table before him. Mr Bumble wiped from his forehead the perspiration which his walk had engendered; glanced at the cocked hat; and smiled. Yes, he smiled. Beadles are but men; and Mr Bumble smiled.

"Now don't you be offended at what I'm a-going to say," observed Mrs Mann with captivating sweetness. "You've had a long walk, you know, or I wouldn't mention it. Will you take a little drop of something, Mr Bumble?"

"Not a drop. Not a drop," said Mr Bumble.

"I think you will," said Mrs Mann, who had noticed the tone of the refusal. "Just a little drop, with a little cold water and a lump of sugar."

Mr Bumble coughed.

"Just a leetle drop," said Mrs Mann persuasively.

"What is it?" inquired the beadle.

"Why, it's what I'm obliged to keep a little of in the house to give the blessed infants when they ain't well, Mr Bumble," replied Mrs Mann as she opened a corner cupboard and took down a bottle and glass. "It's gin. I'll not deceive you, Mr B. It's gin."

"Do you give it to the children, Mrs Mann?" inquired Bumble.

"Ah, bless 'em, that I do, dear as it is," replied the nurse. "I couldn't see 'em suffer before my very eyes."

"No," said Mr Bumble approvingly. "No, you could not. You are a humane woman, Mrs Mann." (Here she set down the glass.) "I shall take an early opportunity of mentioning it to the board, Mrs Mann. (He drew it towards him.) "You feel as a mother, Mrs Mann." (He stirred the gin-and-water.) "I drink your health with cheerfulness." And he swallowed half of it.

"And now about business," said the beadle, taking out a pocket book. "The child that was half-baptized Oliver Twist is nine years old today."

"Bless him!" said Mrs Mann, inflaming her left eye with the corner of her apron.

"And notwithstanding an offered reward of ten pounds, which was afterwards increased to twenty pounds, we have never been able to discover who is his father, or what was his mother's name or condition."

Mrs Mann raised her hands in astonishment, but added, after a moment's reflection, "How comes he to have any name at all then?"

The beadle drew himself up with great pride and said, "I inwented it."

"You, Mr Bumble!"

"I, Mrs Mann. We name our foundlings in alphabetical order. The last was an S — Swubble, I named him. This was a T — Twist I named *him*. The next one as comes will be Unwin, and the next Vilkins."

"Why, you're quite a literary character, sir," said Mrs Mann.

"Well," said the beadle, "perhaps I may be." He finished the gin-and-water and added, "Oliver being now too old to remain here, the·board have determined to have him back into the house. I have come myself to take him there. So let me see him at once."

"I'll fetch him directly," said Mrs Mann.

Oliver, having had as much of the outer coat of dirt, which encrusted his face and hands, removed as could be scrubbed off in one washing, was led into the room.

"Will you go along with me, Oliver?" said Mr Bumble, in a majestic voice.

Oliver was about to say that he would go along with anybody when he caught sight of Mrs Mann, who was shaking her fist at him. He took the hint at once. Hunger and recent ill-usage are great assistants if you want to cry; and Oliver cried very naturally indeed. Mrs Mann gave him a thousand embraces, and, what Oliver wanted a great deal more, a piece of bread and butter. With the slice of bread in his hand, Oliver was led away by Mr Bumble from the wretched home where one kind word or look had never lighted the gloom of his infant years.

9

Oliver had not been within the walls of the workhouse a quarter of an hour when Mr Bumble informed him that the board had said he was to appear before it.

Mr Bumble conducted him into a large whitewashed room, where eight or ten fat gentlemen were sitting around a table. "You know you're an orphan, I suppose?" asked one.

"What's that, sir?" enquired poor Oliver.

"You know you've got no father or mother, and that you were brought up by the parish, don't you?"

"Yes, sir," replied Oliver, weeping bitterly.

"Well! You have come here to be educated and taught a useful trade," said another. "So you'll begin to pick oakum tomorrow morning at six o'clock."

For the combination of both these blessings in the one single process of picking oakum, Oliver bowed low and was then hurried away to a large ward, where, on a rough hard bed, he sobbed himself to sleep.

The room in which the boys were fed was a large stone hall, with a copper at one end; out of which the master ladled the gruel at meal-times. The bowls never wanted washing. The boys polished them with their spoons till they shone again; and when they had performed this operation, they would sit staring at the copper. Oliver Twist and his companions suffered the tortures of slow starvation for three months. At last they got so voracious and wild with hunger that one boy hinted darkly that unless he had another basin of gruel, he might some night happen to eat the boy who slept next to him. He had a wild, hungry eye; and they implicitly believed him. A council was held; lots were cast who should walk up to the master after supper that evening and ask for more; and it fell to Oliver.

The evening arrived, and the boys took their places.

The gruel disappeared; the boys whispered to each other, and winked at Oliver. Child as he was, he was desperate with hunger, and reckless with misery. He rose from the table; and advancing to the master, basin and spoon in hand, said, somewhat alarmed at his own temerity, "Please, sir, I want some more."

The master was a fat, healthy man; but he turned very pale.

"What!" he said in a faint voice.

"Please, sir," said Oliver, "I want some more."

The master aimed a blow at Oliver's head with the ladle and shrieked for the beadle.

The board was sitting when Mr Bumble rushed into the room and said, "I beg your pardon, sir! Oliver Twist has asked for more."

There was a general start. Horror was depicted on every countenance.

Oliver was ordered into instant confinement; and a bill was next morning pasted on the gate, offering a reward of five pounds to anybody who would take Oliver Twist off the hands of the parish.

It was decided that Oliver should go to Mr Sowerberry, the undertaker, as general house-lad, and once more attaching himself to Mr Bumble's coat cuff, he was led away to new suffering.

After eating his supper, scraps put by for the dog, Oliver was shown to his bed under the counter of the shop, among the coffins.

Oliver was awakened in the morning by a loud kicking at the outside of the shop-door. "I suppose yer the new boy, a'n't yer?" said a voice through the keyhole.

Oliver drew back the bolts with a trembling hand and opened the door.

"Yer don't know who I am, I suppose, Work'us?" said

a large boy. "I'm Mister Noah Claypole, and you're under me. Take down the shutters, yer idle young ruffian!"

Noah was a charity-boy, not a workhouse orphan. The shop-boys in the neighbourhood had long been in the habit of branding Noah with the epithets of "leathers", "charity" and the like, and Noah had borne them without reply. But now that fortune had cast in his way a nameless orphan, at whom even the meanest could point the finger of scorn, he retorted on him with interest.

For many months Oliver continued meekly to submit to the domination and ill-treatment of Noah Claypole. Charlotte, the kitchen maid, treated him badly because Noah did, and Mrs Sowerberry was his decided enemy.

One day Oliver and Noah descended into the kitchen at the usual dinner-hour. "Work'us," said Noah, "how's your mother?"

"She's dead," replied Oliver; "don't you say anything about her."

"Yer know, Work'us," said Noah, "it can't be helped now; and I'm very sorry for it; and I'm sure we all are, and pity yer very much. But yer must know, Work'us, yer mother was a regular right-down bad'un."

Crimson with fury, Oliver started up; overthrew the chair and table; seized Noah by the throat; shook him till his teeth chattered in his head; and felled him to the ground.

A minute ago the boy had looked the quiet, mild creature that harsh treatment had made him. But his spirit was roused at last, the cruel insult to his dead mother had set his blood on fire. His breast heaved, his attitude was erect, his whole person changed, as he stood glaring over the cowardly tormentor who now lay crouching at his feet.

"He'll murder me!" blubbered Noah. "Charlotte! Missis! Here's the new boy a-murdering of me! Help! Help! Oliver's gone mad!"

Charlotte and Mrs Sowerberry dragged Oliver into the cellar, and there locked him up, and on Mr Sowerberry's return Oliver was given a good drubbing.

For the rest of the day he was shut up in the back kitchen, and at night Mrs Sowerberry looked into the room, and, amid the jeers and pointings of Noah and Charlotte, ordered him to his bed.

With the first ray of light that struggled through the shutters, Oliver rose, and unbarred the door. One timid look around — one moment's pause of hesitation — he had closed it behind him, and was in the open street.

He looked to the right and to the left, uncertain whither to fly. He remembered to have seen wagons toiling up the hill. He took the same route, and walked quickly on.

Along this same footpath Oliver well remembered he had trotted beside Mr Bumble, when he first carried him to the workhouse from the farm. His way lay directly in front of the cottage. His heart beat quickly when he thought of this, and he half resolved to turn back. He had come a long way, though, and would lose a great deal of time by doing so. Besides, it was so early that there was very little fear of his being seen; so he walked on.

He reached the house. There was no appearance of its inmates stirring at that early hour. Oliver stopped and peeped into the garden. A child was weeding one of the little beds and as he stopped he raised his pale face, and disclosed the features of one of Oliver's former companions. Oliver felt glad to see him for, though younger than himself, he had been his little friend and playmate. They had been beaten and starved, and shut up together, many and many a time.

"Hush, Dick!" said Oliver as the boy ran to the gate and thrust his thin arm through the rails to greet him. "Is anyone up?"

"Nobody but me," replied the child.

"You mustn't say you saw me, Dick," said Oliver. "I am running away. They beat and ill-use me, Dick, and I am going to seek my fortune a long way off. I don't know where. How pale you are!"

"I heard the doctor tell them I was dying," replied the child, with a faint smile. "I am very glad to see you, but don't stop, don't stop!"

"Yes, I will, to say goodbye to you," replied Oliver. "I shall see you again, Dick, I know I shall. You will be well and happy."

"I hope so," replied the child. "After I am dead, but not before. I know the doctor must be right, Oliver, because I dream so much of heaven, and kind faces that I never see when I am awake. Kiss me," said the child, climbing up the low gate and flinging his little arms around Oliver's neck. "Goodbye! God bless you!"

The blessing was from a young child's lips, but it was the first that Oliver had ever heard invoked upon his head; and through all the struggles and sufferings, and troubles and changes, of his after life, he never once forgot it.

Oliver reached the stile at which the footpath terminated and once more gained the high road. It was eight o'clock now. Though he was nearly five miles away from the town, he ran and hid behind hedges, by turns, till noon, fearing that he might be pursued and overtaken. Then he sat down to rest by the side of a milestone and began to think, for the first time, where he had better go and try to live.

The stone by which he was seated said, in large characters, that it was just seventy miles from that spot to London. The name awakened a new train of ideas in the boy's mind. London — that great place! Nobody, not

15

even Mr Bumble, could ever find him there. He had often heard the old men in the workhouse say that no lad of spirit need want in London; that there were ways of living in that vast city that those in country parts had no idea of. It was the very place for a homeless boy. As these things passed through his thoughts he jumped up and again walked forward.

Oliver walked twenty miles that day, and all that time tasted nothing but a crust of dry bread and a few draughts of water which he begged at the cottages by the roadside. When the night came he turned into a meadow and, creeping close under a hayrick, determined to lie there until morning.

He felt cold and stiff when he got up next morning, and so hungry that he exchanged his only penny for a small loaf. He had walked no more than twelve miles when night closed in again; for his feet were sore, and his legs so weak that they trembled beneath him. Another night passed and the bleak, damp air made him worse, and when he set off next morning he could hardly crawl along.

In fact, if it had not been for a good-hearted turnpike man and a benevolent old lady, Oliver's troubles would have been shortened by the very same process which put an end to his mother's: in other words, he would have fallen dead upon the king's highway. But the turnpike man gave him a meal of bread and cheese, and the old lady, who had a shipwrecked grandson wandering barefoot in some distant part of the earth, took pity upon the poor orphan and gave him what little she could afford — and more — with such kind and gentle words, and such tears of sympathy and compassion, that they sank deeper into Oliver's soul than all the sufferings he had ever undergone.

Early on the seventh morning after he had left his

native place, Oliver limped slowly into the little town of Barnet.

He had been crouching on a step for some time, when he was roused by observing that a boy, who had passed him carelessly some minutes before, had returned and was surveying him most earnestly. The boy remained in the same attitude of observation so long that Oliver raised his head, and returned his steady look. Upon this, the boy crossed to Oliver, and said, "Hallo! my covey, what's the row?"

The boy who addressed this enquiry to the young wayfarer was about his own age, but one of the queerest-looking boys that Oliver had ever seen. He was a snub-nosed, flat-browed, common-faced boy, and as dirty a juvenile as one would wish to see; but he had about him all the airs and manners of a man. He was short for his age, with rather bow legs, and little, sharp, ugly eyes. His hat was stuck on the top of his head so lightly that it threatened to fall off every moment — and would have done so very often — if the wearer had not had a knack of every now and then giving his head a sudden twitch, which brought it back to its old place again. He wore a man's coat, which reached nearly to his heels. He had turned the cuffs back, half way up his arm, to get his hands out of the sleeves, apparently with the ultimate view of thrusting them into the pockets of his corduroy trousers, for there he kept them.

"Hallo, my covey! What's the row?" said this strange young gentleman to Oliver.

"I am very hungry and tired," replied Oliver, the tears standing in his eyes as he spoke. "I have walked a long way. I have been walking for seven days."

"Walking for sivin days!" said the young gentleman. "Come, you want grub, and you shall have it. I'm at low-water mark myself, but as far as it goes I'll fork out. Up with you on your pins. There!"

17

Assisting Oliver to rise, the young gentleman took him to a shop where he purchased ham and a loaf, the ham being kept clean by making a hole in the loaf by pulling out a portion of the bread, and stuffing it inside. Taking the bread under his arm, the young gentleman turned into a small public house, and led the way to a room in the rear of the premises. Here a pot of beer was brought in, by direction of the mysterious youth, and Oliver, falling to at his new friend's bidding, made a long and hearty meal, during the progress of which the strange boy eyed him from time to time with great attention.

"Going to London?" said the strange boy when Oliver had finished.

"Yes."

"Got any lodgings?"

"No."

"Money?"

"No."

The strange boy whistled, and put his arms into his pockets as far as the big coat sleeves would let them go.

"Do you live in London?" inquired Oliver.

"Yes, I do, when I'm at home," replied the boy. "I suppose you want some place to sleep in tonight, don't you?"

"I do indeed," answered Oliver. "I have not slept under a roof since I left the country."

"Don't fret your eyelids on that score," said the young gentleman. "I've got to be in London tonight, and I knows a 'spectable old gentleman as lives there, wot'll give you lodgings for nothink, and never ask for the change — that is, if any gentleman he knows interduces you. And don't he know me? Oh, no! Not in the least! By no means! Certainly not!"

The young gentleman smiled as if to show that his

words were playfully ironical, and finished the beer as he did so.

This led to a more friendly dialogue, from which Oliver discovered that his friend's name was Jack Dawkins, and that among his intimate friends he was better known as "The Artful Dodger".

As John Dawkins objected to their entering London before nightfall it was nearly eleven o'clock when they reached the turnpike at Islington. The Dodger scudded along at a rapid pace, directing Oliver to follow close at his heels.

Oliver was just considering whether he hadn't better run away when his conductor, catching him by the arm, pushed open the door of a house and, drawing him into the passage, closed it behind them.

"Now then!" cried a voice from below, in reply to a whistle from the Dodger.

"Plummy and slam!" was the reply.

This seemed to be some watchword or signal that all was right, for the light of a feeble candle gleamed on the wall at the remote end of the passage, and a man's face peeped out from where a balustrade of the old kitchen staircase had been broken away.

"There's two on you," said the man, thrusting the candle further out, and shading his eyes with his hand. "Who's t'other one?"

"A new pal," replied Jack Dawkins, pulling Oliver forward. "Is Fagin upstairs?"

"Yes, he's a sortin' the wipes. Up with you!" The candle was drawn back and the face disappeared.

Oliver, groping his way with one hand, and having the other firmly grasped by his companion, ascended with much difficulty the dark and broken stairs which his conductor mounted with an ease and expedition that showed he was well acquainted with them. He threw open the door of a back room and drew Oliver in after him.

The walls and ceiling of the room were perfectly black with age and dirt. There was a table before the fire upon which were a candle, stuck in a ginger-beer bottle, two or three pewter pots, a loaf and butter, and a plate. In a frying pan, which was on the fire, some sausages were cooking and standing over them, with a toasting fork in his hand, was a very old shrivelled Jew, whose villainous-looking and repulsive face was obscured by a quantity of matted red hair. He was dressed in a greasy flannel gown, and seemed to be dividing his attention between the frying pan and a clothes-horse, over which a great number of silk handkerchiefs were hanging. Several rough beds, made of sacks, were huddled side by side on the floor, and seated around the table were four or five boys, none older than the Dodger, smoking long clay pipes, and drinking spirits with the air of middle-aged men. These all crowded about their associate as he whispered a few words to the Jew, and then turned round and grinned at Oliver, as did the Jew himself, toasting fork in hand.

"This is him, Fagin," said Jack Dawkins. "My friend, Oliver Twist."

The Jew grinned and, making a low bow to Oliver, took him by the hand and hoped he should have the honour of his intimate acquaintance.

Upon this the young gentlemen with the pipes came round him, and shook both his hands very hard, especially the one in which he held his little bundle. One young gentleman was very anxious to hang up his cap for him, and another put his hands in Oliver's pockets in order that, as he was very tired, he might not have the trouble of emptying them himself when he went to bed. These civilities would probably have been extended much further, but for the liberal use of the Jew's toasting fork on the heads and shoulders of the affectionate youths who offered them.

"We are very glad to see you, Oliver — very," said the Jew. "Dodger, take off the sausages and draw a tub near the fire for Oliver. Ah, you're a-staring at the pocket-handkerchiefs, eh, my dear? There are a good many of 'em, ain't there? We've just looked 'em out, ready for the wash, that's all, Oliver — that's all. Ha, ha, ha!"

The latter part of this speech was hailed by a loud shout from all the joyful pupils of the merry old gentleman. In the midst of which they went to supper.

Oliver ate his share, and the Jew then mixed him a glass of hot gin and water, telling him he must drink it off directly, because another gentleman wanted the tumbler. Oliver did as he was desired. Immediately afterwards he felt himself gently lifted on to one of the sacks, and then he sank into a deep sleep.

It was late next morning when Oliver awoke from a

sound long sleep. There was no other person in the room but the old Jew, who was boiling some coffee in a saucepan for breakfast, and whistling softly to himself as he stirred it round and round with an iron spoon.

Although Oliver had roused himself from sleep he was not thoroughly awake.

When the coffee was done the Jew turned round and looked at Oliver, and called his name. He did not answer, and was to all appearance asleep.

The Jew stepped gently to the door, which he fastened. He then drew forth, from some trap in the floor, a small box, which he placed carefully on the table. His eyes glistened as he raised the lid and looked in. Dragging an old chair to the table, he sat down, and took from it a magnificent gold watch, sparkling with jewels.

"Aha!" said the Jew, distorting every feature with a hideous grin. "Lever dogs! Fine fellows!"

He took rings, brooches, bracelets and other articles of jewellery from the box, and surveyed them with equal pleasure.

Then his bright dark eyes fell on Oliver's face. The boy's eyes were fixed on his in mute curiosity. Fagin closed the box with a loud crash and, laying his hand on a bread knife which was on the table, started furiously up. "What do you watch me for?" said the Jew. "What have you seen?"

"I wasn't able to sleep any longer, sir," replied Oliver meekly. "I am very sorry to have disturbed you, sir."

"You were not awake an hour ago?" said the Jew.

"Upon my word I was not, sir," replied Oliver earnestly. "I was not, indeed, sir."

"Tush, tush, my dear!" said the Jew, resuming his old manner. "I know that. I only tried to frighten you. The pretty things are mine, Oliver, my little property. They're all I have to live on in my old age."

Soon after the Dodger returned, accompanied by a very sprightly young friend, who was formally introduced as Charley Bates. The four sat down to breakfast on the coffee, and some hot rolls and ham, which the Dodger had brought home in his hat.

"Well," said the Jew, glancing slyly at Oliver, and addressing himself to the Dodger, "I hope you've been at work this morning, my dears?"

"Hard," replied the Dodger.

"As nails," added Charley Bates.

"Good boys!" said the Jew. "What have you got, Dodger?"

"A couple of pocket books."

"And what have you got, my dear?" said Fagin to Charley Bates.

"Wipes," replied Master Bates, producing four handkerchiefs.

"You'd like to be able to make pocket-handkerchiefs as easy as Charley Bates, wouldn't you, Oliver?" said the Jew.

"Very much indeed, if you'll teach me, sir," replied Oliver.

When the breakfast was cleared away the merry old gentleman and the two boys played at a very curious and uncommon game, which was performed in this way. The merry old gentleman, placing a snuff-box in one pocket of his trousers, a note case in the other, and a watch in his waistcoat pocket, and a mock diamond pin in his shirt, buttoned his coat tight round him and, putting his spectacle-case and handkerchief in his pockets, trotted up and down the room with a stick, in the manner in which old gentlemen walk about the streets any hour of the day. Sometimes he stopped at the fireplace, and sometimes at the door, as if he were staring into shop windows. At such times he would look constantly round him, for fear of thieves, and keep slapping all his pockets in turn, to see that he hadn't lost anything. He did it in such a very funny and natural manner that Oliver laughed till the tears ran down his face.

All this time the two boys followed him closely, getting out of his sight so nimbly, every time he turned round, that it was impossible to follow their motions. At last the Dodger trod upon his toes, or ran upon his boot accidentally, while Charley Bates stumbled up against him, and in that one moment they took from him, with extraordinary rapidity, snuff-box, note case, shirt-pin, pocket handkerchief, watch — even the spectacle-case. If the old gentleman felt a hand in any one of his pockets he cried out here it was, and then the game began all over again.

At length Charley Bates expressed his opinion that it was time to pad the hoof. This, it occurred to Oliver, must be French for going out, for directly afterwards the Dodger and Charley went away together, having been furnished by the amiable old Jew with money to spend.

"There, my dear," said Fagin, "that's a pleasant life, isn't it? They have gone out for the day."

"Have they done with work, sir?" inquired Oliver.

"Yes," said the Jew. "That is, unless they should come across any when they are out; and they won't neglect it, if they do, my dear — depend upon it. Make 'em your models, my dear — make 'em your models. Do everything they bid you, and take their advice in all matters — especially the Dodger's, my dear. He'll be a great man himself, and will make you one, too, if you take pattern by him. Is my handkerchief hanging out of my pocket, my dear?" he added, stopping short.

"Yes, sir," said Oliver.

"See if you can take it out without my feeling it, as you saw them do when we were at play this morning."

Oliver held up the bottom of the pocket with one hand, as he had seen the Dodger hold it, and drew the handkerchief lightly out of it with the other.

"Is it gone?" cried the Jew.

"Here it is, sir," said Oliver, showing it in his hand.

"You're a clever boy, my dear," said the playful old gentleman, patting Oliver on the head approvingly. "I never saw a sharper lad. Here's a shilling for you. If you go on in this way, you'll be the greatest man of the time."

Oliver wondered what picking the old gentleman's pocket in play had to do with his chances of being a great man, but he thought that the Jew, being so much his senior, must know best.

For many days Oliver remained in the Jew's room, sometimes taking part in the game. At length he began to languish for the fresh air, and asked the old gentleman to allow him to go out to work with his two companions.

At length one morning Oliver obtained the permission he had so eagerly sought.

The three boys sallied out, and were just emerging from a narrow court when the Dodger made a sudden stop, and, laying his finger on his lip, drew his companions back again, with the greatest caution. "Do you see that old cove at the book-stall?" he said.

"Yes, I see him," said Oliver.

"He'll do," said the Dodger.

Oliver looked from one to the other with the greatest surprise; but he was not permitted to make any enquiries, for the two boys walked stealthily across the road, and slunk close behind the old gentleman. Oliver stood looking on in silent amazement.

What was Oliver's horror and alarm to see the Dodger plunge his hand into the old gentleman's pocket, and draw from thence a handkerchief; to see him hand the same to Charley Bates; and finally to behold them both running away round the corner at full speed!

In an instant the whole mystery of the handkerchiefs, the watches and the Jew, rushed upon the boy's mind. He stood for a moment, then, confused and frightened, he took to his heels.

In the very instant when Oliver began to run, the old gentleman, missing his handkerchief, turned sharp around, and shouting, "Stop thief!", made off after him.

But the old gentleman was not the only person who raised the hue and cry. The Dodger and Master Bates, unwilling to attract public attention by running down the open street, had merely retired into the very first doorway round the corner. They no sooner heard the cry, and saw Oliver running, than they issued forth, shouting, "Stop thief!" too, and joined in the pursuit like good citizens.

Oliver was not familiar with the axiom that self-preservation is the first law of nature. If he had been, perhaps he would have been prepared for this. Not being prepared, however, it alarmed him the more, so away he went like the wind, with the old gentleman and the two boys roaring and shouting behind him.

Stopped at last! A clever blow! He is down upon the pavement, and the crowd eagerly gather round him, each newcomer jostling and struggling with the others to catch a glimpse.

"Stand aside!"

"Give him a little air!"

"Nonsense! He don't deserve it."

"Where's the gentleman?"

"Here he is, coming down the street."

"Make room there for the gentleman!"

"Is this the boy, sir?"

"Yes."

Oliver lay, covered with mud and dust, and bleeding

from the mouth, looking wildly round upon the heap of faces that surrounded him, when the old gentleman was dragged and pushed into the circle by the foremost of the pursuers.

"Yes," said the gentleman, "I am afraid it is the boy."

"Afraid!" murmured the crowd. "That's a good 'un."

"Poor fellow!" said the gentleman. "He has hurt himself."

"I did that, sir," said a great, lubberly fellow, stepping forward, "And I cut my knuckle agin' his mouth. I stopped him, sir."

A police officer at that moment made his way through the crowd, and seized Oliver by the collar.

"It wasn't me, indeed, sir, it was two other boys," said Oliver, but the police officer escorted him away, the old gentleman at his side.

"I am not sure that this boy actually took the handkerchief. I — I would rather not press the case," said the old gentleman.

"Must go before the magistrate now," said the court official, and the old gentleman and Oliver were ushered into the imposing presence of the renowned Mr Fang.

After hearing the case, Mr Fang was about to commit Oliver to three months hard labour when an elderly man rushed in and advanced towards the bench. "I saw it all. I keep the book-stall," he said. "The robber was another boy."

In short, Oliver was discharged, and the old gentleman, finding Oliver lying on the pavement outside, his shirt unbuttoned, his face a deadly white, and a cold tremble convulsing his whole body, called a coach and took him to his home.

Here a bed was prepared in which the old gentleman, Mr Brownlow, saw his charge comfortably deposited; and here he was tended with a kindness and solicitude that knew no bounds.

But, for many days, Oliver remained insensible to all the goodness of his new friends.

Weak, thin, and pallid, he awoke at last from what seemed to have been a long and troublesome dream. Feebly raising himself in the bed, he looked anxiously round.

"Where have I been brought to?" said Oliver.

A motherly old lady rose from an armchair close by. "Hush, my dear," said the old lady softly. "You must be very quiet, or you will be ill again. Lie down again, there's a dear!"

It had been bright for hours when Oliver opened his eyes again, and he felt cheerful and happy. The crisis of the disease was safely passed.

In three days time he was able to sit in an easy-chair and Mrs Bedwin, the old lady, had him carried downstairs into the little housekeeper's room which belonged to her.

"Are you very fond of pictures, dear?" enquired the old lady, seeing that Oliver had fixed his eyes on a portrait which hung against the wall.

"I don't quite know, ma'am," said Oliver, without taking his eyes from the canvas. "What a beautiful mild face that lady's is!"

There came a soft tap at the door, and in walked Mr Brownlow.

"Poor boy, poor boy!" said Mr Brownlow. "How do you feel, my dear?"

"Very happy, sir," replied Oliver. "And very grateful indeed, sir, for your goodness to me."

"Bedwin, look here!" said the old gentleman. As he spoke, he pointed to the picture above Oliver's head, and then to the boy's face. There was its living copy. The eyes, the head, the mouth — every feature was the same.

Oliver knew not the cause of this sudden exclamation,

for, not being strong enough to bear the start it gave him, he fainted away.

Meanwhile, the Dodger and Charley Bates were busily recounting the story of Oliver's capture to Fagin, and to an acquaintance of his, Bill Sikes.

"I'm afraid," said the Jew, "that he may say something which will get us into trouble."

"If he hasn't peached, and is committed, there's no fear till he comes out again," said Mr Sikes; "and then he must be taken care of."

Another acquaintance, a young lady called Nancy, was persuaded to go to the office where Oliver had been taken, and find out what had happened to him.

Nancy was informed that Oliver had been driven off by an old gentleman towards Pentonville, and she passed on this information to the Jew and Bill Sikes.

"We must know where he is, my dears; he must be found," said the Jew. "He has not peached so far. If he means to blab us among his new friends, we may stop his mouth yet."

The days of Oliver's recovery were happy days. Everything was so quiet, and neat, and orderly, everybody so kind and gentle, that after the noise and turbulence in the midst of which he had always lived, it seemed like heaven itself.

After some days, Mr Grimwig, an old friend of Mr Brownlow's, came to call. He was suspicious of Oliver, and of the story he had told about his former life.

"When are you going to hear a true account of the life and adventures of Oliver Twist?" asked Mr Grimwig. "He is deceiving you, my good friend."

"I'll answer for that boy's truth with my life!" said Mr Brownlow.

As fate would have it, Mr Brownlow wanted some books to be returned to a book-stall.

"Send Oliver with them," said Mr Grimwig, with an ironic smile. "He will be sure to deliver them safely."

"You *shall* go, my dear," said the old gentleman, giving Oliver instructions and directions.

"I won't be ten minutes, sir," replied Oliver eagerly, and he left the room.

"You really expect him to come back, do you?" enquired Mr Grimwig. "He'll join his old friends the thieves, and laugh at you. If ever that boy returns to this house, sir, I'll eat my head."

Meanwhile Oliver Twist was on his way to the book-stall.

He was walking along when he was startled by a young woman screaming out very loud, "Oh, my dear brother!" and he hardly looked up when he was stopped by Nancy's arms thrown tight around his neck.

"What the devil's this?" said Sikes. "Young Oliver! Come home directly."

"I don't belong to them. I don't know them. Help! Help!" cried Oliver.

Weak with recent illness, stupefied by the blows and the suddenness of the attack, terrified by the brutality of the man — what could one poor child do? Darkness had set in; it was a low neighbourhood; no help was near; resistance was useless. In another moment he was dragged away into a labyrinth of dark narrow courts, and forced along them at a pace which rendered the few cries he dared to give utterance to wholly unintelligible.

"So you wanted to get away, did you?" said the Jew, taking up a jagged and knotted club. "Eh?"

The Jew inflicted a smart blow on Oliver's shoulders with the club when the girl, rushing forward, wrested it from his hand. "I won't stand by and see it done, Fagin!"

she cried. "You've got the boy, what more would you have? He's a thief, a liar, a devil, all that's bad from this night forth. Isn't that enough without blows? I thieved for you when I was a child not half as old as this!"

"Well," replied the Jew. "It's your living!"

"Ay, it is!" returned the girl. "It is my living; and the cold, wet, dirty streets are my home; and you are the wretch that drove me to them long ago, and that'll keep me there till I die!"

The girl said nothing more; but tearing her hair and dress in a transport of frenzy, made a rush at the Jew and fainted.

Mr Bumble, on his way to London on certain parochial business, happened upon a piece in the paper, inserted by Mr Brownlow, offering a reward for any information about Oliver Twist.

The sum and substance of Mr Bumble's words was that

Oliver was a foundling, born of low and vicious parents; and that he had, from his birth, displayed no better qualities than malice, ingratitude and treachery.

Mr Brownlow paced the room to and fro for some minutes. At length he stopped and rang the bell violently.

"Mrs Bedwin," said Mr Brownlow, "Oliver is an imposter. Never let me hear the boy's name again."

It was a damp, chill, windy night when the Jew set off for Spitalfields to discuss plans for a robbery with Bill Sikes.

"Now, my dear, about that crib at Chertsey," said the Jew. "When is it to be done, Bill, eh? Such plate, my dear, such plate!"

"It can't be a put-up job, as we expected," said Sykes. "Toby Crackit has been hanging about the place for a fortnight, and he can't get one of the servants into a line. Is it worth fifty shiners extra, if it's done from the outside?"

"Yes, my dear, yes," rejoined the Jew.

"Then," said Sikes, "let it come off as soon as you like. The crib's barred up at night, but there's one part we can crack, safe and softly."

"Is there no help wanted but yours and Toby's?" asked the Jew.

"I want a boy," replied Sikes, "and he mustn't be a big 'un."

"Then Oliver's the boy for you," replied the Jew. "He's been in good training these last few weeks, and it's time he began to work for his bread."

After some discussion, it was decided that Nancy should repair to the Jew's the next evening when the night had set in, and bring Oliver away with her.

"I have come from Bill," said Nancy, when she went the next evening to collect Oliver. "You are to go with me."

33

Nancy looked cautiously round.

"Hush!" she said, stooping over him. "You can't help yourself. I have tried hard for you, but all to no purpose. You are hedged round and round; and if ever you are to get loose from here, this is not the time."

"So you've got the kid," said Sikes when they reached his room. He pulled off Oliver's cap and threw it into a corner; then stood the boy in front of him.

"Do you know wot this is?" enquired Sikes, taking up a pocket-pistol.

Oliver replied in the affirmative.

"Well," said the robber, putting the barrel to his temple, "if you speak a word when you're out with me, that loading will be in your head without notice."

It was a cheerless morning when they went out — blowing and raining hard, and the clouds looking dull and stormy.

After a long and tiring journey, Sikes and Oliver met up with Toby Crackit and, after resting in a ruined house, the two robbers issued forth, with Oliver between them.

It was now intensely dark, and they soon arrived at Chertsey.

They stopped before a detached house surrounded by a wall, to the top of which Toby Crackit, scarcely pausing, climbed in a twinkling.

Before Oliver had time to look round, Sikes had caught him under the arms, and in three or four seconds he and Toby were lying on the grass on the other side. Sikes followed directly. And they stole cautiously towards the house.

And now, for the first time, Oliver, well-nigh mad with grief and terror, saw that housebreaking and robbery, if not murder, were the objects of the expedition. He clasped his hands together and uttered a subdued exclamation of horror.

A window so small that the inmates had probably not thought it worth while to defend, was opened.

"Now listen," whispered Sikes, drawing a lantern from his pocket, and throwing the glare full on Oliver's face, "I'm going to put you through there. Take this light; go softly up the steps afore you, and along the hall to the street door, and let us in."

Sikes put Oliver through the window and, without leaving hold of his collar, planted him on the floor inside.

"Directly I leave go of you, do your work. Hark!" he said.

In the short time he had had to collect his senses, the boy had resolved that, whether he died in the attempt or not, he would make one effort to alarm the family. Filled with this idea, he advanced at once.

"Come back!" Sikes suddenly cried.

Scared by the sudden breaking of the dead stillness and by a loud cry which followed it, Oliver let his lantern fall, and knew not whether to advance or fly.

The cry was repeated — a light appeared — a vision of two terrified, half-dressed men at the top of the stairs swam before his eyes — a flash — a loud noise — smoke — a crash somewhere — and he staggered back.

Sikes had him by the collar before the smoke had cleared away, and dragged the boy up.

Sikes drew him through the window. "Give me a shawl here. They've hit him. Quick! Damnation, how the boy bleeds!"

Then came the loud ringing of a bell, mingled with the noise of fire-arms, and the shouts of men, and the sensation of being carried over uneven ground at a rapid pace. And then the noise grew confused in the distance, and a cold deadly feeling crept over the boy's heart; and he saw and heard no more.

The night was bitter cold. The snow lay on the ground,

frozen into a hard thick crust, and a sharp wind howled.

Such was the aspect when Mrs Corney, the matron of the workhouse to which our readers have already been introduced as the birthplace of Oliver Twist, sat herself down before a cheerful fire in her own little room.

She had just tasted her first cup of tea when she was disturbed by a soft tap at the room door.

"Oh, come in with you!" said Mrs Corney, sharply. "Some of the old women dying, I suppose. They always die when I'm at meals. What's amiss, eh?"

"At your service, ma'am," said Mr Bumble. "This is the port wine, ma'am, that the board ordered for the infirmary — real, fresh, genuine port wine; only out of the cask this forenoon, clear as a bell!"

The matron enquired whether he wouldn't take a cup of tea?

Mr Bumble laid his hat and stick upon a chair, and drew another chair to the table.

"Sweet, Mr Bumble?" enquired the matron, taking up the sugar-basin.

"Very sweet, indeed, ma'am," replied Mr Bumble fixing his eyes on Mrs Corney.

The beadle drank his tea to the last drop, wiped his lips, and deliberately kissed the matron.

"Mr Bumble," cried the discreet lady in a whisper; "Mr Bumble, I shall scream!"

But the exertion was rendered unnecessary by a hasty knocking at the door.

"If you please, mistress," said a withered old female pauper. "Old Sally is a-going fast. She's troubled in her mind — she says she has got something to tell, which you must hear. She'll never die quiet till you come, mistress."

At this intelligence Mrs Corney requested Mr Bumble to stay till she came back, and bidding the messenger walk fast, followed her from the room.

The patient had raised herself upright, and was stretching her arms towards them.

"I'll never lie down again alive!" said the woman. "I *will* tell her! Come here! Nearer! Let me whisper in your ear.

"In this very room — in this very bed — I once nursed a pretty young creatur' that was brought into the house with her feet cut and bruised with walking, and all soiled with dust and blood. She gave birth to a boy, and died. I robbed her, so I did! She wasn't cold when I stole it!"

"Stole what?" cried the matron.

"*It!*" replied the woman. "It was gold, I tell you! — rich gold, that might have saved her life! She charged me to keep it safe and whispered that if her baby was born alive, and thrived, the day might come when it would not feel so much disgraced to hear its poor young mother named."

"The boy's name?" demanded the matron.

"They *called* him Oliver," replied the woman feebly. "The gold I stole was —"

"Yes, yes — what?"

She was bending eagerly over the old woman to hear her reply; but drew back as she once again rose, slowly and stiffly, into a sitting posture, then fell lifeless on the bed.

"Stone dead!" said one of the old women.

"And nothing to tell, after all," rejoined the matron.

"Wolves tear your throats!" muttered Sikes, grinding his teeth.

He rested the body of the wounded boy across his knee, and turned his head to look back at his pursuers.

"Stop, you white-livered hound!" cried the robber to Toby Crackit, who was already ahead. "Stop!"

The repetition of the word brought Toby to a dead standstill.

"Bear a hand with the boy!" roared Sikes, beckoning furiously to his confederate. "Come back!"

"It's all up, Bill!" cried Toby. "Drop the kid, and show 'em your heels." With this parting advice, Mr Crackit darted off at full speed. Sikes clenched his teeth; took one look round; threw over the prostrate form of Oliver the cape in which he had been hurriedly muffled; ran along the front of the hedge, as if to distract the attention of those behind from the spot where the boy lay; paused, for a second before another hedge which met it at right angles; cleared it at a bound, and was gone.

Morning drew on apace.

At length a low cry of pain broke the stillness that prevailed; and uttering it, the boy awoke. His left arm hung heavy and useless at his side; and the bandage was saturated with blood. He was so weak that he could scarcely raise himself into a sitting posture; and when he had done so, he looked round for help, and groaned with pain. Trembling in every joint from cold and exhaustion he made an effort to stand upright; but, shuddering from head to foot, fell on the ground.

After a short return of the stupor in which he had been so long plunged, Oliver, urged by a sickness at his heart which seemed to warn him that if he lay there he must surely die, got upon his feet and essayed to walk. His head was dizzy, and he staggered to and fro like a drunken man.

He saw that at no great distance there was a house, which perhaps he could reach. He summoned up all his strength for one last trial, and bent his faltering steps towards it.

As he drew nearer a feeling came over him that he had seen it before.

That garden wall! It was the very same house they had attempted to rob.

He pushed against the garden-gate; it was unlocked, and swung open. He tottered across the lawn, knocked faintly at the door, and, his whole strength failing him, sunk down.

Mr Giles and Brittles, servants at the house, and the people who had chased the robbers away, were recovering from the night's excitement when they heard the knock at the door.

The door was opened, and they beheld poor little Oliver Twist, speechless and exhausted.

Brittles uttered a loud cry. Mr Giles, seizing the boy by one leg and one arm, lugged him into the hall, and deposited him at full length on the floor.

In the midst of all this noise and commotion there was heard a sweet female voice. "Is the poor creature hurt?"

"Wounded desperate, miss," replied Giles.

"Hush, pray; there's good man!" rejoined the young lady. "Wait while I speak to aunt."

She soon returned, with the direction that the wounded person was to be carried upstairs to Mr Giles's room; and that Brittles was to take himself instantly to Chertsey, from which place he was to despatch a constable and a doctor.

Mr Losberne, the doctor, was absent much longer than either Rose, the young lady, or her aunt, Mrs Maylie, had anticipated.

Oliver's ailings were neither slight nor few. In addition to the pain and delay attendant on a broken limb, his exposure to the wet and cold had brought on fever which hung about him for many weeks, and reduced him sadly. But at length he began to get better, and to be able to say sometimes, in a few tearful words, how deeply he felt the goodness of the two sweet ladies, and how ardently he hoped that, when he grew strong and well again, he could do something to show his gratitude.

"Poor fellow!" said Rose. "You shall have many opportunities of serving us. We are going to the country, and my aunt intends that you shall accompany us. The quiet place, the pure air will restore you in a few days."

But Oliver was still troubled. He could not forget the kindness shown to him by Mr Brownlow and his housekeeper. "If they knew how happy I am now, they would be pleased, I am sure," he said.

"I am sure they would," rejoined Oliver's benefactress: "and Mr Losberne has promised that he will carry you to see them."

In a short time Oliver was sufficiently recovered to undergo this expedition, and one morning he and Mr Losberne set out.

Alas! Mr Brownlow's house was empty, and there was a bill in the window, "To Let".

A servant said that Mr Brownlow had sold off his goods, and gone to the West Indies, six weeks before.

This bitter disappointment caused Oliver much sorrow and grief, even in the midst of his happiness; for he had pleased himself, many times during his illness, with thinking of all that Mr Brownlow and Mrs Bedwin would say to him, and what delight it would be to tell them how many long days and nights he had passed in reflecting on what they had done for him, and in bewailing his cruel separation from them. The hope of clearing himself with them, and explaining how he had been forced away, had sustained him under many of his recent trials; and now the idea that they should have gone so far, and carried with them the belief that he was an imposter and a robber was almost more than he could bear.

When the fine warm weather had begun, Oliver and his benefactors departed to a cottage in the country.

It was a happy time. The days were peaceful and serene; the nights brought with them neither fear nor care, nothing but pleasant thoughts. Every morning he went to a white-headed old gentleman who taught him to read better, and to write; and spoke so kindly, and took such pains, that Oliver could never try enough to please him. Then he would walk with Mrs Maylie and Rose, and hear them talk of books; or perhaps sit near them and listen whilst the young lady read.

So three months glided away.

Spring flew swiftly by, and summer came.

One beautiful night they had taken a longer walk than was customary for them, and when they returned home Rose sat down at the piano and began to play. After a few minutes, she fell into a low and very solemn air; and, as she played they heard her sob, as if she were weeping.

"Rose, my dear!" said the elder lady. "What is this? In tears? My dear child, what distresses you?"

"Nothing, aunt, nothing," replied the young lady and, making an effort, strove to play some livelier tune; but her fingers dropped powerless on the keys, and covering her face with her hands, she sank upon a sofa, and gave vent to the tears which she was now unable to repress.

"My child!" said the elderly lady. "I never saw you thus before."

"I would not alarm you if I could avoid it," rejoined Rose; "but I have tried very hard, and cannot help this. I fear I *am* ill, aunt."

An anxious night ensued. When morning came, Rose was in the first stage of a high and dangerous fever.

"We must be active, Oliver, and not give way to useless grief," said Mrs Maylie. "This letter must be sent to Mr Losberne. It must be carried to the market-town — and thence despatched to Chertsey. The people at the inn will undertake to do this; and I can trust to you to see it done, I know."

42

With these words she gave Oliver her purse, and he started off at the greatest speed he could muster . . .

Oliver hurried up the inn-yard, and was turning out of the gateway when he accidentally stumbled against a tall man wrapped in a cloak.

"Ha!" cried the man, fixing his eyes on Oliver. "What the devil's this?"

"I beg your pardon, sir," said Oliver.

"Death!" muttered the man to himself, glaring at the boy with his large dark eyes. "Who would have thought it? Grind him to ashes! He'd start up from a marble coffin to come in my way!"

The man shook his fist and gnashed his teeth as he uttered these words. He advanced towards Oliver, but fell to the ground, writhing and foaming in a fit.

Oliver gazed for a moment at the struggles of the madman (for such he supposed him to be), and then darted into the house for help. Having seen him carried into the hotel, he turned homewards, running as fast as he could to make up for lost time.

Rose Maylie had rapidly grown worse, and before midnight was delirious. A medical practitioner was in constant attendance and had pronounced her disorder to be one of a most alarming nature. "In fact," he said, "it would be a miracle if she recovered."

How often did Oliver start from his bed that night, and, stealing out with noiseless footstep to the staircase, listen for the slightest noise from the sick chamber! How often did a tremble shake his frame, and cold drops of terror start upon his brow, when a sudden trampling of feet caused him to fear that something too dreadful to think of had occurred!

Morning came, and the cottage was lonely and still. Mr Losberne arrived. "It is hard," said the doctor, "but there is very little hope."

That same evening, a young gentleman arrived with Giles.

"Better or worse?" cried the gentleman.

"Better, much better!" replied Oliver, hastily.

As they walked along, Oliver glanced at the newcomer. He seemed about five-and-twenty years of age, and was of middle height; his countenance was frank and handsome; and his demeanour easy. He bore so strong a resemblance to the old lady, that Oliver would have had no difficulty in imagining their relationship, even if he had not already spoken of her as his mother.

"Mother!" whispered Harry Maylie. "Why did you not write before? If Rose had — I cannot utter that word now — if this illness had terminated differently, how could you ever have forgiven yourself? How could I ever have known happiness again?"

"My dear son," said Mrs Maylie, "if an enthusiastic and ambitious man marry a wife on whose name there is a stain, which, though no fault of hers, may be visited by cold and sordid people upon her, and upon his children also, he may, no matter how generous and good his nature, one day repent of the connection he formed in early life. And she may have the pain and torture of knowing that he does so."

"On Rose, sweet, gentle girl, my heart is set," replied Harry Maylie. "I have no thought, no hope in life, beyond her; and if you oppose me in this, you take my happiness in your hands, and cast them to the wind. Before I leave this place Rose shall hear me."

"She shall," said Mrs Maylie, "but reflect for a few moments on Rose's history, and consider what effect the knowledge of her doubtful birth may have on her decision."

One beautiful evening, Oliver sat at the window, intent upon his books. He had been poring over them for some time, and by slow degrees, he fell asleep.

Oliver knew that he was in his own little room; that his books were lying on the table before him; and that the air was stirring among the plants outside. And yet he was asleep. Suddenly, the air became close and confined; and he thought, with a glow of terror, that he was in the Jew's house again. There sat the hideous old man, pointing at him and whispering to another man.

"Hush, my dear!" he thought he heard the Jew say; "it is he, sure enough. Come away."

"He!" the other man seemed to answer; "could I mistake him? If a crowd of devils were to put themselves into his exact shape, and he stood among them, there is something that would tell me how to point him out. If you buried him fifty feet deep, and took me across his grave, I should know, if there wasn't a mark above it, that he lay buried there!"

The man seemed to say this with such dreadful hatred that Oliver awoke with fear.

There — at the window — so close that he could have almost touched him — there stood the Jew! And beside

him was the scowling man who had accosted him at the inn-yard!

It was but an instant, a glance, a flash, before his eyes; and they were gone. But they had recognised him, and he them. He stood for a moment, and then called for help.

The inmates of the house found him pale and agitated, scarcely able to articulate the words, "The Jew! The Jew!"

"It must have been a dream, Oliver," said Harry Maylie.

"Oh, no, indeed, sir," replied Oliver, "I saw him too plainly for that. I saw them both, as plainly as I see you now."

Meanwhile Rose was recovering rapidly.

But, although this happy change had a visible effect on the little circle, there was at times restraint upon some there, even upon Rose herself, which Oliver could not fail to remark. It became evident that something was in progress which affected the peace of the young lady, and of somebody else besides.

One morning, when Rose was alone in the breakfast-parlour, Harry Maylie entered, and begged permission to speak with her.

"What I have to say has already presented itself to your mind," said Harry. "The most cherished hopes of my heart are not unknown to you, though from my lips you have not yet heard them stated. Rose, my own dear Rose! For years I have loved you; hoping to win my way to fame, and then come proudly home and tell you it had been pursued only for you to share. That time has not arrived; but here, with no fame won, I give to you the heart so long your own, and stake my all upon the words with which you greet the offer."

"You must forget me," said Rose. "Not as your dearly-attached companion, but as the object of your love."

46

"And your reasons, Rose, for this decision?"

"You have a right to know them," rejoined Rose. "I owe it to myself, that I, a friendless girl, with a blight upon my name, should not give your friends reason to suspect that I had fastened myself on all your hopes and projects. The prospect before you is a brilliant one. All the honours to which great talents and powerful connections can help men in public life are in store for you. But those connections are proud; and I will neither mingle with such as hold in scorn the mother who gave me life, nor bring disgrace on the son of her who has so well supplied the mother's place. In a word, there is a stain upon my name."

"One more word, Rose!" cried Harry. "If I had been less fortunate would you have turned from me then?"

"If your lot had been differently cast," rejoined Rose, "if you had been even a little above me I should have been spared this trial. I have every reason to be happy, now: but then, Harry, I should have been happier."

"I ask one promise," said Harry. "Once, and only once more, let me speak to you again on this subject, for the last time."

"Let it be so," rejoined Rose; "it is but one more pang the more, and by that time I may be enabled to bear it better."

She extended her hand again. But the young man caught her to his bosom, and imprinting one kiss on her forehead, hurried from the room.

Mr Bumble sat in the workhouse parlour, with his eyes moodily fixed on the cheerless grate.

Mr Bumble was no longer a beadle. He had married Mrs Corney, and was master of the workhouse.

"And tomorrow two months it was done!" said Mr Bumble, with a sigh. "It seems an age. I sold myself for six teaspoons, a pair of sugar-tongs, and a milk-pot; with a small quantity of secondhand furniture, and twenty pound in money. I went very reasonable. Cheap, dirt cheap!"

Mr Bumble went out of the workhouse and stepped into a public-house. There he met a stranger who asked him if he knew Oliver Twist.

"I remember him, of course," said Mr Bumble.

"It's not of him I want to hear," said the stranger. "It's of the hag that nursed his mother. Where is she?"

"She died last winter," rejoined Mr Bumble.

Mr Bumble well remembered the night of old Sally's death, and although Mrs Corney had never confided to him the disclosure of which she had been the solitary witness, he had heard enough to know that it related to something that had occurred in the old woman's attendance upon the young mother of Oliver Twist.

A meeting was arranged between Mr Bumble and the stranger, Monks, who was very interested to know what old Sally had said.

The next evening, Mr and Mrs Bumble went to a little colony of ruinous houses erected on a low swamp bordering the river.

They were admitted into one of the houses by Monks.

"Now," he said, "what was the nature of the old hag's communication?"

Mrs Bumble told of old Sally's admissions. "She stole from the corpse that which the dead mother had prayed her to keep for the infant's sake. Then she died. But she clutched my gown violently with one hand, and when I saw that she was dead, and so removed the hand by force, I found it clasped a scrap of dirty paper — a pawnbroker's duplicate."

"For what?" demanded Monks.

Mrs Bumble threw upon the table a small kid bag. It

contained a little gold locket, in which were two locks of hair, and a plain gold wedding-ring, engraved "Agnes".

"And this is all," said Monks, and he suddenly wheeled the table aside, and threw back a large trap-door. Turbid water, swollen by heavy rain, was rushing rapidly on below; and all other sounds were lost in the noise of its splashing against the green and slimy piles.

Monks dropped the little packet into the stream. It fell straight, clove the water with a scarcely audible splash, and was gone.

"There!" said Monks, closing the trap-door.

It was a family hotel in a quiet street near Hyde Park. As the lamp which burnt before its door guided Nancy to the spot, the clock struck eleven.

"Now, young woman!" said a smartly-dressed female, "who do you want here?"

"Miss Maylie," said Nancy.

At length Nancy was admitted to a small ante-chamber, where Rose soon joined her.

"It's hard to get to see you, lady," said Nancy.

"I am very sorry if anyone behaved harshly to you," replied Rose. "Tell me why you wished to see me."

"I am about to put my life, and the lives of others, into your hands," replied the girl. "I am the girl that dragged Oliver back to old Fagin's, the Jew's, on the night he went out from the house in Pentonville. I have stolen away from those who would surely murder me if they knew I had been here, to tell you what I have overheard. Do you know a man named Monks?"

"No," said Rose.

"Some time ago, soon after Oliver was put into your house on the night of the robbery, I — suspecting this man — listened to a conversation held between him and Fagin in the dark. I found out that Monks had seen him accidentally with two of our boys on the day we first lost him, and had known him directly to be the same child that he was watching for. A bargain was struck with Fagin, that if Oliver was got back he should have a certain sum; and he was to have more for making him a thief, which this Monks wanted for some purpose of his own.

"Last night he came again," Nancy continued. "The first words I heard Monks say were these: 'So the only proofs of the boy's identity lie at the bottom of the river'. He said that though he had got the young devil's money safely now, he'd rather have had it the other way; for what a game it would have been to have brought down the boast of the father's will, by driving him through every jail in town, and then hauling him up for some felony which Fagin could easily manage, after having made a good profit from him besides. Then he said that if he could gratify his hatred by taking the boy's life, he would. 'In short, Fagin,' he says, 'Jew, you never laid such snares as I'll contrive for my young brother, Oliver'."

"His brother!" exclaimed Rose.

"Those were his words," said Nancy. "It is growing late, and I must get back quickly."

"But what can I do?" said Rose.

"You must have some gentleman about you that will advise you," rejoined the girl.

"But where can I find you again?" asked Rose.

"Every Sunday night, from eleven until twelve," said the girl, "I will walk on London Bridge if I am alive."

Thus speaking, and sobbing aloud, the unhappy creature turned away.

Rose decided to consult Harry, and had taken up the same pen, and laid it down again fifty times, when Oliver entered the room.

"I have seen the gentleman," he said, "the gentleman who was so good to me — Mr Brownlow. I couldn't speak to him, for he didn't see me — I'm going there directly!"

"Quick!" said Rose. "Tell them to fetch a hackney-coach, and be ready to go with me. I will take you there directly."

When they arrived Rose asked to see Mr Brownlow, leaving Oliver in the coach.

Rose related all that had befallen Oliver since he left Mr Brownlow's house, concluding with the assurance that his only sorrow had been not being able to meet with his former benefactor and friend.

Whilst Oliver and Mrs Bedwin were reunited, Rose told Mr Brownlow Nancy's story.

A meeting soon followed, between Rose and Mrs Maylie, Mr Brownlow and Dr Losberne, who had been advised of all that had taken place.

"It is quite clear," said Mr Brownlow, "that we shall have extreme difficulty in getting to the bottom of this mystery, unless we can bring this man Monks upon his knees. That can only be done when he is not surrounded by these people. But before we can resolve upon any course of action, it will be necessary to see the girl, to ascertain whether she will point out this Monks. She cannot be seen until next Sunday night; this is Tuesday. I suggest that in the meantime we remain perfectly quiet, and keep these matters secret even from Oliver himself."

The clock chimed three-quarters past eleven as two figures emerged on London Bridge. One was that of a woman, who looked eagerly about her; the other was that of a man, who slunk along in the deepest shadow, never allowing himself to gain upon her footsteps. At nearly the centre of the bridge she stopped. The man stopped too.

The hour had not struck two minutes when a young lady, accompanied by a grey-haired gentleman, alighted from a hackney-carriage. They had scarcely set foot upon the bridge when the girl started, and immediately made towards them.

"Not here," said Nancy hurriedly. "Come down the steps yonder."

The man followed them and, scarcely breathing, listened attentively.

"I tell you that we propose to extort the secret from this man Monks," said Mr Brownlow. "He must be delivered up by you."

"And what of the others?" asked Nancy.

"If the truth is forced from Monks," Mr Brownlow replied, "they shall go scot free."

Nancy proceeded to describe the public-house and the night and hour on which Monks was most in the habit of frequenting it.

"He is tall," said the girl, "and a strongly made man, but not stout. His lips are often discoloured and disfigured; for he has desperate fits, and sometimes even bites his hands and covers them with wounds. Upon his throat there is —"

"A broad red mark, like a burn or scald!" cried the gentleman.

"How's this!" said the girl. "You know him!"

"I think I do," said the gentleman. "We shall see."

With that, Mr Brownlow and Rose left for their carriage, and Nancy hurried off into the shadows.

Fagin's spy darted away and made for the Jew's house.

The spy told Fagin and Sikes all that he had heard on the bridge, and immediately Sikes rushed out into the silent street.

The robber held his headlong course, nor muttered a word, nor relaxed a muscle, until he reached his own door. Entering his room, he double-locked the door, and drew back the curtain of the bed.

Nancy was lying upon it.

"Get up!" said the man.

"Bill," said the girl, "why do you look like that at me?"

The robber sat regarding her with dilated nostrils and heaving breast; and then, grasping her by the head and throat, dragged her into the middle of the room, and placed his heavy hand upon her mouth.

"You she-devil!" he said. "You were watched tonight; every word you said was heard."

The housebreaker grasped his pistol, and he beat it twice, with all the force he could summon, upon the upturned face that almost touched his own.

Nancy staggered and fell, nearly blinded with the blood that rained down from a deep gash in her forehead.

It was a ghastly figure to look upon. The murderer, staggering backwards to the wall, and shutting out the sight with his hand, seized a heavy club and struck her down.


The twilight was beginning to close in when Mr Brownlow alighted from a hackney-coach at his own door. A sturdy man got out of the coach and stationed himself on one side of the steps, while another man stood upon the other side. They helped out a third man, and hurried him into the house. This man was Monks.

"This is pretty treatment, sir," said Monks, "from my father's oldest friend."

"It is because I was your father's oldest friend that I am moved to treat you gently now," returned Mr Brownlow. "Yes, Edward Leeford, even now. You have a brother."

"I have no brother," replied Monks. "I was an only child."

"I know that of the wretched marriage into which family pride forced your unhappy father, you were the sole issue," said Mr Brownlow. "But I also know that your parents separated, and, when they had been separated for some time, your father fell among new friends, a naval officer whose wife had died and left him with two children. They were both daughters; one a beautiful creature of nineteen, the other a mere child. As the old officer knew your father more and more, he grew to love him. His daughter did the same. The end of a year found him contracted, solemnly contracted, to that daughter; the object of the first, true, ardent, only passion of a guileless untried girl. At length one of the rich relations, to strengthen whose interest your father had been sacrificed in marriage, died, and left your father some money. It was necessary that he should immediately repair for Rome, where this man had died, leaving his affairs in great confusion. He went; was seized with mortal illness there; was followed by your mother. He died the day after her arrival, leaving no will — *no will* — so the whole property fell to her and you.

"Before he went abroad," said Mr Brownlow, "he came to me, and left with me a likeness of this girl he had left behind. He confided in me his intention to settle on his wife and you a portion of the money, then flee the country with the poor girl. Alas, I never saw him more.

"When your brother was rescued by me, his strong resemblance to this picture struck me with astonishment," Mr Brownlow went on. "You *have* a brother; you know it, and him. There was a will, which your mother destroyed, leaving the secret to you at her own death. You repaired to the place of his birth. There existed proofs of his birth and parentage. The proofs were destroyed by you. Unworthy son, coward, liar — you, who hold your councils with thieves and murderers in dark rooms at night — you, whose plots and wiles have brought a violent death upon the head of one worth millions such as you — you, Edward Leeford, do you still brave me?"

"No, no, no!" returned the coward.

"But this is only a partial disclosure of your secrets," replied Mr Brownlow. "Will you now disclose the whole?"

"Yes, I will."

"Set your hand to a statement of truth and facts, and repeat it before witnesses?"

"That I promise, too."

While Monks was pacing up and down, meditating with dark and evil looks on this proposal, the door was unlocked and Mr Losberne entered the room in violent agitation.

"Sikes will be taken!" he cried. "He will be taken tonight!"

"The Jew," said Mr Brownlow; "what of him?"

"He will be. They're sure of him."

Near to that part of the Thames where the buildings on the banks are the dirtiest and the vessels on the river blackest, there exists the filthiest, strangest, the most extraordinary of the many localities that are hidden in London, wholly unknown, even by name, to the great mass of inhabitants.

In such a neighbourhood stands Jacob's Island, surrounded by a muddy ditch eight or six feet deep, known in these days as Folly Ditch.

It was here, to a deserted, ruinous house, that Sikes went for cover and protection, for Toby Crackit and some of his acquaintances were hiding there.

Suddenly Crackit pointed to the window. There were lights gleaming below, voices in loud and earnest conversation, the tramp of hurried footsteps. Then came a loud knocking at the door, and a hoarse murmur from a multitude of angry voices.

"The tide," cried the murderer, "the tide was in as I

came up. Give me a rope, a long rope. They're all in front. I may drop into the Folly Ditch and clear off that way." Sikes, hastily selecting the longest and strongest cord, hurried up to the house-top.

The water was out, and the ditch a bed of mud.

The crowd was hushed, doubtful of his purpose; but the instant they perceived it, they raised a cry of triumphant execration. Again and again it rose. It seemed as though the whole city had poured its population out to curse him.

The man had shrunk down, quelled by the ferocity of the crowd, and the impossibility of escape; but suddenly he sprung upon his feet, determined to make one last effort for his life by dropping into the ditch, and endeavouring to creep away in the darkness and confusion.

Roused into new strength and energy, he set his foot against the stack of chimneys, fastened one end of the rope tightly round it, and with the other made a strong running noose by the aid of his hands and teeth. He could let himself down by the cord to within less distance of the ground than his own height, and had his knife ready in his hand to cut it then and drop.

At the very instant when he brought the loop over his head previous to slipping it beneath his arm-pits — at that very instant the murderer uttered a yell of terror.

"Her eyes again!" he cried, in an unearthly screech.

Staggering as if struck by lightning, he lost his balance and tumbled over the parapet. The noose was at his neck. It ran up with his weight, tight as a bowstring, and swift as the arrow it speeds. He fell for five-and-thirty feet. There was a sudden jerk, a terrific convulsion of the limbs; and there he hung, with the open knife clenched in his stiffening hand.

The old chimney quivered with the shock, but stood it bravely. The murderer swung lifeless against the wall.

Two days later, Oliver found himself in a hotel room in his native town with Mrs Maylie and Rose.

That night Mr Brownlow entered with a man whom they told him was his brother, and it was the man he had met at the market-town, and seen with Fagin at the window.

"This child," said Mr Brownlow, drawing Oliver to him, "is your half-brother; the illegitimate son of your father, my dear friend Edwin Leeford, by poor young Agnes Fleming, who died in giving him birth."

"Yes," said Monks, "that is their child."

Monks revealed the story of how his own mother, hearing that her husband was ill, had gone to him, and discovered a package and a will. The will left Monks and his mother an annuity, but the bulk of his property he divided into two equal portions — one for Agnes Fleming, and the other for their child.

"My mother," said Monks, "did what a woman should have done — she burnt the will. And when she died, I promised that if the child crossed my path, I would hunt it down."

"And the locket?" said Mr Brownlow.

"I bought it from the woman who stole it from the nurse, who stole it from the corpse," answered Monks. "It's at the bottom of the river."

"The father of the unhappy Agnes had *two* daughters," said Mr Brownlow. "What was the fate of the other — the child?"

Monks explained that when the father died, the child was taken in by cottagers who reared it as their own. A widow lady saw the girl by chance, pitied her, and took her home.

"Do you see her now?" asked Mr Brownlow.

"Yes, leaning on your arm."

"But not the less my niece," cried Mrs Maylie, holding

the fainting girl in her arms, "not the less my dearest child. Come, come, my love, remember who this is who waits to clasp you in his arms, poor child! See here look, look, my dear."

"Not aunt," cried Oliver, throwing his arms about her neck; "I'll never call her aunt — sister, my own dear sister, that something taught my heart to love so dearly from the first! Rose, dear, darling Rose!"

Let the tears which fell, and the broken words which were exchanged in the long close embrace between the orphans, be sacred. A father, sister and mother were gained and lost in that one moment. Joy and grief were mingled. But there were no bitter tears, for even grief itself arose so softened, and clothed in such sweet and tender recollections, that it became a solemn pleasure, and lost all character of pain.

They were a long, long time alone. A soft tap at the door at length announced that someone was without. Oliver opened it and gave place to Harry Maylie.

When the two came out again, they were engaged.

The court was paved, from floor to roof, with human faces. Inquisitive and eager eyes peered from every inch of space. All looks were fixed upon one man — the Jew.

At length there was a cry of silence, and a breathless look from all towards the door. The jury returned, and passed him close. Perfect stillness ensued – not a rustle — not a breath — Guilty!

The judge assumed the black cap. The address was solemn and impassive; the sentence fearful to hear.

Fagin was led away to one of the condemned cells, and left there — alone.

It was not until the night of the last awful day, that a withering sense of his desperate state came in its full intensity upon his blighted soul; not that he had ever held any defined or positive hope of mercy, but that he had never been able to consider more than the dim probability of dying so soon.

He cowered down upon his stone bed, and thought of the past.

The space before the prison was cleared, and a few strong barriers, painted black, had been already thrown across the road to break the pressure of the expected crowd when Mr Brownlow and Oliver presented an order of admission to the prisoner.

The condemned criminal was seated on his bed, rocking himself from side to side, with a countenance more like that of a snared beast than the face of a man. His mind was evidently wandering to his old life.

"Here," said the turnkey, "here's somebody wants to see you. Fagin, Fagin! Are you a man?"

"I shan't be long," replied the Jew. As he spoke he caught sight of Oliver and Mr Brownlow. Shrinking to the farthest corner of the seat, he demanded to know what they wanted there.

"You have some papers," said Mr Brownlow, "which were placed in your hands by Monks. You know that Sikes is dead, that Monks has confessed, that there is no hope of further gain. Where are those papers?"

"The papers," said the Jew, drawing Oliver towards him, "are in a canvas bag, in a hole a little way up the chimney in the top front room."

"You had better leave him now, sir," said the turnkey, and the door of the cell was opened.

Before three months had passed, Rose Fleming and Harry Maylie were married and Mrs Maylie took up her abode with her son and daughter-in-law.

It appeared that if the property remaining in the custody of Monks were equally divided between himself and Oliver, it would yield, to each, little more than three thousand pounds.

Monks, still bearing the assumed name, retired with his portion to a distant part of the New World, where, having quickly squandered it, he once more fell into his old courses, and, after undergoing a long confinement for some fresh act of fraud, sank under an attack of his old disorder, and died in prison.

Mr Brownlow adopted Oliver as his own son, removing with him and the old housekeeper to within a mile of his dear friends.

Within the altar of the old church there stands a white marble table, which bears as yet but one word — "Agnes!" There is no coffin in that tomb; but, if the spirits of the dead ever come back to earth to visit spots hallowed by the love of those whom they knew in life, I believe that the shade of Agnes sometimes hovers round that solemn nook. I believe it none the less because that nook is in a church, and she was weak and erring.

# Nicholas Nickleby

# Introducing Mr Ralph Nickleby

Mr Ralph Nickleby was not what you would call a merchant: neither was he a banker, nor an attorney, nor a special pleader, nor a notary. He was certainly not a tradesman, and still less could he lay any claim to the title of a professional gentleman. Nevertheless, as he lived in a spacious house in Golden Square, displaying the word 'Office', it was clear that Mr Ralph Nickleby did, or pretended to do, business of some kind; and the fact was abundantly demonstrated by the attendance, between the hours of half-past nine and five, of a sallow-faced man in rusty brown, who sat upon an uncommonly hard stool in a species of butler's pantry at the end of the passage, and always had a pen behind his ear when he answered the bell. This clerk was a tall man of middle-age with two goggle eyes, and a suit of clothes much the worse for wear, and very much too small.

His name was Newman Noggs and he had kept his horses and hounds once, but he squandered his money, invested it anyhow, borrowed at interest, and in short made first a thorough fool of himself, and then a beggar.

Newman Noggs, being utterly destitute, served Ralph Nickleby for rather less than the usual wages of a boy of thirteen; and his eccentric taciturnity rendered him an especially valuable person in a place where much business was done, of which it was desirable no mention should be made out of doors.

"Ah! Newman," said Mr Nickleby, looking up from his desk. "The letter about the mortgage has come, has it? I thought it would."

"Wrong," replied Newman.

"What *has* come, then?" inquired Mr Nickleby.

"This," said Newman, drawing a sealed letter slowly from his pocket. "Post-mark, Strand, black wax, black

63

border, woman's hand, C. N. in the corner."

"Black wax," said Mr Nickleby, glancing at the letter. "I know something of that hand, too. Newman, I shouldn't be surprised if my brother were dead."

Mr Nickleby snatched the letter from his assistant, opened and read it.

"It is as I expected, Newman," said Mr Nickleby. "He is dead!"

"Children alive?" inquired Noggs.

"Why, that's the very thing," replied Mr Nickleby. "They are both alive.

"And the widow, too," added Mr Nickleby, "and all three in London, confound them; all three here, Newman."

Later, Mr Nickleby made his way to the Strand, and referring to his letter to ascertain the number of the house he wanted, stopped at a private door about half-way down that crowded thoroughfare.

Mr Nickleby gave a double knock, which was answered by a servant girl.

Ralph walked in. "Is Mrs La what's-her-name at home?"

"Creevy – La Creevy," replied a voice, as a yellow head-dress bobbed over the bannisters.

"I infer that the floor above belongs to you, ma'am?" said Mr Nickleby.

Yes it did, Miss La Creevy replied. The upper part of the house belonged to her, and as she had no necessity for the rooms just then, she was in the habit of letting them. Indeed, there was a lady from the country and her two children in them.

Climbing up a perpendicular flight, Mr Ralph Nickleby stopped on the landing, when he was overtaken by the handmaid.

"What name?" said the girl.

"Nickleby," replied Ralph.

"Oh! Mrs Nickleby," said the girl, throwing open the

door, "here's Mr Nickleby."

A lady in deep mourning rose, but, incapable of advancing to meet him, leant upon the arm of a slight but very beautiful girl of about seventeen, who had been sitting by her. A youth, who appeared a year or two older, stepped forward and saluted Ralph as his uncle.

"You are Nicholas, I suppose?" growled Ralph.

"That is my name, sir," replied the youth.

"I hoped," faltered Mrs Nickleby, "that you might have an opportunity of doing something for your brother's children. It was his dying wish that I should appeal to you on their behalf."

"Well, well," said Ralph. "Have you ever done anything, sir?" turning to his nephew.

"No," replied Nicholas, bluntly.

"Are you willing to work, sir?"

"Of course I am," replied Nicholas haughtily.

Mr Ralph Nickleby took a newspaper from his pocket, and looking for a short time among the advertisements, read as follows:

"EDUCATION. – At Mr Wackford Squeers's Academy, Dotheboys Hall, at the delightful village of Dotheboys, near Greta Bridge in Yorkshire. Youth are boarded, clothed, booked, furnished with pocket-money, provided with all necessaries, instructed in all languages, living and dead, mathematics, orthography, geometry, astronomy, trigonometry, the use of the globes, algebra, single stick (if required), writing, arithmetic, fortification, and every other branch of classical literature. Terms, twenty guineas per annum. No extras, no vacations, and diet unparalleled. Mr Squeers is in town, and attends daily, from one till four, at the Saracen's Head, Snow Hill. N.B. An able assistant wanted. Annual salary £5. A Master of Arts would be preferred."

"There," said Ralph. "Let him get that situation, and his

fortune is made."

"But the salary is so small, and it is such a long way off, uncle!" faltered Kate.

"I say," repeated Ralph, tartly, "let him get that situation, and his fortune is made."

"If I am fortunate enough to be appointed to this post, sir, for which I am so imperfectly qualified, what will become of those I leave behind?" asked Nicholas.

"Your mother and sister, sir," replied Ralph, "will be provided for."

"Then," said Nicholas, starting gaily up, and wringing his uncle's hand, "I am ready to do anything you wish me. Let us try our fortune with Mr Squeers at once; he can but refuse."

"He won't do that," said Ralph.

Nicholas having carefully copied the address of Mr Squeers, the uncle and nephew issued forth together in quest of that accomplished gentleman; Nicholas firmly persuading himself that he had done his relative great injustice in disliking him at first sight, and Mrs Nickleby being at some pains to inform her daughter that she was sure he was a much more kindly disposed person than he seemed, which Miss Nickleby dutifully remarked he might very easily be.

## Mr Wackford Squeers

Mr Squeers's appearance was not prepossessing. He had but one eye, and the popular prejudice runs in favour of two. The eye he had was unquestionably useful, but decidedly not ornamental, being of a greenish grey, and in shape resembling the fanlight of a street door. The blank side of his face was much wrinkled and puckered up, which gave him a very sinister appearance, especially when he smiled, at which times his expression bordered closely on the villainous. His hair was very flat and shiny, save at the ends, where it was brushed stiffly up from a low protruding forehead, which assorted well with his harsh voice and coarse manner. He was about two or three and fifty, and a trifle below the middle size. He wore a white neckerchief with long ends, and a suit of scholastic black, but his coat sleeves being a great deal too long, and his trousers a great deal too short, he appeared ill at ease in his clothes.

"How do you do, sir?" said Squeers.

"Perhaps you recollect me?" said Ralph, looking narrowly at the schoolmaster.

"You paid me a small account at each of my half-yearly visits to town, for some years, I think, sir," replied Squeers.

"I did," rejoined Ralph.

"For the parents of a boy named Dorker, who unfortunately —"

"— unfortunately died at Dotheboys Hall," said Ralph, finishing the sentence.

"And now," said Ralph, "we had better transact our business. You have advertised for an able assistant, sir?"

"Precisely so," said Squeers.

"Here he is," said Ralph. "My nephew Nicholas, hot from school, with everything he learnt there fermenting in his head, and nothing fermenting in his pocket, is just the man you want."

"I am afraid," said Squeers, "I am afraid the young man won't suit me."

"Let me have two words with you," suggested Ralph.

The two words were had apart, and in a couple of minutes Mr Wackford Squeers announced that Mr Nicholas Nickleby was from that moment first assistant master at Dotheboys Hall.

## The Arrival

The school was a long cold-looking house, one storey high, with a few straggling outbuildings behind, and a barn and stable adjoining. It was dark when Nicholas arrived with Mr Squeers. Presently a tall lean boy, with a lantern in his hand, issued forth.

"Is that you, Smike?" cried Squeers.

"Yes, sir," replied the boy.

Mr Squeers, having bolted the door, ushered Nicholas into a small parlour scantily furnished with a few chairs and a couple of tables.

A female bounced into the room, and seizing Mr Squeers by the throat gave him two loud kisses. The lady, who was of a large raw-boned figure, was about half a head taller than Mr Squeers.

"This is the new young man, my dear."

"Oh," replied Mrs Squeers, nodding her head at Nicholas, and eyeing him coldly from top to toe.

A young servant girl brought in a Yorkshire pie and some cold beef, and Smike appeared with a jug of ale.

Nicholas considered the boy more attentively, and was surprised to observe the extraordinary mixture of garments which formed his dress. Although he could not have been less than eighteen or nineteen years old, and was tall for that age, he wore a skeleton suit, such as is usually put upon very little boys, and which, though most absurdly short in the arms and legs, was quite wide enough for his attenuated frame. He had a very large pair of boots, too patched and tattered for a beggar. God knows how long he had been there, but he still wore the same linen which he had first taken down; for round his neck was a tattered child's frill, only half concealed by a coarse man's neckerchief. He was lame; and as he feigned to be busy in arranging the table, glanced at the letters with a look so

keen, and yet so dispirited and hopeless, that Nicholas could hardly bear to watch him.

"Have you – did anybody – has nothing been heard – about me?" he asked Squeers.

"Not a word," resumed Squeers, "and never will be. Now, this is a pretty sort of thing, isn't it, that you should have been left here all these years and no money paid after the first six – nor no notice taken, nor no clue to be got who you belong to?"

"How's the steak, Squeers?" said Mrs S.

"Tender as a lamb," replied Squeers. "Have a bit."

"I couldn't eat a morsel," replied his wife. "What'll the young man take, my dear?"

"I'll take a little of the pie, if you please," replied Nicholas. "A very little, for I'm not hungry."

"Well, it's a pity to cut the pie if you're not hungry, isn't it?" said Mrs Squeers.

"Whatever you please," replied Nicholas abstractedly.

At length Mr Squeers yawned and opined that it was high time to go to bed.

Nicholas, being left alone, sat himself down in a chair and mentally resolved that, come what might, he would endeavour for a time to bear whatever wretchedness might be in store for him, and that, remembering the helplessness of his mother and sister, he would give his uncle no plea for deserting them in their need. He even hoped that affairs at Dotheboys Hall might yet prove better than they promised.

He was preparing for bed when a sealed letter fell from his coat pocket.

It was directed to himself, was written upon very dirty paper, and in such cramped and crippled writing as to be almost illegible. After great difficulty he contrived to read as follows:

"My dear young Man.

"If ever you want a shelter in London, I live at the sign of the Crown, in Silver Street, Golden Square. You can come at night. Excuse errors.           NEWMAN NOGGS."

After he had folded this letter and placed it in his pocket-book, Nicholas Nickleby's eyes were dimmed with a moisture that might have been taken for tears.

## At Dotheboys Hall

Mr and Mrs Squeers viewed the boys as their natural enemies; and considered that their business and profession was to get as much from every boy as could be screwed out of him.

"There," said the schoolmaster as they stepped in together; "this is our shop, Nickleby."

The pupils – the young noblemen! How the last faint traces of hope, the remotest glimmering of any good to be derived from his efforts in this den, faded from the mind of Nicholas as he looked in dismay around! Pale and haggard faces, lank and bony figures, children with the countenances of old men, deformities with irons upon their limbs, boys of stunted growth, and others whose long meagre legs would hardly bear their stooping bodies, all crowded on the view together; there were the bleared eye, the hare-lip and crooked foot, and every ugliness or distortion that told of unnatural aversion conceived by parents for their offspring, or of young lives which, from the earliest dawn of infancy, had been one horrible endurance of cruelty and neglect. With every kindly sympathy and affection blasted in its birth, with every young and healthy feeling flogged and starved down, with every revengeful passion that can fester in swollen hearts, eating its evil way to their core in silence, what an incipient hell was breeding there!

There was none of the noise and clamour of a school-room, none of its boisterous play or hearty mirth. The children sat crouching and shivering together, and seemed to lack the spirit to move about.

A few slovenly lessons were performed through the day; and then Squeers retired to his fireside, leaving Nicholas to take care of the boys in the school-room, which was very cold, and where a meal of bread and cheese was served out shortly after dark.

Nicholas sat down, so depressed and self-degraded by the consciousness of his position that if death could have come upon him at that time he would have been almost happy to meet it. The cruelty of which he had been an unwilling witness that day, the coarse and ruffianly behaviour of Squeers, the filthy place, the sights and sounds about him, all contributed to this state of feeling.

But the resolution he had formed on the preceding night remained undisturbed. He had written to his mother and sister, announcing the safe conclusion of his journey, and saying as little about Dotheboys Hall, and saying that little as cheerfully, as he possibly could. He hoped that by remaining where he was, he might do some good, even there, and at all events others depended too much on his uncle's favour to admit of awakening his wrath.

All at once he encountered the upturned face of Smike. He had paused to steal a look at Nicholas, and when he saw that he was observed, shrunk back as if expecting a blow.

"You need not fear me," said Nicholas kindly. "Are you cold?"

"I am not cold," replied Smike quickly. "I am used to it."

Nicholas could not help exclaiming, "Poor fellow!"

If he had struck the drudge, he would have slunk away without a word. But now he burst into tears.

"Oh dear, oh dear!" he cried, covering his face with his

cracked and horny hands. "My heart will break. It will, it will."

The bell rang and the boy crept away as if anxious to avoid notice. It was with a heavy heart that Nicholas soon afterwards – no, not retired; there was no retirement there – followed – to his dirty and crowded dormitory.

## Smike Finds a Friend

The wretched creature, Smike, since the night Nicholas had spoken kindly to him in the school-room, had followed him to and fro with an ever restless desire to serve or help him, content only to be near him. He was an altered being; he had an object now, and that object was to show his attachment to the only person – that person a stranger – who had treated him like a human creature.

But upon this poor being all the spleen and ill-humour of Squeers that could not be vented on Nicholas were unceasingly bestowed. Drudgery would have been nothing – he was well used to that. Buffetings inflicted without cause would have been equally a matter of course, for to them also he had served a long and weary apprenticeship; but it was no sooner observed that he had become attached to Nicholas than stripes and blows, stripes and blows, morning, noon, and night, were his only portion. Squeers was jealous of the influence which his man had so soon acquired, and Smike paid for both. Nicholas saw it, and ground his teeth at every repetition of the savage and cowardly attack.

"But for you," said the outcast, "I should die. They would kill me."

"You will do better, poor fellow," replied Nicholas, "when I am gone."

"Tell me," said the boy imploringly. "Oh do tell me, *will* you go – *will* you?"

"I shall be driven to that at last!" said Nicholas. "The world is before me, after all."

"Should I ever meet you there?" demanded the boy.

"You would," replied Nicholas, "and I would help and aid you, and not bring fresh sorrow on you as I have done here."

## Smike Runs Away

"Smike!" shouted Squeers.

"He is not here, sir," replied Nicholas.

There was a general hum in the midst of which one shrill voice was heard to say, "Please, sir, I think Smike's run away, sir."

"If I catch him," said Squeers, "I'll only stop short of flaying him alive, I give you notice, boys."

After a very hasty breakfast, Squeers started forth in the ponychaise, intent upon discovery and vengeance.

Another day came, and Nicholas was scarcely awake when he heard the wheels of a chaise approaching the house. It stopped. The voice of Mrs Squeers was heard, and in exultation, ordering a glass of spirits for somebody, which was in itself a sufficient sign that something extraordinary had happened. Nicholas hardly dared to look out of the window, but he did so, and the very first object that met his eyes was the wretched Smike.

To all appearance more dead than alive, he was brought in the house and securely locked up in a cellar, until such time as Mr Squeers should operate upon him in presence of the assembled school.

The news that Smike had been caught and brought back in triumph, ran like wild-fire through the hungry community, and expectation was on tiptoe all the morning. On tiptoe it was destined to remain, however, until afternoon; when Squeers, having refreshed himself with

his dinner, made his appearance with a countenance of portentous import, and a fearful instrument of flagellation, strong, supple, wax-ended, and new – in short, purchased that morning expressly for the occasion.

"Nickleby! To your desk, sir."

Squeers left the room, and shortly afterwards returned dragging Smike by the collar.

Squeers caught the boy firmly in his grip; one desperate cut had fallen on his body – he was wincing from the lash and uttering a scream of pain – it was raised again, and again about to fall – when Nicholas Nickleby suddenly starting up, cried, "Stop!" in a voice that made the rafters ring.

"Sit down, beggar!" screamed Squeers, almost beside himself with rage, and seizing Smike as he spoke.

"Wretch," rejoined Nicholas, fiercely, "touch him at your peril!"

"Stand back," cried Squeers, brandishing his weapon.

"I have a long series of insults to avenge," said Nicholas, flushed with passion; "and my indignation is aggravated by the dastardly cruelties practised on helpless infancy in this foul den. Have a care; for if you do raise the devil within me, the consequences shall fall heavily upon your own head."

Squeers spat upon him, and struck him across the face. Nicholas sprang upon him, and beat the ruffian till he roared for mercy.

Having brought affairs to this happy termination, and ascertained that Squeers was only stunned, and not dead, Nicholas left, packed up a few clothes and marched boldly out by the front door.

He did not travel far. He stumbled upon an empty barn within a couple of hundred yards of the roadside, in a warm corner of which he stretched his weary limbs, and soon fell asleep.

When he awoke the next morning, he sat up, rubbed his eyes and stared at some motionless object which seemed to be stationed within a few yards in front of him.

It was Smike.

"May I – may I go with you?" asked Smike, timidly. "I will be your faithful hard-working servant, I will, indeed. I want no clothes," added the poor creature, drawing his rags together; "these will do very well. I only want to be near you."

"And you shall," cried Nicholas. "And the world shall deal by you as it does by me, till one or both of us shall quit it for a better. Come!"

## Nicholas Seeks his Fortune

It was a cold, dry, foggy morning in early spring.

"Now listen to me, Smike," said Nicholas, as they trudged with stout hearts onwards. "We are bound for Portsmouth. Portsmouth is a seaport town, and if no other employment is to be obtained, I should think we might get on board some ship. I am young and active, and could be useful in many ways. So could you."

"I am very willing," said Smike, brightening up.

They walked many miles that day and twilight had closed in when they turned off the path to the door of a roadside inn, yet twelve miles short of Portsmouth.

A glance at the toil-worn face of Smike determined Nicholas, so without any further consideration he made up his mind to stay where he was.

The landlord led them into the kitchen.

"What can you give us for supper?" was Nicholas's natural question.

"I'll tell you what," rejoined the landlord. "There's a gentleman in the parlour that's ordered a hot beef-steak pudding and potatoes at nine. There's more of it than he can manage, and I have very little doubt that if I ask leave, you can sup with him. I'll do that in a minute."

"No, no," said Nicholas, detaining him. "You see that I am travelling in a very humble manner, I think, that the gentleman may not relish my company."

"Lord love you," said the landlord, "it's only Mr Crummles; *he* isn't particular."

He had already thrown open the door of the room; into which Nicholas, followed by Smike straightway repaired.

"Mr Vincent Crummels," said the landlord with an air of great deference. "This is the young gentleman."

Mr Vincent Crummels received Nicholas with an inclination of the head.

"What's the matter?" he asked Nicholas.

Nicholas could not refrain from smiling at the abruptness of the question, but owned that he was under some apprehension lest he might not succeed in the object which had brought him to that part of the country.

"And what's that?" asked the manager.

"Getting something to do which will keep me and my poor fellow-traveller in the common necessaries of life," said Nicholas.

"What's to be got to do at Portsmouth more than anywhere else?" asked Mr Vincent Crummles.

"There are many vessels leaving the port, I suppose," replied Nicholas. "I shall try for a berth in some ship or other. There is meat and drink there, at all events. I can rough it, I believe, as well as most men of my age and previous habits."

"You need be able to," said the manager, "if you go on board ship; but you won't."

"Why not?"

"Because there's not a skipper or mate that would think you worth your salt, when he could get a practised hand," replied the manager.

There was a pause. Nicholas gazed ruefully at the fire.

"Does no other profession occur at you, which a young man of your figure and address could take up easily, and see the world to advantage in?" asked the manager.

"No," said Nicholas.

"The theatrical profession," said Mr Vincent Crummles. "I am in the theatrical profession myself, my wife is in the theatrical profession, my children are in the theatrical profession. I'll bring you out, and your friend too. Say the word. I want a novelty."

Nicholas hesitated.

"You can be useful to us in a hundred ways," said Mr Crummles.

"What should I get?" inquired Nicholas. "Could I live by it?"

"Live by it!" said the manager. "Like a prince! You'd make a pound a week!"

Nicholas shrugged his shoulders, but sheer destitution was before him; and if he could summon fortitude to undergo the extremes of want and hardship, for what had he rescued his helpless charge if it were only to bear as hard a fate as that from which he had wrested him? What if he went abroad, and his mother or Kate were to die the while?

Without more deliberation he hastily declared that it was a bargain, and gave Mr Vincent Crummles his hand upon it.

Giving Smike his arm, Nicholas accompanied Mr Crummles up High Street on their way to the theatre.

"Here we are," said Mr Crummles.

It was not very light, but Nicholas found himself close to the first entrance on the prompter's side, among bare walls, dusty scenes, mildewed clouds, heavily daubed draperies, and dirty floors. He looked about him; ceiling, pit, boxes, gallery, orchestra, fittings, and decorations of every kind – all looked coarse, cold, gloomy, and wretched.

"Is this a theatre?" whispered Smike, in amazement; "I thought it was a blaze of light and finery."

"Why, so it is," replied Nicholas, hardly less surprised; "but not by day, Smike – not by day."

"Let me introduce Mrs Vincent Crummles."

"I am glad to see you, sir," said Mrs Vincent Crummles, in a sepulchral voice.

Then there bounded on to the stage a little girl in a dirty white frock with tucks up to the knees, short trousers, sandaled shoes, white bodice, pink gauze bonnet, green veil and curl-papers.

"This, sir," said Mr Vincent Crummles, bringing the maiden forward, "this is the infant phenomenon – Miss Ninetta Crummles."

"Your daughter?" inquired Nicholas.

"My daughter – my daughter," replied Mr Vincent Crummles; "the idol of every place we go into, sir. We have had complimentary letters about this girl, sir, from the nobility and gentry of almost every town in England."

"May I ask how old she is?" inquired Nicholas.

"She is ten years of age, sir."

"Dear me!" said Nicholas, "it's extraordinary."

It was; for the infant phenomenon, though of short stature, had a comparatively aged countenance. She had been kept up late every night, and put upon an unlimited allowance of gin-and-water from infancy, to prevent her growing tall.

"Mr Folair," said the manager, presenting him to Nicholas.

"Happy to know you, sir." Mr Folair touched the brim of his hat with his forefinger, and then shook hands.

The gentleman was a dark-complexioned man,

inclining indeed to sallow, with long thick black hair, and whiskers of the same deep shade. His age did not appear to exceed thirty, although many at first sight would have considered him much older, as his face was long and very pale, from the constant application of stage paint.

"Well, Tommy," said this gentleman, "what's the news?"

"A new appearance, that's all," replied Mr Folair, looking at Nicholas.

"Do the honours, Tommy, do the honours."

"This is Mr Lenville, who does our first tragedy," said the pantomimist.

A pretty general muster of the company had by this time taken place; for besides Mr Lenville and his friend Tommy, there was present a slim young gentleman with weak eyes, who played the low-spirited lovers and sang tenor songs, and who had come arm-in-arm with the comic countryman – a man with a turned-up nose, large mouth, broad face, and staring eyes. Making himself very amiable to the infant phenomenon was an inebriated elderly gentleman in the last depths of shabbiness, who played the calm and virtuous old men; and paying especial court to Mrs Crummles was another elderly gentleman, a shade more respectable, who played the irascible old men. Besides these, there was a roving-looking person in a rough great-coat, who strode up and down in front of the lamps, flourishing a dress-cane, and a little group of three or four young men, with lantern jaws and thick eyebrows.

The ladies were gathered in a little knot by themselves round a rickety table. There was Miss Snevellicci, who could do anything from a medley dance to Lacy Macbeth, her friend Miss Ledrook, and Miss Belvawney, who seldom aspired to speaking parts.

"Ladies and gentlemen," said Mr Vincent Crummles, "on Monday morning we shall read a new piece, the name's not known yet, but everybody will have a good part. Nicholas will take care of that."

"Upon my word," said Nicholas, taking the manager aside, "I don't think I can be ready by Monday."

"Pooh, pooh," replied Mr Crummles.

"But really I can't," returned Nicholas; "my invention is not accustomed to these demands."

"Invention! What the devil's that got to do with it!" cried the manager. "Do you understand French? There, just turn that into English, and put your name on the title-page."

Nicholas smiled, and pocketed the play.

## The Play

Nicholas worked away at the piece, which was speedily put into rehearsal, and then worked away at his own part, which he studied with great perseverance and acted – as the whole company said – to perfection. And at length the great day arrived. The crier was sent round in the morning to proclaim the entertainments with sound of bell in all the thoroughfares; extra bills of three feet long by nine inches wide were dispersed in all directions, flung down all the areas, thrust under all the knockers, and developed in all the shops.

At half-past five there was a rush of four people to the gallery-door; at a quarter before six there were at least a dozen; at six o'clock the kicks were terrific; and when the elder master Crummles opened the door, he was obliged to run behind it for his life. Fifteen shillings were taken in the first ten minutes.

At last the orchestra left off, and the curtain rose upon the new piece. The first scene passed off calmly enough, but when Miss Snevellicci went on in the second, accompanied by the phenomenon as child, what a roar of applause broke out!

And when Nicholas came on for his scene with Mrs Crummles, what a clapping of hands there was!

In short, the success both of new piece and new actor was complete, and when Miss Snevellicci was called for at the end of the play, Nicholas led her on, and divided the applause.

The new piece, being a decided hit, was announced for every evening of performance until further notice, and the evenings when the theatre was closed were reduced from three in the week to two. Nor were these the only tokens of extraordinary success; for on the succeeding Saturday Nicholas received no less than thirty shillings.

The unexpected success and favour with which his experiment at Portsmouth had been received induced Mr Crummles to prolong his stay in that town for a fortnight beyond the period he had originally assigned for the duration of his visit, during which time Nicholas personated a vast variety of characters with undiminished success, and attracted so many people to the theatre who had never been seen there before, that a contract was considered by the manager a very promising speculation. Nicholas assenting to the terms proposed, the contract was had, and by it he realized no less a sum than twenty pounds.

Possessed of this unexpected wealth, Nicholas forwarded one half of the sum he had realized to Newman Noggs, entreating him to take an opportunity of handing it to Kate in secret, and conveying to her the warmest assurances of his love and affection. He further entreated that worthy friend to write full particulars of the situation of his mother and sister, and an account of all the grand things that Ralph Nickleby had done for them.

"You are out of spirits," said Smike, on the night after the letter had been despatched.

"I was thinking about my sister, Smike."

"Is she like you?" inquired Smike.

"A great deal handsomer."

"She must be *very* beautiful," said Smike. "Shall I ever see your sister?"

"To be sure," cried Nicholas; "we shall all be together one of these days – when we are rich, Smike."

"How is it that you, who are so kind and good to me, have nobody to be kind to you?" asked Smike.

"Why, it is a long story," replied Nicholas, "and one you would have some difficulty in comprehending, I fear. I have an enemy – he is rich, and not so easily punished as *your* old enemy, Mr Squeers. He is my uncle, but he is a villain, and has done me wrong."

## A Letter for Nicholas

"Well, Smike," said Nicholas one morning, "is there any letter yet?"

"Yes," replied Smike, "I got this one from the post-office."

"From Newman Noggs," said Nicholas.

Newman took upon himself to send back the ten pounds, observing that he had ascertained that neither Mrs Nickleby nor Kate was in actual want of money at the moment, and that a time might shortly come when Nicholas might want it more. He entreated him not to be alarmed at what he was about to say – there was no bad news – they were in good health – but he thought circumstances might occur, or were occurring, which would render it absolutely necessary that Kate should have her brother's protection, and if so, Newman said, he would write to him to that effect.

Nicholas read this passage very often, and the more he thought of it the more he began to fear some treachery upon the part of Ralph. Once or twice he felt tempted to leave for London without an hour's delay, but a little reflection assured him that if such a step were necessary, Newman would have spoken out and told him so at once.

"At all events I should prepare them here for the possiblity of my going away suddenly," said Nicholas.

With the post next morning came a letter from Newman Noggs, very inky, very short, very dirty, very small, and very mysterious, urging Nicholas to return to London instantly; not to lose an instant; to be there that night if possible.

"What can have happened? Smike, my good fellow, here – take my purse. Put our things together, and pay what little debts we owe – quick, and we shall be in time for the morning coach. I will only tell them that we are going, and will return to you immediately."

Everything was soon ready for their departure, and it was not long before they were on the coach and entering London.

Nicholas engaged beds for himself and Smike at the inn where the coach stopped, and left, without the delay of another moment, to the lodgings of Newman Noggs; for his anxiety and impatience had increased with every succeeding minute, and were almost beyond control. But Newman was not there.

Nicholas tried to remain quietly where he was, but he felt so nervous and excited that he could not sit still.

He strolled westward along one of the thoroughfares which lie between Park Lane and Bond Street, past a handsome hotel, before which he stopped mechanically.

Nicholas walked into the coffee-room.

There was a rather noisy party of four gentlemen by the fire-place.

He was half-dozing, when he was startled by the mention of his sister's name. "Little Kate Nickleby" were the words that caught his ear.

What he heard need not be repeated here. Suffice it that

as the wine went round he heard enough to acquaint him with the characters and designs of those whose conversation he overheard; to possess him with the full extent of Ralph's villainy, and the real reason of his own presence being required in London. He heard all this and more. He heard his sister's sufferings derided, and her virtuous conduct jeered at and brutally misconstrued; he heard her name bandied from mouth to mouth, and herself made the subject of coarse and insolent wagers, free speech, and licentious jesting.

## Nicholas Takes Charge

Smike and Newman Noggs, sat before the fire, listening anxiously to every footstep on the stairs, for the approach of Nicholas.

At length a coach was heard to stop, and Newman ran out to light Nicholas up the stairs.

"I know all," said Nicholas; "I have heard a part, and guessed the rest."

Next morning, Nicholas sprang out of bed as the clock struck seven. Calling a hackney-coach he bade the man drive to the direction which Newman had given him on the previous night.

It was not a quarter to eight when they reached Cadogan Place. Nicholas began to fear that no one might be stirring at that early hour, when he was relieved by the sight of a female servant, employed in cleaning the door-steps.

"Say to Miss Nickleby that her brother is here, and in great haste to see her," said Nicholas.

He soon heard a light footstep which he well knew, and before he could advance to meet her, Kate had fallen on his neck and burst into tears.

"I have been so unhappy here, dear brother," sobbed poor Kate; "so very, very, miserable. Do not leave me here, dear Nicholas, or I shall die of a broken heart."

"I will leave you nowhere," answered Nicholas, "never again, Kate."

To the City they went, with all the speed the hackney-coach could make.

Nicholas sent Kate upstairs a few minutes before him, that his appearance might not alarm his mother, then presented himself with much duty and affection. Newman had not been idle, for there was a little cart at the door, and their belongings were hurrying out already.

Having seen everything safely out, discharged the servant, and locked the door, Nicholas jumped into a cabriolet and drove to a place near Golden Square where he had appointed to meet Noggs. It was barely half past nine when he reached the place of meeting.

"Here is the letter for Ralph," said Nicholas, "and here the key."

Newman reached the office, hung his hat on its accustomed peg, laid the letter and key upon the desk, and waited impatiently until Ralph Nickleby should appear. After a few minutes, the well-known creaking of his boots was heard on the stairs, and then the bell rung.

"Any other letters?"

"One." Newman eyed him closely, and laid it on the desk.

Ralph opened the letter, and read as follows: "You are known to me now. There are no reproaches I could heap upon your head which would carry with them one thousandth part of the grovelling shame that this assurance will awaken even in your breast. Your brother's widow and her orphan child spurn the shelter of your roof, and shun you with disgust and loathing. Your kindred renounce you, for they know no shame but the ties of blood which bind them in name with you. You are an old man, and I leave you to the grave. May every recollection of your life cling to

your false heart, and cast their darkness on your death-bed."

## Smike Meets Mrs Nickleby and Kate

Having established his mother and sister in the apartments of the kind-hearted miniature painter again, Nicholas turned his thoughts to poor Smike, who, after breakfasting with Newman Noggs, had remained in a disconsolate state at that worthy creature's lodgings, waiting with much anxiety for further intelligence of his protector.

"I was afraid," said Smike, overjoyed to see his friend again, "that you had fallen into some fresh trouble; the time seemed so long at last, that I almost feared you were lost."

"Lost!" replied Nicholas gaily. "You will not be rid of me so easily, I promise you. But come; my errand here is to take you home."

"Home!" faltered Smike, drawing timidly back.

"Aye," rejoined Nicholas, taking his arm. "Why not?"

"I had such hopes once," said Smike; "day and night, day and night, for many years. I longed for home till I was weary, and pined away with grief, but now —"

"What now, old friend?"

"I could not part from you to go to any home on earth," replied Smike, pressing his hand; "except one, except one. I shall never be an old man; and if your hand placed me in the grave, and I could think before I died that you would come and look upon it sometimes with one of your kind smiles, and in the summer weather, when everything was alive – not dead like me – I could go to that home almost without a tear."

"Why, here's a dismal face for ladies' company – my pretty sister too, whom you have so often asked me about. For shame! for shame!"

So saying, Nicholas took his companion by the arm, and led the way to Miss La Creevy's house.

"And this, Kate," said Nicholas, entering the room where his sister sat alone, "is the faithful friend and affectionate fellow-traveller whom I prepared you to receive."

Poor Smike was bashful and awkward and frightened enough at first, but Kate advanced towards him kindly, and said how anxious she had been to see him after all her brother had told her, and how much she had to thank him for having comforted Nicholas so greatly in their very trying reverses.

Miss La Creevy was very kind too.

At length the door opened again, and a lady in mourning came in. Nicholas kissed her affectionately.

"You are always kind-hearted, and anxious to help the oppressed, my dear mother," said Nicholas, "so you will be favourably disposed towards him, I know."

"I am sure, my dear Nicholas," replied Mrs Nickleby, "any friend of yours has a great claim upon me; there can be no doubt about that."

Thus the little circle remained, on the most amicable and agreeable footing, until the Monday morning, when Nicholas withdrew himself from it for a short time, seriously to reflect upon the state of his affairs, and to determine, if he could, upon some course of life which would enable him to support those who were so entirely dependent upon his exertions.

What could he do? "Egad!" said Nicholas, "I'll try the Register Office."

As Nicholas stopped to look in at the window an old gentleman happened to stop too, a sturdy old fellow in a broad-skirted blue coat, made pretty large, to fit easily; his bulky legs clothed in drab breeches and high gaiters, and his head protected by a low-crowned broad-brimmed white hat. He wore his coat buttoned; and his dimpled double-chin rested in the folds of a white neckerchief. But what principally attracted the attention of Nicholas was the old gentleman's eye – never was such a clear, twinkling, honest, merry, happy eye as that. And there he stood, with such a pleasant smile playing about his mouth that Nicholas would have been content to have stood there and looked at him until evening.

"A great many opportunities here, sir," Nicholas said.

"A great many people willing and anxious to be employed have seriously thought so very often, I dare say," replied the old man. "Poor fellows, poor fellows!"

"I almost hoped – I mean to say, thought – you had some object in consulting those advertisements."

"Ha! ha!" laughed the old gentleman, rubbing his hands and wrists as if he were washing them. "A very natural thought at all events, after seeing me gazing at those bills. I thought the same of you at first, upon my word I did."

"If you had thought so at last, too, sir, you would not have been far from the truth," rejoined Nicholas.

"What's the matter – what is it – how did it all come about?" said the old man, laying his hand on the shoulder of Nicholas, and walking him up the street.

"My father," replied Nicholas.

"Ah!" said the old gentleman quickly. "Bad thing for a young man to lose his father. Widowed mother, perhaps?"

Nicholas sighed.

"Brothers and sisters too – eh?"

"One sister," rejoined Nicholas.

"Don't say another word – not another word," said he. "Come along with me. We mustn't lose a minute."

The old gentleman hurried him along until they at length emerged in a quiet shady little square. Into the oldest and cleanest-looking house of business in the square, he led the way. The only inscription on the door-post was

'Cheeryble Brothers'; from a hasty glance at some packages which were lying about, Nicholas supposed that the Brothers Cheeryble were merchants.

Passing through a warehouse which presented every indication of a thriving business, Mr Cheeryble (for such Nicholas supposed him to be, from the respect which had been shown him by the warehousemen and porters whom they passed) led him into a little partitioned-off counting-house like a large glass case, in which counting-house there sat a fat, elderly, large-faced clerk, with silver spectacles and a powdered head.

"Is my brother in his room, Tim?" said Mr Cheeryble.

"Yes he is, sir," replied the fat clerk.

"Brother Ned," said Mr Cheeryble, "are you busy, my dear brother, or can you spare time for a word or two with me?"

"Brother Charles, my dear fellow," replied a voice from the inside; so like in its tones to that which had just spoken that Nicholas started, and almost thought it was the same. "Don't ask me such a question, but come in directly."

They went in. What was the amazement of Nicholas when his conductor advanced and exchanged a warm greeting with another old gentleman, the very type and model of himself – the same face, the same figure, the same coat, waistcoat, and neckcloth, the same breeches and gaiters.

As they shook each other by the hand, the face of each lighted up by beaming looks of affection, nobody could have doubted their being twin brothers.

"Brother Ned," said Nicholas's friend, "here is a young friend of mine that we must assist."

"It is enough, my dear brother, that you say we should," returned the other. "He *shall* be assisted. What are his necessities, and what does he require? Where is Tim Linkinwater? Let us have him here."

"Stop, stop, stop," said brother Charles, taking the other aside. "I've a plan, my dear brother, I've a plan. Tim is getting old, and Tim has been a faithful servant, brother Ned. If we could lighten Tim's duties, and prevail upon him to go into the country now and then, and sleep in the fresh air, old Tim Linkinwater would grow young again."

The twins pressed each other's hands in silence, and, in his own homely manner, brother Charles related the particulars he had heard from Nicholas. The conversation which ensued was a long one, and when it was over a secret conference of almost equal duration took place between brother Ned and Tim Linkinwater in another room.

"Tim," said brother Charles, "you understand that we have an intention of taking this young gentleman into the counting-house?"

Brother Ned remarked that Tim was aware of that intention, and quite approved of it; and Tim having nodded, and said he did, drew himself up and looked particularly fat and very important.

"And I think, my dear brother," said Nicholas's first friend, "that if we were to let them that little cottage at Bow which is empty, at something under the usual rent, now – eh, brother Ned?"

"For nothing at all," said brother Ned.

And in one short week Nicholas took possession of the stool, and Mrs Nickleby and Kate took possession of the house; and all was hope, bustle, and light-heartedness.

## A Tea Party

Morning came as usual and with it business-hours, and with them Mr Frank Cheeryble, and with him a long train of smiles and welcomes to them from the worthy brothers, and a more grave and clerk-like, but scarcely less hearty

reception, from Mr Timothy Linkinwater.

Frank Cheeryble was a sprightly, good-humoured, pleasant fellow, with much both in his countenance and disposition that reminded Nicholas very strongly of the kind-hearted brothers. His manner was as unaffected as theirs, he was good-looking and intelligent, had a plentiful share of vivacity, and was extremely cheerful.

"Mr Nickleby," said brother Charles, calling him aside later, and taking him kindly by the hand, "I – I – am anxious, my dear sir, to see that you are properly and comfortably settled in the cottage. I wish, too, to see your mother and sister – to know them, Mr Nickleby, and have an opportunity of relieving their minds by assuring them that any trifling service we have been able to do them is a great deal more than repaid by the zeal and ardour you display. Not a word, my dear sir, I beg. Tomorrow is Sunday. I shall make bold to come out at tea-time, and take the chance of finding you at home."

There was a mighty bustle that night, and a vast quantity of preparation.

About six o'clock in the afternoon Mrs Nickleby was thrown into a great flutter of spirits by the long-expected knock at the door, nor was this flutter at all composed by the audible tread of two pair of boots in the passage, which Mrs Nickleby augured, in a breathless state, must be "the two Mr Cheerybles" as it certainly was, though not the two Mrs Nickleby expected, because it was Mr Charles Cheeryble, and his nephew, Mr Frank.

At the tea-table there was plenty of conversation on a great variety of subjects.

After tea there was a walk in the garden. Kate went first, leaning upon her brother's arm, and talking with him and Mr Frank Cheeryble; and Mrs Nickleby and the elder gentleman followed at a short distance. Smike (who, if he had ever been an object of interest in his life, had been one that day) accompanied them, joining sometimes one group and sometimes the other, as brother Charles, laying his hand upon his shoulder, bade him walk with him, or Nicholas, looking smilingly round, beckoned him to come and talk with the old friend who understood him best.

At length the two gentlemen took their leave. There was one circumstance in the leave-taking which occasioned a vast deal of smiling and pleasantry, and that was, that Mr Frank Cheeryble offered his hand to Kate twice over, quite forgetting that he had bade her adieu already.

## Madeline Bray

"I am about to employ you, my dear sir, on a confidential and delicate mission. The object of this mission is a young lady. You accidentally saw a young lady in this room one morning, my dear sir, in a fainting fit. Do you remember? Perhaps you have forgotten —" said Mr Cheeryble.

"Oh no," replied Nicholas, hurriedly. "I – I – remember it very well indeed."

"She is the daughter," said Mr Cheeryble, "of a lady who, when she was a beautiful girl herself, and I was very many years younger, I – it seems a strange word for me to utter now – I loved very dearly."

"My dear brother Ned," continued Mr Cheeryble, "was to have married her sister, but she died. She is dead too now, and has been for many years. She married – her choice; and I wish I could add that her after-life was as happy, as God knows I ever prayed it might be!"

A short silence intervened.

"It will be enough to say that this was not the case – that she was not happy – that they fell into complicated distresses and difficulties – that she came, twelve months before her death, to appeal to my old friendship; sadly changed, sadly altered, broken-spirited from suffering and

97

ill-usage, and almost broken-hearted. In those times this young lady was a mere child. I never saw her again until that morning when you saw her also. Her father lay in some secret place to avoid his creditors, reduced, between sickness and poverty, to the verge of death, and she, a child, who should have blessed a better man, was steadily braving privation, degradation, and everything most terrible to such a young and delicate creature's heart, for the purpose of supporting him."

Then it came out by little and little, how the twins had been revolving in their good old heads plans and schemes for helping this young lady in the most delicate and considerate way, so that her father should not suspect the source whence the aid was derived. They had at last come to the conclusion that the best course would be to make a feint of purchasing her little drawings and ornamental work at a high price, and keeping up a constant demand for the same. It was necessary that somebody should represent the dealer in such commodities, and after great deliberation they had pitched upon Nicholas to support this character.

"Cannot she be persuaded to –" Nicholas hesitated.

"To leave him?" said brother Charles. "Who could entreat a child to desert her parent?"

"Is he kind to her?" said Nicholas. "Does he requite her affection?"

"True kindness, considerate self-denying kindness, is not in his nature," returned Mr Cheeryble. "The mother, although he wounded her from their marriage till her death as cruelly and wantonly as ever man did, never ceased to love him. She commended him on her death-bed to her child's care. Her child has never forgotten it, and never will."

To the row of houses indicated to him by Mr Charles Cheeryble, Nicholas then directed his steps.

Opening the rickety gate Nicholas knocked at the street door with a faltering hand.

Upstairs he went, and into a front room he was shown. Seated at a little table by the window, on which were drawing materials with which she was occupied, sat the beautiful girl who had so engrossed his thoughts since he first saw her, and who seemed now, in his eyes, a thousand times more beautiful.

But how the graces and elegancies which she had dispersed about the poorly-furnished room, went to the heart of Nicholas! Flowers, plant, birds, the harp, the old piano whose notes had sounded so much sweeter in bygone times – how many struggles had it cost her to keep these two last links of that broken chain which bound her yet to home!

It is not to be supposed that he took in everything at one glance, for he had as yet been unconscious of the presence of a sick man propped up with pillows in an easy-chair who, moving restlessly and impatiently in his seat, attracted his attention.

He was scarce fifty, perhaps, but so emaciated as to appear much older. His features presented the remains of a handsome countenance, but one in which the embers of strong and impetuous passions were easier to be traced than any expression which would have rendered a far plainer face much more prepossessing.

"Madeline, who is this – what does anybody want here – who told a stranger we could be seen? What is it?"

By this time Nicholas had recovered sufficient presence of mind to speak for himself, so he said that he had called about a pair of hand-screens, and some painted velvet for an ottoman. He had also to pay for the two drawings, with many thanks, and, advancing to the little table, he laid upon it a bank note, folded in an envelope and sealed.

Madeline was so busily employed in arranging the

pillows that Nicholas could not see her face, but as she stooped he thought he saw a tear fall.

Nicholas bowed low to the young lady and retired.

He heard a light footstep above him as he descended the stairs, and looking round saw that the young lady was standing there, and glancing timidly towards him, seemed to hesitate whether she should call him back or no.

"You have but to hint a wish," said Nicholas fervently, "and I would hazard my life to gratify it."

"You speak hastily, sir."

"Truly and sincerely," rejoined Nicholas, his lips trembling as he formed the words, "if ever man spoke truly yet I am not skilled in disguising my feelings, and if I were, I could not hide my heart from you. Dear madam, as I know your history, and feel as men and angels must who hear and see such things, I do entreat you to believe that I would die to serve you."

She waved her hand, entreating him to be gone, but answered not a word. Nicholas could say no more, and silently withdrew. And thus ended his first interview with Madeline Bray.

## Poor Smike

While Nicholas, absorbed in the one engrossing subject of interest which had recently opened upon him, occupied his leisure hours with thoughts of Madeline Bray, and, in execution of the commissions which the anxiety of Brother Charles on her behalf imposed upon him, saw her again and again, and each time with greater danger to his peace of mind and a more weakening effect upon the lofty resolutions he had formed, Mrs Nickleby and Kate continued to live in peace and quiet, agitated by no other cares than Smike, whose health, long upon the wane, occasioned both them and Nicholas considerable uneasiness, and even alarm.

It was no complaint or murmur on the part of the poor fellow himself that thus disturbed them. Ever eager to be employed in such slight services as he could render, and always anxious to repay his benefactors with cheerful and happy looks, less friendly eyes might have seen in him no cause for any misgiving. But there were times – and often too – when the sunken eye was too bright, the hollow cheek too flushed, the breath too thick and heavy in its course, the frame too feeble and exhausted, to escape their regard and notice.

Nicholas comforted himself with the hope that his poor friend would soon recover. This hope his mother and sister shared with him; and as the object of their joint solicitude seemed to have no uneasiness or despondency for himself, but each day answered with a quiet smile that he felt better than he had upon the day before, their fears abated, and the general happiness was by degrees restored.

If the Brothers Cheeryble, as they found Nicholas worthy of trust and confidence, bestowed upon him every day some new and substantial mark of kindness, they were not less mindful of those who depended on him. If Brother Charles and Brother Ned failed to look in for at least a few minutes every Sunday, or one evening in the week, there was Mr Tim Linkinwater constantly coming and going in his evening walks, and stopping to rest; while Mr Frank Cheeryble happened, by some strange conjunction of circumstances, to be passing the door on some business or other at least three nights in the week.

"He is the most attentive young man *I* ever saw, Kate," said Mrs Nickleby to her daughter, one evening.

"Surely you are not serious," returned Kate, colouring.

"Not serious!" returned Mrs Nickleby; "why shouldn't I be serious? I'm sure I never was more serious. Where is Mr

101

Smike? He was here this instant."

Upon further inquiry, it turned out, to the good lady's unbounded astonishment, that Smike had that moment gone upstairs to bed.

"Well now," said Mrs Nickleby, "he is the strangest creature! Last Tuesday – was it Tuesday? Yes to be sure it was; you recollect, Kate, my dear, the very last time young Mr Cheeryble was here – last Tuesday night he went off in just the same strange way, at the very moment the knock came to the door. And the strangest thing is, that he does not go to bed, because my room is the next one, and when I went upstairs last Tuesday, hours after him, I found that he had not even taken his shoes off; and he had no candle, so he must have sat moping in the dark all the time. Now, that's very extraordinary!"

Nearly three hours later Nicholas returned, and Kate told him about Smike.

"Poor fellow," said Nicholas, tapping gently at his door, "what can be the cause of all this!"

Smike, very pale and haggard, and completely dressed, confronted them.

"And have you not been to bed?" said Nicholas.

"I could not sleep."

"Then why do you give way to these fits of melancholy?" inquired Nicholas, in his kindest manner. "Or why not tell us the cause? You grow a different creature, Smike."

"I do; I know I do," he replied. "I will tell you the reason one day, but not now."

## A Crisis for Madeline

Bray and his daughter were sitting alone. It was nearly three weeks since he had seen her last, but there was a change in the lovely girl before him which told Nicholas, in

startling terms, what mental suffering had been compressed into that short time.

"Now, sir, what do you want? I suppose you think now," said Bray, wheeling his chair round and confronting Nicholas, "that but for such pitiful sums as you bring her because my daughter has chosen to employ her time as she has, we should starve?"

"I have not thought about it," returned Nicholas.

"Then you may tell your master," said Bray, "that my daughter condescends to employ herself no longer in such labours as these; that she is not at his beck and call as he supposes her to be; that we don't live upon his money as he flatters himself we do; that he may give whatever he owes us to the first beggar that passes his shop, or add it to his own profits next time he calculates them; and that he may go to the devil, for me."

"And this is the independence of a man who would sell his daughter in marriage as he has sold that weeping girl!" thought Nicholas indignantly.

Bray fell into a paroxysm of his disorder, so violent that for a few moments Nicholas was alarmed for his life; but finding that he began to recover, he withdrew, after signifying by a gesture to the young lady that he had something important to communicate, and would wait for her outside the room.

She attempted to pass, but Nicholas gently detained her.

"Leave me, sir, pray."

"I cannot, will not leave you thus," returned Nicholas. I must beseech you to contemplate again the fearful course to which you have been impelled."

"What course is this you speak of, sir?"

"I speak of this marriage," returned Nicholas, "of this marriage, fixed for tomorrow, the history of which is known to me."

Before Nicholas ceased to speak, the young lady buried her face in her hands, and gave her tears free way.

"I will not disguise from you, sir that I have undergone great pain of mind, and have been nearly broken-hearted since I saw you last. I do *not* love this gentleman; the difference between our ages, tastes, and habits, forbids it. This he knows, and knowing, still offers me his hand. By accepting it, and by that step alone, I can release my father, who is dying in this place, prolong his life, perhaps, for many years, restore him to comfort and relieve a generous man from the burden of assisting one by whom, I grieve to say, his noble heart is little understood. Do not think so poorly of me as to believe that I feign a love I do not feel. If I cannot in reason or in nature love the man who pays this price for my poor hand, I can discharge the duties of a wife: I can be all he seeks in me, and will. The interest you take in one so friendless and forlorn as I, the delicacy with which you have discharged your trust, the faith you have kept with me, have my warmest thanks, and move me to tears, as you see. But I do not repent, nor am I unhappy."

At that moment a heavy body fell with great violence on the floor above, and an instant afterwards was heard a most appalling and terrific scream.

They stood still and gazed upon each other. Scream succeeded scream; a heavy pattering of feet succeeded; and many shrill voices clamouring together were heard to cry, "He is dead!"

Nicholas burst from the room, and darting upstairs to the quarter from whence the noise proceeded, forced his way through a crowd of persons who quite filled a small bed chamber, and found Bray lying on the floor quite dead.

"Who is the owner of this house?" said Nicholas, hastily.

An elderly woman was pointed out to him; and to her he said, as he knelt down and gently unwound Madeline's arms from the lifeless mass round which they were entwined: "I represent this lady's nearest friends and must remove her from this dreadful scene. My name and address are upon that card, and you shall receive from me all necessary directions for the arrangements that must be made. Stand aside, every one of you, and give me room and air for God's sake!"

Nicholas, taking his beautiful burden in his arms, rushed violently out. No one cared to stop him, if any were so disposed. Making his way through a mob of people, whom a report of the circumstances had attracted round the house, and carrying Madeline in his great excitement as easily as if she were an infant, he reached the coach, jumped up beside the coachman and bade him drive away.

## The Illness of Dear Friends

The brothers Cheeryble, on being told of these events, bestowed much commendation upon Nicholas for the part he had taken.

The sudden and terrible shock she had received, combined with the great affliction and anxiety of mind which she had for a long time endured, proved too much for Madeline's strength. Recovering from the state of stupefaction into which the sudden death of her father happily plunged her, she only exchanged that condition for one of dangerous and active illness.

At times when Nicholas came home at night, he would be accompanied by Mr Frank Cheeryble, who was commissioned by the brothers to inquire how Madeline was that evening. On such occasions Mrs Nickleby deemed it of particular importance that she should have her wits about her; for from certain signs and tokens which had attracted her attention, she shrewdly suspected that Mr Frank, interested as his uncles were in Madeline, came quite as much to see Kate as to inquire after her; the more especially as the brothers were in constant communication with the medical man, came backwards and forwards very frequently themselves, and received a full report from Nicholas every morning.

Then Smike became alarmingly ill; so reduced and exhausted that he could scarcely move from room to room without assistance, and so worn and emaciated that it was painful to look upon him. Nicholas was warned that the last chance and hope of his life depended on his being instantly removed from London. That part of Devonshire in which Nicholas had been himself bred when a boy was named as the most favourable spot; but this advice was cautiously coupled with the information that whoever accompanies him thither must be prepared for the worst, for every token of rapid consumption had appeared, and he might never return alive.

Nicholas was summoned by brother Charles into his private room, and thus addressed: "My dear sir, no time must be lost. This lad shall not die if such human means as we can use can save his life; neither shall he die alone, and in a strange place. Remove him tomorrow morning, see that he has every comfort that his situation requires, and don't leave him – don't leave him, my dear sir, until you know that there is no longer any immediate danger."

Next morning Nicholas and his feeble companion began their journey.

He never left Smike; to encourage and animate him, administer to his wants, support and cheer him to the utmost of his power was now his constant and unceasing occupation.

They procured a humble lodging in a small farm-house, surrounded by meadows.

At first, Smike was strong enough to walk about for short distances at a time. Nothing appeared to interest him so much as visiting those places which had been most familiar to his friend in bygone days.

Nicholas would point out some tree that he had climbed a hundred times to peep at the young birds in their nest, and the branch from which he used to shout to little Kate. There was the old house too, which they would pass every day, looking up at the tiny window through which the sun used to stream in and wake him on the summer mornings – the hedgerows where the brother and sister had so often gathered wild flowers together, and the green fields and shady paths where they had so often strayed.

One of these expeditions led them through the churchyard where was his father's grave. "Even here," said Nicholas, softly, "we used to loiter before we knew what death was. Once Kate was lost, and after an hour of fruitless search, they found her fast asleep under that tree which shades my father's grave. He was very fond of her, and said when he took her up in his arms, still sleeping, that whenever he died he would wish to be buried where his dear little child had laid her head. You see his wish was not forgotten."

That night, Smike started up from what had seemed to be a slumber, and prayed, as the tears coursed down his face, that Nicholas would make him one solemn promise.

"Promise me that when I die, I shall be buried near – as near as they can make my grave – to the tree we saw today."

Nicholas gave the promise.

In a fortnight's time, Smike became too ill to move about. There was an old couch in the house which was his favourite resting-place by day; when the sun shone, and the weather was warm, Nicholas had this wheeled into a little orchard which was close at hand, and his charge being well wrapped up and carried out to it, they used to sit there sometimes for hours together.

It was on one of these occasions that a circumstance took place which Nicholas at the time thoroughly believed to be the mere delusion of an imagination affected by disease, but which he had afterwards too good reason to know was of real and actual occurrance.

He had brought Smike out in his arms – to see the sunset – and, having arranged his couch, had taken his seat beside it. He had been watching the whole of the night before and, being greatly fatigued, fell asleep.

He could not have closed his eyes five minutes, when he was awakened by a scream, and saw to his great astonishment that his charge had struggled into a sitting posture, and with eyes almost starting from their sockets, was shrieking to him for help.

"Hold me tight. Don't let me go. There – there – behind the tree."

Nicholas followed his eyes. But there was nothing there.

"Do you remember," said Smike, in a low voice, and glancing fearfully round, "do you remember my telling you of the man who first took me to the school?"

"Yes, surely."

"I raised my eyes just now towards that tree – that one with the thick trunk – and there, with his eyes fixed on me, he stood, leaning upon his stick and looking at me, exactly as I told you I remembered him. He was dusty with walking, and poorly dressed – I think his clothes were ragged – but directly I saw him, the wet night, his face when he left me, the parlour I was left in, and the people that were there, all seemed to come back together. When he knew I saw him, he looked frightened, for he started and shrank away. I have thought of him by day, and dreamt of him by night. He looked in my sleep when I was quite a little child, and has looked in my sleep ever since, as he did just now."

Nicholas applied himself to calming the fears of Smike,

which after some time he partially succeeded in doing, though not in removing the impression upon his mind, for he still declared again and again in the most solemn and fervid manner, that he had positively seen what he described.

On a fine, mild autumn day, when all was tranquil and at peace, Nicholas sat in his old place by the bedside, and knew that the time was nearly come.

The dying boy turned towards him, and putting his arm about his neck, said, "I shall soon be there! But I must tell you something first. I should not have a secret from you. You would not blame me at a time like this, I know."

The words which followed were feebly and faintly uttered, and broken by long pauses; but from them Nicholas learnt, for the first time, that the dying boy, with all the ardour of a nature concentrated on one absorbing, hopeless, secret passion, loved him sister Kate.

He had procured a lock of her hair, which hung at his breast, folded in one or two slight ribands she had worn. He prayed that when he was dead, Nicholas would take it off, so that no eyes but his might see it, and that when he was laid in his coffin and about to be placed in the earth, he would hang it round his neck again, that it might rest with him in the grave.

Upon his knees Nicholas gave him this pledge, and promised again that he should rest in the spot he had pointed out. They embraced, and kissed each other on the cheek.

He fell into a slight slumber, and waking, smiled as before; then spoke of beautiful gardens, which he said stretched out before him, and were filled with figures of men, women, and many children, all with light upon their faces; then whispered that it was Eden — and so died.

## Ralph Hears a True Story

Ralph Nickleby sat alone in the solitary room where he was accustomed to take his meals, and to sit of nights when no profitable occupation called him abroad; before him was an untasted breakfast.

That he laboured under some mental or bodily indisposition, and that it was one of no slight kind so to affect a man like him, was sufficiently shown by his haggard face, jaded air, and hollow, languid eyes.

"What is this," he said, "that hangs over me, and I cannot shake off?"

He despatched the woman who kept his house to Newman's lodging, to inquire if he were ill, and why he had not come. She brought back answer that he had not been home all night, and that no one could tell her anything about him.

"But there is a gentleman, sir," she said, "below, who was standing at the door when I came in, and he says –"

"Well," said Ralph, "I'll see him."

"Mr Nickleby, there is terrible news for you, and I am sent to beg you will come with me directly," said a voice he seemed to recognise: Tim Linkinwater.

Tim well remembered afterwards, that as Ralph Nickleby left the house he saw him reel and stagger like a drunken man. He well remembered, too, that when he had placed his foot upon the coach steps, he turned round and looked upon him with a face so ashy pale and so very wild and vacant that it made him shudder, and almost afraid to follow. People were fond of saying that he had some dark presentiment upon him.

Arrived at their place of destination, Ralph entered a room where the brothers Cheeryble were. He was so astounded, not to say awed, by something of a mute compassion for himself which was visible in their manner and in that of the old clerk, that he could scarcely speak.

"Who's that yonder?" he said.

The figure that he had seen so dimly rose, and came slowly down.

Ralph had no reason that he knew, to fear this man; he had never feared him before; but the pallor which had been observed in his face when he issued forth that night, came upon him again; he was seen to tremble, and his voice changed as he said, keeping his eyes upon him, "What does this fellow here? Do you know he is a convict – a felon – a common thief!"

"That boy," said the man, "that these gentlemen have been talking of –"

"That boy," repeated Ralph, looking vacantly at him.

"Whom I saw stretched dead and cold upon his bed, and who is now in his grave."

"Who is now in his grave," echoed Ralph, like one who talks in his sleep.

The man raised his eyes, and clasped his hands solemnly together: "– Was your only son, so help me God in heaven!"

In the midst of a dead silence, Ralph sat down, pressing his two hands upon his temples. He removed them after a minute, and never was there seen such a ghastly face as he then disclosed. He looked fixedly at the man called Brooker, but did not say one word or make the slightest sound or gesture.

"Gentlemen," said the man, "I offer no excuses for myself. I am long past that. If in telling you how this has happened, I tell you that I was harshly used and perhaps driven out of my real nature, I do it only as a necessary part of my story, and not to shield myself; I am a guilty man."

He stopped as if to recollect, and looking away from Ralph and addressing himself to the brothers, proceeded in a subdued and humble tone: "Among those who once

113

had dealings with this man, gentlemen – that's from twenty to five-and-twenty years ago – there was one, a rough, fox-hunting, hard-drinking gentleman, who had run through his own fortune, and wanted to squander away that of his sister; they were both orphans, and she lived with him and managed his house. He, (pointing to Ralph), used to go down to the house in Leicestershire pretty often, and stop there many days at a time. The gentlewoman was not a girl, but she was, I have heard say, handsome, and entitled to a pretty large property. In course of time he married her. The same love of gain which led him to contract this marriage, led to its being kept strictly private, for a clause in her father's will declared that if she married without her brother's consent, the property, in which she had only some life interest while she remained single, should pass away altogether to another branch of the family. The result of this private marriage was a son. The child was put out to nurse a long way off, his mother never saw him but once or twice and then by stealth, and his father – so eagerly did he thirst after the money which seemed to come almost within his grasp now, for his brother-in-law was very ill, and breaking more and more every day – never went near him, to avoid raising any suspicion. The brother lingered on, Mr Nickleby's wife constantly urged him to avow their marriage, he peremptorily refused. She remained alone in a dull country house, seeing little or no company but riotous, drunken sportsmen. He lived in London and clung to his business. Angry quarrels and recriminations took place, and when they had been married nearly seven years, and were within a few weeks of the time when the brother's death would have adjusted all, she eloped with a younger man and left him.

"It was then that I became acquainted with these circumstances from his own lips. There were no secrets then, for the brother and others knew them, but they were communicated to me not on this account, but because I was wanted. He followed the fugitives, he didn't find them, and she died not long after. I don't know whether he began to think he might like the child, or whether he wished to make sure that it should never fall into its mother's hands, but before he went, he entrusted me with the charge of bringing it home. And I did so. He had used me ill – cruelly – and I hated him. I brought the child home to his own house and lodged him in the front garret. Neglect had made him very sickly, and I was obliged to call in a doctor, who said he must be removed for change of air or he would die. I think that first put it in my head. I did it then. He was gone six weeks, and when he came back, I told him that the child was dead and buried. He *was* grieved at *that*, and I was confirmed in my design of opening up the secret one day, and making it a means of getting money from him. I had heard, like most other men, of Yorkshire schools. I took the child to one kept by a man named Squeers, and left it there. I gave him the name of Smike. I paid twenty pounds a year for him for six years, never breathing the secret all the time, for I had left his father's service after more hard usage, and quarrelled with him again. I was sent away from this country. I have been away nearly eight years. Directly I came home again I travelled down into Yorkshire, made inquiries about the boys at the school, and found that this one, whom I had placed there, had run away with a young man bearing the name of his own father. All this time I had never seen the boy. At length I heard that he was very ill, and where he was. I travelled down there that I might recall myself, if possible, to his recollection and confirm my story. I came upon him unexpectedly; but before I could speak he knew me – he had good cause to remember me, poor lad – and I would have sworn to him if I had met him in the Indies; I knew the

115

piteous face I had seen in the little child. After a few days' indecision, I applied to the young gentleman in whose care he was, and I found that he was dead. This is my story."

He had hardly spoken, when the lamp, which stood upon the table close to where Ralph was seated, and which was the only one in the room, was thrown to the ground and, left them in utter darkness. There was some trifling confusion in obtaining another light; the interval was a mere nothing; but when it appeared, Ralph Nickleby was gone.

Creeping from the house and slinking off like a thief: groping with his hand when first he got into the street as if he were a blind man, and looking often over his shoulder while he hurried away, as though he were followed in imagination or reality by someone anxious to question or detain him, Ralph Nickleby left the city behind him and took the road to his own home.

He groped his way up the echoing stair to the front garret – where he closed the door behind him, and remained.

It was a mere lumber-room now, but it yet contained an old dismantled bedstead: the one on which his son had slept, for no other had ever been there.

He tore a rope from one of the old trunks and hanged himself on an iron hook immediately below the trap-door in the ceiling – in the very place to which the eyes of his son, a lonely, desolate, little creature, had so often been directed in childish terror fourteen years before.

## Conclusion

When her term of mourning had expired, Madeline gave her hand and fortune to Nicholas, and on the same day and at the same time Kate became Mrs Frank Cheeryble.

The money which Nicholas acquired in right of his wife

he invested in the firm of Cheeryble Brothers, in which Frank had become a partner. Before many years elapsed, the business began to be carried on in the names of 'Cheeryble and Nickleby'.

The twin brothers retired. Who needs to be told that they were happy? They were surrounded by happiness of their own creation, and lived but to increase it.

The first act of Nicholas, when he became a rich and prosperous merchant, was to buy his father's old house. As time crept on, and there came gradually about him a group of lovely children, it was altered and enlarged, but none of the old rooms were ever pulled down, no old tree was rooted up, nothing with which there was any association of bygone times was ever removed or changed.

Within a stone's-throw was another retreat, enlivened by children's pleasant voices too, and here was Kate, with many new cares and occupations, and many new faces courting her sweet smile.

The grass was green above Smike's grave, and trodden by feet so small and light, that not a daisy drooped its head beneath their pressure. Through all the spring and summer-time, garlands of fresh flowers wreathed by infant hands rested upon the stone, and when the children came to change them lest they should wither and be pleasant to him no longer, their eyes filled with tears, and they spoke low and softly of the poor dead cousin.

# A Tale of
# Two Cities

## Book the First: Recalled to Life

## The Period

It was the best of times, it was the worst of times; it was the age of wisdom, it was the age of foolishness; it was the spring of hope, it was the winter of despair; we had everything before us, we had nothing before us. It was the year one thousand seven hundred and seventy-five.

## The Preparation

On a Friday night late in November, Mr Jarvis Lorry, of Tellson's Bank, London, arrived at Dover on the mail coach. He waited in the Royal George hotel for his guest, Miss Manette.

Miss Lucie Manette was a young lady of not more than seventeen, a short, slight figure with golden hair and blue eyes. As his eyes rested on her a vivid likeness passed before Mr Lorry of a child he had held in his arms on a passage across the Channel from France many years before.

"I received a letter from the Bank respecting the property of my poor father," said Miss Manette, "whom I never saw – so long dead. It said I should go to Paris with you, and that you would explain the details of the business."

Mr Lorry began the story of one of his customers. "He was a French gentleman, a doctor of Beauvais, who married an English lady."

"But this is my father's story," said Miss Manette, "and I think that when I was left an orphan by my mother's surviving my father only two years, it was you who brought me to England."

"It *was* I," said Mr Lorry. "You have been the ward of Tellson's since."

Then Mr Lorry continued. "So far," he said, "this is the story of your father. Now comes the difference. If he had not died; if he had suddenly and silently disappeared to the oblivion of a prison; if his wife had implored in vain for any tidings of him – then the history of your father would have been the history of this unfortunate gentleman. This doctor's wife had suffered so intensely before her child was born that she determined to rear her in the belief that her father was dead. Your mother took this course with you. But your father has been found. He is alive. He is with an old servant in Paris, and we are going there. But this is a secret. All is comprehended in the one line: 'Recalled to Life'."

## The Wine Shop

In a wine shop in the suburb of Saint Antoine, Paris, sat Mr Lorry and Miss Manette.

Mr Lorry spoke to Monsieur Defarge, the owner. Their conference was very short, but very decided, and soon all three went out, leaving Madame Defarge knitting, seeing nothing.

Monsieur Defarge led the way to the top room of a house. The garret was dim and dark; inside a white-haired man sat on a low bench, making shoes.

## The Shoemaker

"Good day!" said Monsieur Defarge. "You are hard at work?"

After a long silence the man's voice replied, "Yes – I am working."

The man had a white beard, raggedly cut, a hollow face, and exceedingly bright eyes. His shirt lay open and showed his body to be withered and worn.

"Tell your visitor what kind of shoe you make, and the maker's name," said Monsieur Defarge.

"It is a lady's shoe," said the man. "And my name? One Hundred and Five, North Tower." And with a weary sound that was not a sigh, nor a groan, he bent to work again.

Miss Manette moved and stood beside him.

"What is this?" he said and, advancing his hand little by little, he took up her golden hair and looked at it. Then he put his hand to his neck and took off a blackened string with a scrap of rag attached to it. It contained two long golden hairs. "It is the same," he said. "How can it be! She laid her head upon my shoulder that night when I was summoned, and in the North Tower I found the hairs upon my sleeve. How was this? Was it you? No, no – that was long ago. What is your name?"

His daughter fell upon her knees. "Oh, sir, at another time you shall know my name," she said. "But I cannot tell you at this time, here. Your agony is over; I have come to take you to England."

Mr Lorry and Monsieur Defarge made ready for the journey and the man, long accustomed to obey, boarded the coach.

## Book the Second: The Golden Thread

### Five Years Later

Tellson's Bank was an old-fashioned place, even in the year one thousand seven hundred and eighty. It was very small, very dark, and very ugly.

Outside Tellson's sat an odd-job-man, an occasional porter and messenger never absent during business hours, unless upon an errand, and then he was represented by his son: a grisly urchin of twelve, his express image. The man's name was Jerry Cruncher.

## A Sight

One March morning Jerry was told to take a message to Mr Lorry at the Old Bailey courts, where a treason case was being tried.

At the Bailey, Jerry watched as the prisoner was brought in. He was a young man of about five-and-twenty, well-grown and well-looking. His condition was that of a young gentleman. He was plainly dressed and his hair, which was long and dark, was gathered in a ribbon.

Silence in the court! Charles Darnay had pleaded Not Guilty to an indictment denouncing him as a traitor to the King, by having assisted Lewis, the French King, in his wars against the said King, by wickedly, traitorously revealing what forces our King had ready to send to Canada and North America.

The accused was quiet and attentive, until he glimpsed two persons upon whom his look immediately rested, a young lady of little more than twenty, and a gentleman, evidently her father, a man of remarkable appearance in respect of the absolute whiteness of his hair and intensity of face. They were witnesses against the prisoner.

## A Disappointment

Mr Attorney-General had to inform the jury that the prisoner, though young in years, was old in treasonable practices. That it was certain that the prisoner had been in the habit of passing between France and England on secret business of which he could give no honest account. That a person who was beyond reproach had ferreted out the nature of the prisoner's schemes. That this patriot would be produced. That he had been the prisoner's friend, but had caused the prisoner's servant to examine his master's drawers and pockets, and secrete his papers. That the prisoner had been furnished with lists of His

Majesty's forces, their disposition and preparation, and had conveyed such information to a hostile power. That the proof would go back five years. That the jury must positively find the prisoner guilty, and make an end of him.

When the Attorney-General ceased, the patriot appeared in the witness box, John Barsad by name. Having released his noble bosom of its burden, the wigged gentleman sitting not far from Mr Lorry begged to ask him a few questions.

Had he ever been a spy himself? No. What did he live upon? His property. Where was his property? He didn't precisely remember. Ever been in prison, debtor's prison? Yes. How many times? Two or three times. Not five or six? Perhaps. Ever borrow money from the prisoner? Yes. Ever pay him back? No. Sure he saw the prisoner with the lists? Certain. Had not procured them himself? No. No motives but motives of patriotism? None whatsoever.

The servant, Roger Cly, swore his way through the case at a great rate. He had taken service with the prisoner four years ago. He began to have suspicions of the prisoner, and to keep an eye upon him, soon afterwards. He had seen lists. He had seen the prisoner show these lists to French gentlemen in Calais. He had known the last witness seven or eight years; that was mere coincidence.

Mr Attorney-General called Mr Jarvis Lorry. "Mr Lorry, look upon the prisoner," he said. "Have you seen him before?"

"I have. I was returning from France and at Calais he came on board and made the voyage with me."

"Were you travelling alone?"

"No, with two companions. A gentleman and lady. They are here."

"Miss Manette!" the Attorney-General called. "Have you seen the prisoner before?"

"Yes, on the ship just referred to."

"Had you any conversation with the prisoner?"

"Yes, my Lord. He noticed that my father was much fatigued and was so good as to shelter him from the wind and weather."

"Had he come on board alone?"

"No, two French gentlemen were with him. They conferred until the last moment."

"Had any papers been handed about among them?"

"Some, but I don't know what papers."

"Now, to the prisoner's conversation, Miss Manette," the Attorney-General continued.

"The prisoner was open in his confidence with me. He told me that he was travelling on delicate business, which might get people into trouble. He said this business had taken him to France, and might take him backwards and forwards between England and France for a long time to come. He was kind and good. I hope," she added, bursting into tears.

Mr Attorney-General now called for Doctor Manette. "Have you ever seen the prisoner before?" he asked.

"Once, when he called at my lodgings some three years ago."

"Can you identify him as your fellow passenger on the boat?"

"Sir, I can do neither."

"Is there a special reason for your being unable to do so?"

"A long imprisonment," he answered.

"Have you no memory of the occasion?"

"None. My mind is a blank. I have no remembrance."

A singular circumstance then arose in the case. The object being to show that the prisoner had travelled to a garrison and dockyard and there collected information, a witness was called.

The witness was quite sure.

"Did you ever see anybody very like the prisoner?"

Not so like (the witness said) that he could be mistaken.

"Look well upon my learned friend there," he said, pointing to his colleague, Sydney Carton, "and then look upon the prisoner. Are they very like each other?"

Allowing for my learned friend's appearance being careless and slovenly, they were sufficiently like each other to surprise not only the witness, but everybody present.

Mr Stryver (the prisoner's counsel) asked the witness if what had happened once, might happen twice. The upshot of which was to smash this witness like a crockery pot.

Mr Stryver now addressed the jury, showing them how the patriot, Barsad, was a hired spy and traitor, one of the greatest scoundrels on earth. How the servant, Cly, was his friend and partner; how their watchful eyes had rested on the prisoner as a victim because some family affairs in France required his making those passages across the Channel, though what those affairs were he could not disclose.

And now the jury retired. Mr Lorry beckoned to Jerry Cruncher. "You will be here when the jury come in. I want you to take the verdict back to the bank."

An hour and a half limped heavily away and the messenger had dropped into a doze when a loud murmur woke him.

Mr Lorry handed him a paper. Hastily written on it was the word ACQUITTED.

## Congratulatory

Doctor Manette, Lucie, Mr Lorry and Mr Stryver stood around Mr Charles Darnay – just released – congratulating him on his escape from death.

Mr Darnay kissed Lucie's hand fervently and gratefully,

and turned to Mr Stryver, whom he warmly thanked.

Lucie and her father departed in a carriage, and Mr Stryver made his way to the robing-room. Another person, who had been leaning against the wall where its shadow was blackest, now stepped up. Nobody had made any acknowledgement of Mr Carton's part in the day's proceedings; nobody had known of it.

Mr Lorry set off for Tellson's, and Carton turned to Darnay. "This is a strange chance that throws you and me together," he said. "This must be strange to you, standing alone with your counterpart."

He led Darnay to a little room in a tavern where Charles was soon recruiting his strength with dinner and wine.

"Do you feel that you belong to this terrestrial scheme again, Mr Darnay?" Carton asked.

"I am confused regarding time and place; but I am so far mended as to feel that."

"As to me, the greatest desire I have is to forget that I belong to it. It has no good in it for me – except wine like this – nor I for it. So we are not much alike in that particular. I think we are not much alike in any particular. Why don't you give a toast?"

"Miss Manette, then!"

"That's a fair young lady to be wept for by! Is it worth being tried for one's life to be the object of such evident sympathy and compassion, Mr Darnay?"

Darnay did not answer, but thanked Carton for his assistance.

"I neither want any thanks, nor merit any," was the careless rejoinder. "I don't know why I did it. Do you think I particularly like you?"

"You have acted as if you do; but I don't think you do."

"I don't think I do," said Carton.

Charles Darnay rose and wished him goodnight.

When he was alone Carton went to a glass on the wall.

"Do you particularly like the man?" he muttered at his own image. "Why should you like a man who resembles you? There is nothing in you to like. Change places with him, and would you have been looked at by those blue eyes as he was, and commiserated by that agitated face as he was? Come on, have it out in plain words! You hate the fellow."

## Hundreds of People

On the afternoon of a certain fine Sunday Mr Jarvis Lorry walked along sunny streets to dine at the lodgings of Doctor Manette.

The Doctor and Miss Lucie were out, but expected home, and Mr Lorry waited inside, where he spoke to Miss Pross, a wild red woman who was Miss Lucie's companion. She was one of those unselfish creatures who will, for pure love, bind themselves willing slaves, to youth when they have lost it, to beauty they never had, to bright hopes that never shone upon their own lives.

"I am very much put out about my Ladybird," she said. "I don't want dozens of people who are not at all worthy of her to come here looking for her."

"Do dozens come?" asked Mr Lorry.

"Hundreds," said Miss Pross.

Soon Doctor Manette and Lucie returned, but no Hundreds of People came to see the sights.

Dinner time, and still no Hundreds of People.

After dinner, Lucie proposed that they should sit outside. Mr Darnay presented himself as they sat, but he was the only one. Doctor Manette received him kindly, and so did Lucie. But Miss Pross suddenly became afflicted with a twitching in the head and body, and retired to the house.

"Have you seen much of the Tower, Doctor?" asked Mr Darnay. "I have been there, as you remember, and they told me a curious thing. In making alterations workmen came upon an old dungeon. Every stone of its wall was covered by inscriptions carved by prisoners – dates, names, prayers. Upon a corner stone were three letters: D I G. There had been no prisoner with these initials, and it was suggested that the letters were the complete word, DIG. Under a stone in the floor were found the ashes of a paper, mingled with the ashes of a small leather bag. What the unknown prisoner had written will never be read."

Doctor Manette suddenly started up, with his hand to his head. His manner and look terrified them all. "There are large drops of rain falling, and they made me start," he said. "We had better go in."

He recovered himself almost instantly, and said not a word about the discovery that he had been told of.

Tea-time, and Miss Pross making tea, with another fit of the jerks, yet no Hundreds of People. Mr Carton had arrived, but he made only two.

They all moved to one of the windows and looked out into the heavy twilight.

There was a great hurry of people in the streets, speeding away to shelter before the storm broke; the house resounded with the echoes of footsteps.

"There is a great crowd coming into our lives," said Sydney Carton. "Are they to come to all of us, or are we to divide them among us?"

"I have imagined them the footsteps of the people who are to come into my life, and my father's."

"I hear them!" said Carton, after a peal of thunder and a vivid flash of lightning. "Here they come, fast, fierce and furious!"

It was one in the morning when Mr Lorry, Mr Darnay and Mr Carton made their way home together. "Goodnight," said Mr Lorry. "Shall we ever see such a night again, together!"

Perhaps. Perhaps, see the great crowd of people bearing down upon them, too.

## Monseigneur in Town

Monseigneur, one of the great lords at the Court, held his reception in his grand hotel in Paris.

Monseigneur had one truly noble idea of general public business, which was to let everything go on in its own way. Monseigneur had the other truly noble idea that it must all go his way – tend to his own power and pocket. Of his pleasures, Monseigneur had the other truly noble idea that the world was made for them.

In his rooms were military officers, destitute of military knowledge; naval officers with no idea of a ship; brazen ecclesiastics; all totally unfit for their callings, all lying horribly in pretending to belong to them.

Bestowing a word here and a smile there Monseigneur passed through them, the show being over, there was one person left, who passed among the mirrors on his way out. "I demote you," said this person, "to the Devil!"

He was about sixty, handsomely dressed, haughty in manner, with a face like a fine mask.

He got into his carriage and drove away with a wild rattle and clatter, the common people dispersing before his horses, barely escaping being run down. At last, swooping at a corner, one of the wheels came to a jolt and the horses reared and plunged.

"What has gone wrong?" said Monsieur.

"Pardon, Monsieur the Marquis!" said a ragged man. "It is a child."

A tall man bent over the tiny bundle. "Killed!" he shrieked. "Dead!"

The people closed round and looked at the Marquis. He threw out a gold coin. "It is extraordinary," he said, "that

130

you cannot take care of your children. How do I know what injury you have done to my horses?"

The tall man called out again, "Dead!"

He was stopped by the arrival of Monsieur Defarge, who spoke to him. "Be a brave man, my Gaspard!" he said. "It is better for the poor thing to die so, than to live. Could it have lived an hour as happily?"

"Pick up that, philosopher," said the Marquis, throwing another coin.

He was being driven away when a coin flew into his carriage. "Hold!" he said. "Who threw that? If I knew which rascal threw, and if that brigand were sufficiently near it, he should be crushed under the wheels."

Not a voice, or a hand, or even an eye was raised, and the Marquis drove on.

## Monseigneur in the Country

At the top of a steep hill the Marquis's carriage halted for an adjustment to be made to the wheels, then travelled on to a poor village, where the Marquis pointed out one of the peasants. "I passed you on the hill?" he asked.

"I had the honour of being passed on the road," said the road mender.

"What did you look at so fixedly?"

"I looked at the man," he said, pointing under the carriage. "He swung there by a chain."

"Who was he?"

"I never saw him before. He was whiter than the miller, all covered with dust, tall as a spectre!"

"Did he run away, when we stopped?"

"He went over the hill-side head first."

"Bah!" said the Marquis. "Drive on!"

At the great door of his chateau he stopped. "Monsieur Charles, whom I expect; is he arrived from England?"

"Not yet."

A little later the nephew arrived. He had been known in England as Charles Darnay.

"You have been a long time coming," said the Marquis.

"I have been detained by – various business. I have come back, sir, pursuing the object that took me away. It carried me into great and unexpected peril; but it is a sacred object, and if it had carried me to death I hope it would have sustained me."

"Not to death," said the uncle.

"I believe it to be your bad fortune, and my good fortune, that has kept me out of prison here. I believe that if you were not in disgrace with the Court, a letter would have sent me to some fortress indefinitely."

"It is possible," said the uncle, "for the honour of the family."

"I believe our name to be detested more than any name in France."

"A compliment," said the Marquis, "to the grandeur of the family. The dark deference of fear and slavery will keep the dogs obedient to the whip."

"We have done wrong," said the nephew, "and are reaping the fruits of wrong."

"We have done wrong?"

"Our family; whose honour is of so much account to both of us, in such different ways. Even in my father's time we did a world of wrong. Can I separate my father's twin brother, inheritor and successor, from himself?"

"Death has done that!" said the Marquis.

"And has left me," answered the nephew, "bound to a system that is frightful to me, but powerless in it; seeking to execute the last request of my dear mother, which implored me to have mercy and redress."

"Seeking them from me," said the Marquis, "you will forever seek them in vain. I will die perpetuating the system

132

under which I have lived. And you," he added, "how do you, under your new philosophy, intend to live?"

"I must do what others of my countrymen may have to do some day – work. In England. The family honour is safe from me in this country. The family name can suffer from me in no other, for I bear it in no other."

"England is the refuge of many. Do you know a doctor and his daughter who have found refuge there?"

"Yes."

"Yes," repeated the Marquis. "So commences the new philosophy! Goodnight. Light my nephew to his chamber, there! And burn him in his bed," he added to himself.

Next morning the chateau woke gradually and surely. But why did the great bell ring? Why did figures run here and there, and horses ride away?

It portended that there was one stone face too many at the chateau. It lay back on the pillow of Monsieur the Marquis. It was like a fine mask. Driven home into the heart of the figure was a knife. Round its hilt was a paper on which was scrawled: *Drive him fast to his tomb. This, from JACQUES".*

## Two Promises

Twelve months had come and gone, and Mr Charles Darnay was established in England as a teacher of French. With great perseverance and untiring industry, he prospered. He had expected labour and he found it, and did it, and made the best of it.

He had loved Lucie Manette from the hour of his danger. He had never heard a sound so dear as the sound of her compassionate voice; had never seen a face so beautiful as hers.

One day he determined to open his mind to Doctor Manette when he knew Lucie to be out with Miss Pross.

He found the doctor reading at a window. "Dear Doctor Manette, I love your daughter," he said, "fondly, dearly, devotedly. If ever there were love in the world, I love her."

"I do not doubt your loving Lucie," said the doctor. "Have you spoken to Lucie?"

"No."

"Have you any reason to believe that Lucie loves you?"

"None. As yet, none."

"I give a promise," said the doctor. "If she should ever tell me that you are essential to her perfect happiness, I will give her to you."

"Your confidence in me ought to be returned with full confidence on my part," said Darnay. "My present name is not my own. I wish to tell you what that is, and why I am in England."

"Stop!" said the doctor of Beauvais. "Tell me when I ask you, not now. If Lucie should love you, tell me on your marriage morning. Do you promise?"

"Willingly."


## The Fellow of No Delicacy

If Sydney Carton shone anywhere, he certainly never shone in the house of Doctor Manette. He had been there often, and had always been the same moody and morose lounger there.

And yet he did care something for the streets that environed that house. Many a night he vaguely wandered there; many a dreary daybreak revealed his solitary figure lingering there.

One day in August he went to the doctor's house and found Lucie alone. She had never been quite at ease with him, and received him with some little embarrassment. "I fear you are not well, Mr Carton!" she observed.

"The life I lead is not conducive to health."

"Is it not a pity to live no better life?" asked Lucie, who was surprised to see that there were tears in his eyes.

"It is too late for that. I shall never be better than I am. I shall sink lower, and be worse. Pray forgive me. I break down before the knowledge of what I want to say to you. If it had been possible that you could have returned the love of the man you see before you – wasted, drunken creature as you know him to be – he would have been conscious, in spite of his happiness, that he would bring you to misery, blight you, disgrace you. I wish you to know that you have been the last dream of my soul. Since I knew you I have been troubled by a remorse that I thought would never reproach me again. I distress you; I draw fast to an end. Will you let me believe that the last confidence of my life lies in your innocent breast, and will be shared by no one?"

"Mr Carton," Lucie answered, "the secret is yours, not mine; and I promise to respect it."

He put her hand to his lips, and moved towards the door. "In the hour of my death I shall hold sacred that my last avowal of myself was made to you, and that my name, and faults, and miseries were gently carried in your heart."

He was so unlike what he had ever shown himself to be, and it was so sad to think how much he had thrown away, that Lucie wept for him.

"Be comforted!" he said. "I am not worth such feeling. Within myself I shall always be what I am now, though outwardly I shall be what you have seen before. For you, and for any dear to you, I would do anything. The time will not be long in coming when new ties will be formed about you – the dearest ties that will grace and gladden you. Oh, Miss Manette, think now and then that there is a man who would give his life, to keep a life you love beside you!"

## The Honest Tradesman

One day Jerry Cruncher observed a funeral. "Who is it?" he asked.

"Spy!" said a spectator. "Old Bailey spy! Roger Cly."

"Why, to be sure!" exclaimed Jerry, recalling the trial he had witnessed. "I've seen him."

The large crowd that had gathered jeered and shouted, and the coach doors were opened. The one mourner scuffled out and in a moment was away up a by-street.

The dead man disposed of, the crowd eventually dispersed, their sport over; Mr Cruncher remained behind to confer with the undertakers.

That night Jerry said that he was going fishing, and at one o'clock he opened a locked cupboard and brought forth a sack, a crowbar, a rope and chain, and other fishing tackle of that nature.

Young Jerry, his son, had been ordered to bed, but was not long after his father, who soon collected two other fishermen.

The three scaled an iron gate, then moved away on their hands and knees. They were in a churchyard.

They fished with a spade first, then there was a screwing and complaining sound down below and the figures were strained, as if by a weight. By slow degrees the weight came to the surface. Young Jerry knew what it would be, but when he saw it, he was so frightened that he ran all the way home.

There was no fish for breakfast, but Mr Cruncher was washed and brushed at the usual hour, and set off with his son for Tellson's.

Young Jerry, his cunning now fresh with the day, asked, "Father, what's a Resurrection-Man?"

"Well," returned Mr Cruncher, "he's a tradesman."

"What's the goods?"

136

"His goods is a branch of scientific goods."

"Persons' bodies, ain't it?" asked Young Jerry. "I should like to be a Resurrection-Man when I'm quite growed up!"

## Knitting

There had been earlier drinking than usual in the wine-shop of Monsieur Defarge, though the master was not visible.

It was high noontide when two dusty men entered: one was Monsieur Defarge, the other a mender of roads.

The man was taken outside, up a steep staircase into a garret – the garret where a white-haired man had sat on a bench, making shoes.

Defarge closed the door, and spoke to three other men who had gathered there. "Jacques One, Jacques Two, Jacques Three! This is the witness encountered by me, Jacques Four. He will tell you all. Speak, Jacques Five!"

"I saw him," began the mender of roads, "a year ago, underneath the carriage of the Marquis, hanging by the chain. This tall man is lost – and he is sought ten, eleven months when I see him again with six soldiers. I follow. They bring him up to the prison. In the morning I see him, high up, behind the bars of a lofty iron cage; he regards me like a dead man."

Defarge and the three glanced darkly at one another.

"He remains there for some days. They whisper that he will not be executed; petitions have been presented to the King himself. Again they whisper that he will be executed. On Monday morning there is raised a gallows. He is hanged there – and is left hanging. I left at sunset and walked until I met this comrade."

"How say you?" demanded Number One. "To be registered?"

"To be registered as doomed to destruction," returned

Defarge. "The chateau and all the race. Extermination."

"Are you sure that the register is safe? Shall we always be able to decipher it – or will she?"

"Knitted in her own stitches and her own symbols it will always be as plain to her as the sun. Confide in Madame Defarge."

"Is this rustic to be sent back soon?" asked another.

"He knows nothing," said Defarge. "He wishes to see the King, the Queen and Court; let him see them on Sunday."

"What?" exclaimed the man.

"Show a cat milk if you wish her to thirst for it," said Defarge. "Show a dog his natural prey if you wish him to bring it down one day."

## Still Knitting

The road mender returned to his village and Madame Defarge and her husband to the wine-shop. "There is another spy in our quarter," said Defarge. "John Barsad. Age, about forty years; height, about five feet nine; black hair, complexion dark; nose not straight."

"He shall be registered tomorrow," said Madame.

Next noontide saw her knitting when a stranger entered. "Good day," she said, but added to herself: "About forty, black hair. JOHN BARSAD."

"A bad business, Gaspard's execution," said Barsad.

"If people use knives, they have to pay," returned Madame. "He has paid the price."

Barsad turned to Monsieur Defarge. "I know of some interesting connections with your name," he said. "When Doctor Manette was released, you, his old domestic, had the charge of him. It was to you that his daughter came. I have known them, in England. Miss Manette is going to be married – to the nephew of the Marquis; in other words, the present Marquis. He lives unknown in England; he is Mr Charles Darnay. D'Aulnais is the name of his mother's family."

Madame Defarge knitted steadily, but the intelligence had a palpable effect on her husband, and the spy saw it.

When Barsad had left, Defarge turned to his wife. "Can .it be true? Her husband's name is on the register?"

## Nine Days

On Lucie's marriage-day she, Miss Pross and Mr Lorry waited outside the Doctor's room where he was speaking with Charles Darnay. When the Doctor appeared he was deadly pale.

Charles and Lucie were married, and set off for the country, but when Mr Lorry returned to visit the Doctor he was stopped by a low sound of knocking.

"All is lost!" said Miss Pross. "He doesn't know me, and is making shoes!"

Mr Lorry went into the Doctor's room. The shoemaker was very busy, but would not speak. He worked, and worked, and words fell on him as they would have fallen on the air.

The time went very slowly, and Mr Lorry's hope darkened, and his heart grew heavier every day, six days, seven days, eight days, nine days.

## An Opinion

On the tenth morning Mr Lorry found the tools out aside, and the Doctor reading. He supposed that Lucie's wedding had taken place yesterday.

"My dear Manette," said Mr Lorry, "I am anxious to have your opinion on a very curious case, the case of an old and a prolonged shock. A shock from which he has recovered. But unfortunately there has been a slight relapse."

The Doctor asked, "Of how long?"

"Nine days and nights."

"Does his daughter know of the relapse?"

"No," replied Mr Lorry. "How does this relapse come about?"

"I believe," returned Doctor Manette, "that there had been a strong revival of the remembrance that was the first cause of the malady."

"As to the future," hinted Mr Lorry.

"As to the future, I should hope that the worst is over."

On the three following days the Doctor remained well, and on the fourteenth day he went to join Lucie and her husband for the rest of their holiday.

## A Plea

When the newly-married pair came home, Sydney Carton spoke to Darnay. "You remember a certain occasion when I was more drunk then usual?" he said. "I was insufferable about liking you and not liking you. I wish you would forget it."

"I forgot it long ago," Darnay replied. "Have I had nothing more important to remember? The great service you rendered me that day?"

"Well, if you could endure to have a worthless fellow coming and going, I ask that I be permitted to come and go as a privileged person here."

Darnay agreed, and when Sydney had gone, made some mention of the conversation, and spoke of Sydney as a problem of carelessness and recklessness.

Later Lucie spoke to him. "I think poor Mr Carton deserves more consideration and respect," she said. "Be very generous with him always. He has a heart he very seldom reveals, and there are deep wounds in it. I have seen it bleeding. I am sure that he is capable of good things,

141

even magnanimous things."

## Echoing Footsteps

Some years passed. Darnay was prosperous, and Lucie the happy mother of a daughter of six.

On a night in mid-July, 1789, Mr Lorry came late from Tellson's. "There is such uneasiness in Paris," he said. "Our customers over there cannot confide their property to us fast enough. There is a mania for sending it to England."

Saint Antoine had been, that morning, a vast mass of scarecrows with gleams of light above the heads, where steel blades and bayonets shone in the sun.

"Come!" cried Defarge. "Patriots and friends, we are ready! The Bastille!"

With a roar that sounded as if all the breath in France had been shaped into the detested word, a living sea rose and overflowed the city to that point.

The attack began. Deep ditches, double drawbridge, massive stone walls, cannon, muskets, fire and smoke. Flashing weapons, blazing torches, bravery without stint, the furious sound of the living sea. Then a white flag from the fortress – suddenly the sea was over the drawbridge, past the stone walls. The Bastille surrendered!

"The prisoners!" was the cry taken up by the sea that rushed in, and Defarge went to the North Tower, to One Hundred and Five.

There was a small unglazed window high in the wall so that the sky could only be seen by stooping low and looking up. There was a stool, a table, a straw bed and four blackened walls. A.M. was scratched on one. "Alexandre Manette," said Defarge.

They searched the cell, found nothing, and left the tower.

# Fire Rises

There was a change in the village where the mender of roads went forth daily. Far and wide lay a ruined country. Every green leaf, every blade of grass and blade of grain was as shrivelled and poor as the miserable people.

As the mender of roads worked he viewed a figure approaching on foot, a shaggy haired man, tall, in wooden shoes, steeped in the mud and dust of many highways.

"How goes it, Jacques?" the man said.

"Ah, well, Jacques."

They joined hands.

"Tonight?" said the mender of roads.

"Tonight," said the man.

That night, when the village had taken its poor supper, it did not creep to bed, but came out of doors again. A curious whispering was upon it, and all looked expectantly at the sky in one direction only.

The night deepened. The trees around the old chateau moved in a rising wind. Uneasy rushes went through the hall, and shook the curtain of the bed where the last Marquis had slept.

Presently the chateau began to make itself visible by some light of its own. Soon flames burst forth, and soared higher.

The chateau was left to itself to flame and burn, and four figures trudged away to their next destination.

In such risings of fire three years of tempest were consumed. Three more birthdays of little Lucie had been woven into the peaceful tissue of the life of her home.

Monseigneur, as a class, took to his noble heels.

The August of the year one thousand seven hundred and ninety-two was come, and Monseigneur was by this time scattered far and wide.

The great gathering-place of Monseigneur, in London, was Tellson's Bank.

143

On a steaming, misty afternoon, Mr Lorry sat at his desk, and Charles Darnay stood leaning on it, talking with him in a low voice.

"Although you are the youngest man that ever lived," said Charles, "I must still suggest."

"That I am too old?" said Mr Lorry.

"A long journey, a disorganised country, a city that may not be even safe for you."

"My dear Charles," said Mr Lorry, "it is safe enough for me. If I were not prepared to submit myself to a few inconveniences for the sake of Tellson's, who ought to be?"

A clerk approached Mr Lorry, and laying a soiled and unopened letter before him, asked if he had yet discovered any traces of the person to whom it was addressed? Darnay saw his own right name. The address, turned into English, ran: "Very pressing. To Monsieur heretofore the Marquis St Evrémonde, of France. Confided to the cares of Messrs Tellson and Co., Bankers, London, England."

Dr Manette had made it his one urgent request that the secret of this name should be kept between them. Nobody else knew it to be his name.

"No," said Mr Lorry, in reply to the clerk.

Darnay said, "I know the fellow."

"Will you take charge of the letter?" said Mr Lorry. "You know where to deliver it?"

"I do. I will come back to see you off."

Very ill at ease with himself, Darnay opened the letter, and read it:

Prison of the Abbaye, Paris
June 21, 1792

Monsieur heretofore the Marquis,

After having long been in danger of my life at the hands of

144

the village, I have been seized, and brought a long journey on foot to Paris. On the road I have suffered a great deal.

The crime for which I am imprisoned, and for which I shall lose my life is, treason against the majesty of the people, in that I have acted against them for an emigrant. It is in vain I represent that I have acted for them, and not against, according to your commands. It is in vain that I had collected no rent. The only response is, where is that emigrant? I cry in my sleep where is he? I demand of Heaven, will he not come to deliver me?

GABELLE.

The uneasiness in Darnay's mind was roused to life by this letter. The peril of an old servant whose only crime was fidelity to his family, stared him reproachfully in the face. He must go to Paris.

Neither Lucie nor her father must know of it until he was gone.

He walked until it was time to return to Tellson's and take leave of Mr Lorry. As soon as he arrived in Paris he would present himself to this old friend, but he must say nothing of his intention now.

"I have delivered that letter," said Charles Darnay. "I would not consent to your being charged with any written answer, but perhaps you will take a verbal one? It is to a prisoner in the Abbaye, Gabelle."

"Gabelle. And what is the message?"

"Simply, that he has received the letter, and will come. He will start upon his journey tomorrow night."

## Book the Third: The Track of a Storm

## In Secret

The traveller fared slowly who fared towards Paris from

England in the autumn of the year one thousand seven hundred and ninety-two. Every town-gate had its band of citizen-patriots, who stopped all comers and goers, inspected their papers, turned them back, or sent them on.

Darnay had been days upon his journey when he was awakened at the small inn to which he had been remitted until morning, in the middle of the night. Awakened by a timid local functionary and three armed patriots.

"Emigrant," said the functionary, "I am going to send you on to Paris, under an escort."

The escort were two mounted patriots in red caps who rode one on either side of him. When they came to the town of Beauvais the aspect of affairs was very alarming. An ominous crowd gathered to see him dismount and voices called out, "Down with the emigrant! He is a traitor since the decree. His life is forfeit to the people. His cursed life is not his own!"

Daylight found them before the wall of Paris. The barrier was closed and strongly guarded.

"Where are the papers of this prisoner?" demanded a resolute-looking man.

The patriot produced them. Casting his eyes over Gabelle's letter, the same personage in authority left without saying a word, and went into the guard-room.

After a half-hour, the man in authority directed the guard to open the barrier. The two patriots turned and rode away.

Darnay accompanied his conductor into a guard-room, where certain soldiers and patriots, asleep and awake, drunk and sober, were standing and lying about. Some registers were lying open on a desk, and an officer of a coarse, dark aspect, presided over these.

"Citizen Defarge," said he to Darnay's conductor. "Is this the emigrant Evrémonde?"

"This is the man."

"You are consigned, Evrémonde, to the prison of La

146

Force."

"Just Heaven!" exclaimed Darnay. "Under what law, and for what offence?"

"We have new laws, Evrémonde, and new offences, since you were here." He said it with a hard smile.

"Is it you," said Defarge, in a low voice, as they went down the guard-house steps, "who married the daughter of Doctor Manette, once a prisoner in the Bastille?"

"Yes," replied Darnay, looking at him with surprise.

"My name is Defarge, and I keep a wine-shop."

"My wife came to your house to reclaim her father? Yes!"

"In the name of that sharp female newly born, and called La Guillotine, why did you come to France?"

"Will you render me a little help?"

"None." Defarge spoke.

"Will you answer me a single question?"

"Perhaps."

"In this prison that I am going to so unjustly, shall I have some free communication with the world outside?"

"You will see."

"I am not to be buried there, prejudged?"

"You will see. Other people have been similarly buried in worse prisons, before now."

"But never by me, Citizen Defarge."

The prison of La Force was a gloomy prison, dark and filthy.

"Come!" said the gaoler, taking up his keys. "Come with me, emigrant."

Through the dismal prison twilight, his new charge accompanied him, many doors clanging and locking behind them, until they came to a large, low, vaulted chamber, crowded with prisoners.

Charles Darnay crossed to a grated door which closed under the gaoler's hand.

The wicket opened on a stone staircase, leading upward. When they had ascended forty steps the gaoler opened a low black door, and they passed into a solitary cell. It struck cold and damp, but was not dark.

"Yours," said the gaoler, and went out.

"Five paces by four and a half, five paces by four and a half." The prisoner walked to and fro in his cell, counting its measurement. "He made shoes, he made shoes, he made shoes."

## The Grindstone

Tellson's Bank in Paris was in a wing of a large house, approached by a court-yard and shut off from the street by a high wall and a strong gate.

Mr Jarvis Lorry sat by a fire and on his honest and courageous face there was a shade of horror.

On the opposite side of the court-yard was a large grindstone, which appeared to have hurriedly been brought there.

From the streets beyond the high wall and the strong gate, there came the usual night hum of the city, with now and then an indescribable ring in it, weird and unearthly.

"Thank God," said Mr Lorry, clasping his hands, "that no one near and dear to me is in this dreadful town tonight!" His door suddenly opened, and two figures rushed in, at sight of which he fell back in amazement.

Lucie and her father!

"What is this?" cried Mr Lorry, breathless and confused. "Lucie! Manette! What has happened?"

"Charles. Here."

"Here, in Paris?"

"Has been here some days – three or four – I don't know how many. An errand of generosity brought him here unknown to us; he was stopped and sent to prison."

The old man uttered an irrepressible cry. Almost at the same moment, a loud noise of feet and voices came pouring into the court-yard.

"What is that noise?" said the Doctor.

"Don't look!" cried Mr Lorry.

The Doctor turned, and said, with a cool bold smile: "My dear friend, I have a charmed life in this city. I have been a Bastille prisoner. There is no patriot in France, who, knowing me to have been a prisoner in the Bastille, would touch, except to overwhelm me with embraces. My old pain has given me a power that has gained us news of Charles and brought us here."

"What prison is he in?" said Mr Lorry.

"La Force!"

"La Force! Lucie, my child, you cannot possibly stir out. You must be obedient, still, and quiet. You must let me put you in a room at the back here. You must leave your father and me alone."

"I will be submissive to you. I know you are true."

The old man came hurrying back to the Doctor, and looked out with him into the court-yard. Looked out upon a throng of men and women: forty or fifty in all. They had rushed in to work at the grindstone; it had evidently been set up there for their purpose.

But, such awful workers, and such awful work! Hatchets, knives, swords, all brought to be sharpened.

"They are," Mr Lorry whispered, "murdering the prisoners. If you really have the power you think you have – make yourself known to these devils, and get taken to La Force. It may be too late, I don't know, but let it not be a minute later!"

Doctor Manette hastened out of the room.

His streaming white hair, his remarkable face, and the confidence of his manner, carried him in an instant to the heart of the concourse at the stone.

## The Shadow

Mr Lorry removed Lucie, her child and Miss Pross to a lodging, and left Jerry with them.

He was again alone in his room when he heard a foot upon the stair. In a few moments, a man stood in his presence, who addressed him by his name.

"I have seen you somewhere," said Mr Lorry.

"Perhaps at my wine-shop?"

Mr Lorry said: "You come from Doctor Manette? What does he send me?"

Defarge gave him a scrap of paper: *Charles is safe, but I cannot safely leave this place yet. The bearer has a short note from Charles to his wife. Let the bearer see his wife.*

"Will you accompany me," said Mr Lorry, "to where his wife resides?"

"Yes," returned Defarge. They went down into the court-yard. There, they found two women; one, knitting.

"Madame Defarge, surely!" said Mr Lorry. "Does Madame go with us?"

"Yes. That she may be able to recognise the persons. It is for their safety."

They were admitted by Jerry, and found Lucie weeping. She read the note: *Dearest, Take courage. I am well, and your father has influence around me. You cannot answer this. Kiss our child for me.*

"Is that his child?" said Madame Defarge, stopping in her work and pointing her knitting-needle at little Lucie as if it were the finger of Fate.

"Yes, madame," answered Mr Lorry.

The shadow attendant on Madame Defarge seemed to fall, threatening and dark, on the mother and child.

"It is enough, my husband," said Madame Defarge. "I have seen them. We may go."

## Calm in Storm

Doctor Manette did not return until the morning of the fourth day of his absence.

The crowd had taken him through a scene of carnage to the prison of La Force, where he had found a Tribunal sitting. He had announced himself by name and profession as having been for eighteen years a secret and unaccused prisoner in the Bastille.

He had ascertained that his son-in-law was among the living prisoners, and had pleaded hard to the Tribunal for his life and liberty.

The Doctor also pleaded for permission to remain, and obtained the permission.

The Doctor used his personal influence so wisely that he

was soon the inspecting physician of three prisons, among them La Force.

But, though the Doctor never ceased trying to get Charles Darnay set at liberty, the public current of the time set too strong and fast for him.

Prisons gorged with people who had committed no offence, and could obtain no hearing; these things became the established order and nature of things. Above all, one hideous figure grew familiar – the figure of the sharp female called La Guillotine.

It sheared off heads so many, that it, and the ground it polluted, were a rotten red. It hushed the eloquent, struck down the powerful, abolished the beautiful and good.

Among these terrors, the Doctor walked with a steady head, never doubting that he would save Lucie's husband at last. Yet the current of the time swept time away so fiercely, that Charles had lain in prison one year and three months.

## The Wood-sawyer

One year and three months. During all that time Lucie was never sure but that the Guillotine would strike off her husband's head the next day. Every day, through the stony streets, the tumbrils now jolted heavily, filled with Condemned, all red wine for La Guillotine.

Her father said to her, on coming home one evening. "My dear, there is an upper window in the prison, to which Charles can sometimes gain access at three in the afternoon. He might see you in the street, he thinks, if you stood in a certain place."

From that time, in all weathers, she waited there two hours. As the clock struck two, she was there, and at four she turned away. She never missed a single day.

It was the dark corner of a small street. The hovel of a

cutter of wood was the only house. "Walking here again, citizeness?"

"You see me, citizen!"

The wood-sawyer, who had once been a mender of roads, pointed at the prison. "But it's not my business," said he.

Thenceforth, to secure his good will, Lucie always spoke to him first, and often gave him drink-money.

He was an inquisitive fellow, and sometimes when she had forgotten him in gazing at the prison she would find him looking at her. "But it's not my business!" he would say.

These occupations brought her round to the December month, wherein her father walked among the terrors with a steady head. On a lightly snowing afternoon she arrived at the usual corner. Presently she heard a troubled movement and a shouting which filled her with fear. A throng of people came pouring round the corner, in the midst of whom was the wood-sawyer. There could not be fewer than five hundred people, and they were dancing like five thousand demons. There was no other music than their own singing. They danced to the popular Revolution song, keeping a ferocious time that was like a gnashing of teeth. They advanced, retreated, struck at one another's hands, clutched at one another's heads, spun round alone, caught one another and spun round in pairs, until many of them dropped. No fight could have been half so terrible as this dance. This was the Carmagnole.

It passed, leaving Lucie frightened and bewildered.

"O my father!" for he stood before her when she lifted up the eyes she had darkened with her hand; "such a cruel, bad sight."

A footstep in the snow. Madame Defarge. "I salute you, citizeness," from the Doctor.

"I salute you, citizen." This in passing. Nothing more.

Madame Defarge gone.

"Give me your arm, my love. Charles is summoned for tomorrow. He has not received the notice yet, but I know that he will be removed to the Conciergerie. He shall be restored to you within a few hours. I must see Lorry."

It was almost dark when they arrived at the Bank.

Who could that be with Mr Lorry – the owner of the riding-coat upon the chair – who must not be seen? From whom newly arrived, did he come out? To whom, raising his voice and turning his head towards the door of the room from which he had issued, did he say: "Removed to the Conciergerie, and summoned for tomorrow?"

## Triumph

The dread Tribunal of five Judges, Public Prosecutor, and determined Jury, sat every day. Their lists went forth every evening, and were read out by the gaolers of the various prisons to their prisoners.

"Charles Evrémonde, called Darnay," was at length arraigned.

Looking at the Jury and the turbulent audience, he might have thought that the usual order of things was reversed, and that the felons were trying the honest men. The lowest, cruellest, and worst populace of a city were the directing spirits of the scene, noisily commenting, applauding, disapproving, without a check. Of the men, the greater part were armed; of the women, some wore knives, some ate and drank, many knitted. Among these last, was one, with a spare piece of knitting under her arm as she worked. She was by the side of a man whom he remembered as Defarge.

Charles Evrémonde, called Darnay, was accused by the public prosecutor as an emigrant, whose life was forfeit to the Republic, under the decree which banished all emigrants on pain of Death. His head was demanded.

"Take off his head!" cried the audience.

The President asked the prisoner whether he had lived many years in England? Was he not an emigrant then? What did he call himself?

Not an emigrant, he hoped, because he had voluntarily relinquished a title that was distasteful to him, and a station that was distasteful to him, and had left his country to live by his own industry in England, rather than on the industry of the overladen people of France.

But he had married in England? Her name and family?

"Lucie Manette, only daughter of Doctor Manette, the good physician who sits there."

This answer had a happy effect upon the audience. Cries in exaltation of the well-known good physician rent the hall.

The President asked, why had he returned to France?

He had returned on the written entreaty of a French citizen, who represented that his life was endangered by his absence. He had come back to save a citizen's life. Was that criminal in the eyes of the Republic?

The populace cried enthusiastically, "No!"

The President required the name of that citizen. The accused explained that the citizen was Gabelle.

Citizen Gabelle was called to confirm it, and did so.

At every vote (the Jurymen voted aloud and individually), the populace set up a shout of applause. All the voices were in the prisoner's favour, and the President declared him free.

## A Knock at the Door

One evening a blow struck upon the door of the lodging, and four rough men in red caps, armed with sabres and pistols, entered the room. "The Citizen Evrémonde, called

Darnay," said the first. "You are again the prisoner of the Republic. You return straight to the Conciergerie, and are summoned for tomorrow."

Dr Manette asked, "How does this happen?"

"Citizen Doctor," said the first, "he is accused by Saint Antoine."

"Will you tell me who denounced him?"

"It is against rule. But he is denounced by the Citizen and Citizeness Defarge. And by one other."

"What other?"

"You will be answered tomorrow. Now, I am dumb!"

## A Hand at Cards

Happily unconscious of the new calamity at home, Miss Pross crossed the river, reckoning in her mind the number of indispensable purchases she had to make. Mr Cruncher walked at her side. Miss Pross bethought herself of the wine they wanted.

As their wine was measuring out, a man parted and rose to depart. No sooner did he face her, than Miss Pross uttered a scream, and clapped her hands.

"What is the matter?" said the man who had caused Miss Pross to scream; speaking in a vexed, abrupt voice (though in a low tone), and in English.

"Oh, Solomon, dear brother!" cried Miss Pross.

"Don't call me Solomon. Do you want to be the death of me?" asked the man in a frightened way. "Come out, if you want to speak to me."

"Now," said Solomon, stopping at the dark street corner, "if you expect me to be surprised, I am not surprised; I knew you were here; I know of most people who are here. Go your way as soon as possible, and let me go mine. I am busy. I am an official."

Mr Cruncher, interposed with the following singular

question: "I say! Might I ask the favour? As to whether your name is John Solomon, or Solomon John? She calls you Solomon, and she must know, being your sister. And *I* know you're John. And regarding that name of Pross. That warn't your name over the water. You was a spy-witness at the Bailey. What was you called at that time?"

"Barsad," said another voice.

The speaker was Sydney Carton.

"Don't be alarmed," he said. "I arrived at Mr Lorry's yesterday evening; I present myself here to talk with your brother. I wish for you sake he was not a spy of the Prisons. I lighted on you, Mr Barsad, coming out of the prison of the Conciergerie an hour or more ago. I remember faces well. I walked into the wine-shop close after you, and sat near you. I had no difficulty in deducing the nature of your calling. Could you favour me with some minutes of your company – at the office of Tellson's Bank?"

"I'll hear what you have got to say. Yes, I'll go with you."

Mr Lorry turned his head as they entered, and showed the surprise with which he saw a stranger.

"Miss Pross's brother, sir," said Sydney. "Mr Barsad. Witness at that trial."

"Mr Barsad has been recognised by Miss Pross," said Sydney, "and has acknowledged the relationship. I pass to worse news. Darnay has been arrested again. When was it done, Mr Barsad?"

"Just now."

"I am shaken, Mr Lorry, by Doctor Manette's not having had the power to prevent this arrest," said Sydney. "This is a desperate time, when desperate games are played for desperate stakes. The stake I have resolved to play for is a friend in the Conciergerie. And the friend I purpose to myself to win, is Mr Barsad."

"You need have good cards, sir," said the spy.

"I'll see what I hold."

"Mr Barsad, spy and secret informer, represents himself to his employers under a false name. That's a very good card. Mr Barsad, now in the employ of the French was formerly in the employ of the aristocratic English government, the enemy of France. That's an excellent card. Inference clear as day that Mr Barsad is the spy of Pitt, the English traitor and agent of all mischief so much spoken of and so difficult to find. That's a card not to be beaten. I play my Ace, Denunciation of Mr Barsad to the nearest Section Committee. Look over your hand, Mr Barsad, and see what you have."

It was a poor hand. Mr Barsad saw losing cards in it. Thrown out of employment in England, he had crossed the Channel, and accepted service in France: first, as a tempter and an eavesdropper among his own countrymen there: gradually, as a tempter and an eavesdropper among the natives. He knew that under the overthrown government he had been a spy upon Saint Antoine and Defarge's wine-shop.

"I have a strong impression that I have another good card here," said Carton. "That friend and fellow-spy, who was he? Cly! Disguised, but the same man."

"Now you are hasty, sir," said Barsad. "Cly has been dead several years. I helped to lay him in his coffin."

Mr Cruncher rose and stepped forward. "That there Roger Cly, master," he said. "Cly was never in that there coffin. You buried paving-stones and earth in that coffin. Me and two more knows it."

Barsad turned to Sydney Carton. "It has come to a point. I go on duty soon, and can't overstay my time. You told me you had a proposal; what is it?"

"You are a turnkey at the Conciergerie?"

"I can pass in and out when I choose."

"So far, we have spoken before these two," said Carton. "Come into the dark room here, and let us have one final word alone."

## The Game Made

Sydney Carton and the spy returned from the dark room. "Adieu, Mr Barsad," said the former.

When they were alone, Mr Lorry asked him what he had done?

"Not much. If it should go ill with the prisoner, I have ensured access to him, once. It is all I could do," said Carton.

Carton left and stopped at a chemist's shop, laying a scrap of paper before him. "Whew!" the chemist whistled softly. "You will be careful to keep them separate, citizen? You know the consequences of mixing them?"

"Perfectly."

Certain small packets were made and given to him.

Next morning the court was all astir and a-buzz when Carton took his place. Mr Lorry was there, and Doctor Manette was there. Lucie was there, sitting beside her father.

Charles Evrémonde, called Darnay. Released yesterday. Reaccused and retaken yesterday. Suspected and denounced enemy of the Republic, one of a family of tyrants, one of a race proscribed.

The President asked, was the Accused openly denounced? By whom?

"Three voices. Ernest Defarge, Thérèse Defarge, his wife, Alexandre Manette, physician."

A great uproar took place in the court, and in the midst of it, Doctor Manette was seen, pale and trembling, standing where he had been seated. "President, I indignantly protest to you that this is a forgery and a fraud."

Defarge was produced, and expounded the story of the imprisonment, and of the release, and of the state of the prisoner when released and delivered to him.

"You did good service at the taking of the Bastille, citizen?"

"I believe so. I knew that this prisoner had been confined in a cell known as One Hundred and Five, North Tower. I resolved to examine that cell. In a hole in the chimney I find a written paper. This is that written paper, the writing of Doctor Manette."

## The Substance of the Shadow

"I, Alexandre Manette, unfortunate physician, native of Beauvais, write this in the Bastille, during the last month of the year 1767. One cloudy moonlight night, in the third week of December in the year 1757, I was walking by the Seine when a carriage came along, driven very fast. A head was put out at the window, and a voice called to the driver to stop. The same voice called to me by my name. I answered, and two gentlemen alighted. They were both wrapped in cloaks, and appeared to conceal themselves. As they stood side by side I also observed that they were greatly alike, in stature, manner, voice, and (as far as I could see) face too. Almost like twin brothers.

"'Doctor Manette, formerly of Beauvais, the young physician, originally an expert surgeon, who has a rising reputation in Paris? Will you please to enter the carriage?'

"The carriage stopped at a solitary house. I heard cries proceeding from an upper chamber. I was conducted to this chamber, the cries growing louder as we ascended the stairs, and I found a patient in a high fever of the brain, lying on a bed.

"The patient was a woman of great beauty, and young; assuredly not much past twenty. Her hair was torn and ragged, and her arms were bound to her sides with sashes. On one of them I saw the armorial bearings of a Noble, and the letter E.

"Her eyes were wild, and she constantly uttered piercing shrieks, and repeated the words, 'My husband, my father, and my brother!' and then counted up to twelve, and said, 'Hush!' For an instant, she would pause to listen, and then the piercing shrieks would begin again, and she would repeat the cry.

"'She has a husband, a father, and a brother?' I asked.

"'A brother.'

"'She has some association with the number twelve?'

"'With twelve o'clock.'

"I made the patient swallow some medicine and waited.

"'There is another patient,' said the elder brother.

"The other patient lay in a back room, a handsome peasant-boy of not more than seventeen. The wound was a sword-thrust. He was dying fast.

"'How has this been done, monsieur?' said I to the elder brother.

"'A crazed young common dog! Forced my brother to draw upon him, and has fallen by my brother's sword.'

"The boy's eyes slowly moved to me. 'Doctor, they are very proud, these Nobles; but we common dogs are proud too, sometimes. She – have you seen her, Doctor?'

"I said, 'I have seen her.'

"'She is my sister, Doctor. She was a good girl. We were all tenants of that man who stands there.'

"'Doctor, my sister married. She had not been married many weeks, when that man's brother saw her and admired her, and asked that man to lend her to him. To persuade her husband they harnessed him to a cart and drove him. They kept him out at night, and ordered him back into his harness in the day. But he was not persuaded. No! taken out of harness one day at noon, to feed – if he could find food – he sobbed twelve times, once for every stroke of the bell, and died on her bosom.'

"'Then, with that man's permission his brother took her away. I took my young sister (for I have another) to a place beyond the reach of this man, then I tracked the brother here. Where is the man who was here? Turn my face to him. Marquis,' said the boy, 'in the days when all these things are to be answered for, I summon you and yours, to the last of your bad race, to answer for them.'

"I laid him down dead and when I returned to the bedside of the young woman, I found her raving in precisely the same order and continuity.

"This lasted twenty-six hours when she began to falter, and lay like the dead. It was then that I knew her condition to be that of one in whom the first expectations of being a mother have arisen.

"She lingered for a week. 'At last she is dead?' said the elder.

"'She is dead,' said I. He gave me gold. I took it from his hand, but laid it on the table.

"'Pray excuse me,' said I. 'Under the circumstances, no.' We parted without another word on either side.

"Early in the morning, the gold was left at my door. I decided to write privately to the Minister, stating the nature of the two cases to which I had been summoned. I wished to relieve my own mind. The letter was lying before me just completed, when I was told that a lady wished to see me.

"The lady was the wife of the Marquis St Evrémonde. I connected the title by which the boy had addressed the elder brother, with the initial letter embroidered on the scarf. She had discovered the main facts of the cruel story. She had reasons for believing that there was a young sister living, and her greatest desire was, to help that sister. I could tell her nothing but that there was such a sister; beyond that, I knew nothing. When I handed her down to the door, there was a child, two to three years old, in her carriage.

"'For his sake, Doctor,' she said, 'I would do all I can to make what poor amends I can. He will never prosper in his inheritance otherwise.'

"She kissed the boy, and said, 'It is for thine own dear sake. Thou wilt be faithful, little Charles?' The child answered her bravely, 'Yes!' I never saw her more.

"I sealed my letter and delivered it myself that day.

"That night, the last night of the year, towards nine o'clock, a man in a black dress rang at my gate.

"'An urgent case', he said. He had a coach in waiting.

"When I was clear of the house, a black muffler was drawn over my mouth and my arms were pinioned. The two brothers identified me with a single gesture. The Marquis took from his pocket the letter I had written, burnt it in the light of a lantern and extinguished the ashes with his foot. Not a word was spoken. I was brought here, I was brought to my living grave.

"Them and their descendants, to the last of their race, I, Alexandre Manette, unhappy prisoner, do this last night in the year 1767, denounce to the times when all these things shall be answered for. I denounce them to Heaven and to earth."

A terrible sound arose when the reading of this document was done.

At every juryman's vote, there was a roar. Another and another. Roar and roar.

Unanimously voted. Back to the Conciergerie, and Death within four-and-twenty hours!

## Dusk

The tribunal adjourned. Lucie stood stretching out her arms towards her husband. "If I might embrace him once!"

Barsad proposed, "Let her embrace him."

Her father followed her, and would have fallen on his knees, but that Darnay seized him, crying: "No, no! What have you done, that you should kneel to us! We know now, what you underwent when you suspected my descent, and when you knew it. It was the always-vain endeavour to discharge my poor mother's trust that first brought my fatal presence near you. Be comforted, and forgive me. Heaven bless you!"

Sydney Carton came and took her up, carried her lightly to the door, and laid her tenderly down in a coach.

When they arrived he lifted her again, and laid her down on a couch, where her child and Miss Pross wept over her.

"Oh, Carton, Carton, dear Carton!" cried little Lucie. "Now that you have come, I think you will do something to help mamma, something to save papa! Can you, of all people who love her, bear to see her so?"

"Before I go," he said, and paused – "I may kiss her?"

It was remembered afterwards that he murmured some words. The child, heard him say, "A life you love."

When he had gone out into the next room, he turned suddenly on Mr Lorry and her father, and said, "You had great influence yesterday, Doctor Manette; let it at least be tried. The hours between this and tomorrow afternoon are few and short, but try."

"I intend to try. I will not rest a moment."

"It will be dark soon after four. If I go to Mr Lorry's at nine, shall I hear what you have done?"

"Yes."

## Darkness

Sydney Carton paused in the street, and turned towards Saint Antoine.

He went direct to Defarge's, and went in.

165

There happened to be no customer in the shop but Jacques Three, in conversation with the Defarges.

Carton walked in, took his seat and asked (in very indifferent French) for a small measure of wine.

"English?" asked Madame Defarge.

"Yes, madame, yes. I am English!"

Madame Defarge returned to her counter and he heard her say, "I swear to you, like Evrémonde!"

After a silence of a few moments, during which they all looked towards him, they resumed their conversation.

"It is true what madame says," observed Jacques Three. "Why stop?"

"Well, well," reasoned Defarge, "but one must stop somewhere."

"At extermination," said madame.

"Extermination is good doctrine," said Defarge. "But this Doctor has suffered much; you observed his face when the paper was read."

"I have observed his face!" repeated madame. "I have observed his face to be not the face of a true friend of the Republic! For other crimes as tyrants and oppressors, I have this race a long time on my register, doomed to destruction and extermination. That peasant family so injured by the two Evrémonde brothers, is my family, that sister of the mortally wounded boy was my sister, that husband was my sister's husband, that unborn child was their child, that brother was my brother, that father was my father, those dead are my dead, and that summons to answer for those things descends to me!"

Customers entered, and the group was broken up. The English customer asked to be directed towards the National Palace.

He was soon swallowed up in the shadow of the prison

wall. At the appointed hour, he presented himself in Mr Lorry's room again.

The instant Doctor Manette entered the room, it was plain that all was lost. They asked him no question, for his face told them everything.

"Where is my bench?" he said. "What have they done with my work? Time presses: I must finish those shoes."

They looked at one another, and their hearts died within them. Lost utterly lost!

Carton was the first to speak: "The last chance is gone; he had better be taken to her. But, before you go, will you, steadily attend to me? Don't ask me why I exact the promise I am going to exact; I have a reason – a good one."

"I don't doubt it," answered Mr Lorry. "Say on."

"First," he put his hand in his coat, and took a paper from it, "that is the certificate which enables me to pass out of this city. Keep it for me, and this similar certificate, enabling Doctor Manette and his daughter and her child, to pass the barrier and the frontier. "They are in great danger. They are in danger of denunciation by Madame Defarge. I have seen the spy. He confirms me. This new denunciation will not take place until after tomorrow. Buy the means of travelling to the coast as quickly as the journey can be made. Early tomorrow have your horses ready, so that they may start at two o'clock in the afternoon. Have all these arrangements made in the court-yard here, even to the taking of your own seat in the carriage. The moment I come to you, take me in, and drive away. Wait for nothing but to have my place occupied, and then for England! Now goodbye!"

## The Exchange

In the black prison of the Conciergerie, the doomed of the

day awaited their fate.

The hours went on and the clocks struck the numbers Darnay would never hear again. Nine gone for ever, ten gone for ever, eleven gone for ever, twelve gone for ever. The final hour was Three, and he knew he would be summoned earlier, as the tumbrils jolted heavily and slowly through the streets.

One struck. "There is but another now," he said.

Footsteps in the stone passage outside. He stopped.

The key was put in the lock, and turned. Before the door was opened, a man said in English: "He has never seen me here. Go in alone; I wait near. Lose no time!"

The door was opened and closed, and there stood Sydney Carton.

"I am possessed of a power over one of the keepers here, and in virtue of it I stand before you. I come from your wife, dear Darnay," said Carton. "I bring you a request from her. You must comply with it — take off those boots you wear, and draw on these of mine."

"Carton, there is no escaping from this place; it never can be done. You will only die with me. It is madness."

"It would be madness if I asked you to escape; but do I? Change that cravat for this of mine, that coat for this of mine. While you do it, let me take this ribbon from your hair, and shake out your hair like this of mine!"

"Write what I shall dictate. Quick, friend, quick! 'If you remember,'" said Carton, dictating, "'the words that passed between us, long ago, you will readily comprehend this when you see it.'"

He was drawing his hand from his breast; the prisoner saw it. "Is that a weapon in your hand?" he asked.

"No. Write on. 'I am thankful that the time has come, when I can prove them.'" As he said these words his hand slowly moved down close to the writer's face.

The pen dropped from Darnay's fingers on the table, and he looked about him vacantly.

"What vapour is that?" he asked.

For a few seconds he faintly struggled with the man who had come to lay down his life for him; but, within a minute he was stretched insensible on the ground.

Quickly Carton dressed himself in the clothes the prisoner had laid aside. Then he called, "Come in!" and the Spy presented himself.

"Take him to the coach," said Carton. "Say that I was weak and faint when you brought me in, and I am fainter now you take me out. The parting interview has overpowered me. Quick!"

The door closed, and Carton was left alone. He listened for any sound that might denote suspicion or alarm. There was none. Breathing more freely in a little while, he sat down at the table, and listened again until the clock struck Two.

Several doors were opened in succession, and finally his own. A gaoler looked in, merely saying, "Follow me, Evrémonde!" and he followed into a large dark room, where others were brought to have their arms bound. The majority were silent and still, looking fixedly at the ground.

The same shadows that are falling on the prison, are falling, in that same hour of the early afternoon, on the Barrier when a coach going out of Paris drives up to be examined.

"Who goes here? Papers!" The papers are handed out, and read. "Alexandre Manette. Physician. Lucie. His daughter. Lucie, her child. Sydney Carton. Advocate. English. Which is he?"

He lies in the corner of the carriage. He is pointed out.

"Jarvis Lorry. Banker. English. Which is he?"

"I am he."

"Behold your papers, Jarvis Lorry, countersigned.

Forward! A good journey!"

"I salute you, citizens. And the first danger passed!"

## The Knitting Done

Madame Defarge held darkly ominous council with Jacques Three of the Revolutionary Jury.

"Defarge," said Jacques Three, "is undoubtedly a good Republican? Eh?"

"My husband, fellow-citizen, is a good Republican and a bold man. But my husband has his weaknesses, and he is so weak as to relent towards this Doctor. But, the Evrémonde people are to be exterminated, and the wife and child must follow the husband and father. My husband has not my reason for pursuing this family to annihilation. I must act for myself, therefore. She will now be at home, awaiting the moment of his death. She will be mourning and grieving. She will be in a state of mind to impeach the justice of the Republic. I will go to her."

When the journey had been planned last night, the difficulty of taking Miss Pross in it had much engaged Mr Lorry's attention. It was not merely desirable to avoid overloading the coach, but it was of the highest importance that the time occupied in examining its passengers, should be reduced to the utmost. Finally, he had proposed that Miss Pross and Jerry, who were at liberty to leave the city, should leave at three o'clock in the lightest-wheeled conveyance. They would soon overtake the coach, and, would greatly facilitate its progress during the precious hours of the night.

Miss Pross and Jerry were concluding their arrangements to follow the coach as Madame Defarge drew nearer.

"Take me in to the carriage near the great cathedral door between the two towers at three o'clock," said Miss Pross, and Mr Cruncher went out and left her by herself to follow as she had proposed.

She looked at her watch, and it was twenty minutes past two. She had no time to lose. Miss Pross got a basin of cold water and began laving her eyes, which were swollen and red, but constantly paused and looked round to see that there was no one watching her. In one of those pauses she cried out, for she saw a figure standing in the room.

Madame Defarge said, "The wife of Evrémonde; where is she?"

Miss Pross placed herself before the door of the chamber which Lucie had occupied.

Madame Defarge raised her voice and called out, "Citizen Doctor! Wife of Evrémonde! Child of Evrémonde! Any person answer the Citizeness Defarge!"

Perhaps the following silence whispered to Madame Defarge that they were gone. Three doors she opened swiftly, and looked in.

"I will have you from that door," said Madame Defarge, and made at the door.

Miss Pross seized her round the waist in both her arms, and held her tight.

Madame Defarge's hands were at her bosom. Miss Pross saw the loaded pistol, struck at it, struck out a flash and a crash, and stood alone.

All this was in a second. Madame Defarge's body lay lifeless on the ground.

Miss Pross arrived at the cathedral, where the escort took her in, and took her away.

## The Footsteps Die Out For Ever

Along the Paris streets, the death-carts rumble, hollow and harsh. Six tumbrils carry the day's wine to La Guillotine.

The clocks are on the stroke of three. In front of the

Guillotine, seated in chairs, are a number of women, busily knitting.

"Thérèse!" cries one. "Who has seen her? Thérèse Defarge!"

"She never missed before," says another. "Evrémonde will be despatched in a wink, and she not here!"

The tumbrils begin to discharge their loads. Crash! A head is held up, and the knitting-women count One.

The supposed Evrémonde descends – is gone. Twenty-three.

* * *

They said of him, about the city that night, that it was the peacefullest man's face ever beheld there. Many added that he looked prophetic.

One of the most remarkable sufferers by the same axe – a woman – had asked at the foot of the same scaffold, not long before, to be allowed to write down the thoughts that were inspiring her. If he had given an utterance to his, and they were prophetic, they would have been these:

"I see Barsad, and Cly, Defarge, the Juryman, long ranks of the new oppressors who have risen on the destruction of the old, perishing by this instrument, before it shall cease out of its present use. I see a beautiful city and a brilliant people rising from this abyss. I see the evil of this time gradually making expiation for itself and wearing out.

"I see the lives for which I lay down my life, peaceful, useful, prosperous and happy, in that England which I shall see no more.

"I see that I hold a sanctuary in their hearts, and in the hearts of their descendants, generations hence. I see Lucie, an old woman, weeping for me on the anniversary of this day.

"It is a far, far better thing that I do, than I have ever done; it is a far, far better rest that I go to than I have ever known."

# A Christmas Carol

## Christmas Eve

Marley was dead, to begin with. There is no doubt whatever about that. The register of his burial was signed by the clergyman, the clerk, the undertaker, and the chief mourner. Scrooge signed it.

Old Marley was as dead as a door-nail.

Scrooge knew he was dead? Of course he did. How could it be otherwise? Scrooge and he were partners for I don't know how many years. Scrooge was his sole executor, his sole administrator, his sole assign, his sole residuary legatee, his sole friend, and sole mourner.

Scrooge never painted out Old Marley's name. There it stood, years afterwards, above the warehouse door; Scrooge and Marley.

Oh! but he was a tight-fisted hand at the grindstone. Scrooge! a squeezing, wrenching, grasping, scraping, clutching, covetous, old sinner! Hard and sharp as flint, from which no steel had ever struck out generous fire; secret, and self-contained, and solitary as an oyster. The cold within him froze his old features, nipped his pointed nose, shrivelled his cheek, stiffened his gait; made his eyes red, his thin lips blue; and spoke out shrewdly in his grating voice.

Once upon a time – of all the good days in the year, on Christmas Eve – old Scrooge sat busy in his counting-house. It was cold, bleak, biting weather; and he could hear the people in the court outside, go wheezing up and down, beating their hands upon their breasts, and stamping their feet upon the pavement stones to warm them. The city clocks had only just gone three, but it was quite dark already – it had not been light all day – and candles were flaring in the windows of the neighbouring offices, like ruddy smears upon the palpable brown air. The fog came pouring in at every chink and keyhole, and was so dense without, that although the court was of the narrowest, the houses opposite were mere phantoms.

The door of Scrooge's counting-house was open that he might keep his eye upon his clerk, who in a dismal little cell beyond, a sort of tank, was copying letters. Scrooge had a very small fire, but the clerk's fire was so very much smaller that it looked like one coal. But he couldn't replenish it, for Scrooge kept the coal-box in his own room; and so surely as the clerk came in with the shovel, the master predicted that it would be necessary for them to part. Wherefore the clerk put on his white comforter, and tried to warm himself at the candle.

"A merry Christmas, uncle! God save you!" cried a cheerful voice. It was the voice of Scrooge's nephew, who came upon him so quickly that this was the first intimation he had of his approach.

"Bah!" said Scrooge, "Humbug!"

He had so heated himself with rapid walking in the fog and frost, this nephew of Scrooge's, that he was all in a glow; his face was ruddy and handsome; his eyes sparkled, and his breath smoked again.

"Christmas a humbug, uncle!" said Scrooge's nephew. "You don't mean that, I am sure?"

"I do," said Scrooge. "Merry Christmas! What right have you to be merry? What reason have you to be merry? You're poor enough."

"Come, then," returned the nephew gaily. "What right have you to be dismal? What reason have you to be morose? You're rich enough."

Scrooge having no better answer ready on the spur of the moment, said, "Bah!" again; and followed it up with, "Humbug."

"Don't be cross, uncle!" said the nephew.

"What else can I be," returned the uncle, "when I live in such a world of fools as this? Merry Christmas! What's

Christmas time to you but a time for paying bills without money; a time for finding yourself a year older, but not an hour richer. If I could work my will," said Scrooge indignantly, "every idiot who goes about with "Merry Christmas" on his lips should be boiled with his own pudding, and buried with a stake of holly through his heart. He should!"

"Uncle!" pleaded the nephew.

"Nephew!" returned the uncle, sternly, "keep Christmas in your own way, and let me keep it in mine."

"Keep it!" repeated Scrooge's nephew. "But you don't keep it."

"Let me leave it alone, then," said Scrooge. "Much good may it do you! Much good it has ever done you!"

"There are many things from which I might have derived good, by which I have not profited, I dare say," returned the nephew. "Christmas among the rest. But I am sure I have always thought of Christmas time, when it has come round, as a good time; a kind, forgiving, charitable, pleasant time; the only time I know of, in the long calendar of the year, when men and women seem by one consent to open their shut-up hearts freely, and to think of people below them as if they really were fellow-passengers to the grave, and not another race of creatures bound on other journeys. And therefore, uncle, though it has never put a scrap of gold or silver in my pocket, I believe that it *has* done me good, and *will* do me good; and I say, God bless it!"

The clerk in the tank involuntarily applauded. Becoming immediately sensible of the impropriety, he poked the fire, and extinguished the last frail spark for ever.

"Let me hear another sound from *you*," said Scrooge, "and you'll keep your Christmas by losing your situation! You're quite a powerful speaker, sir," he added, turning to his nephew. "I wonder you don't go into Parliament."

"Don't be angry, uncle. Come! Dine with us tomorrow."

Scrooge said that he would see him – yes, indeed he did. He said that he would see him in hell first.

"I want nothing from you; I ask nothing of you; why cannot we be friends?"

"Good afternoon," said Scrooge.

"I am sorry, with all my heart, to find you so resolute. We have never had any quarrel, to which I have been a party. But I have made the trial in homage to Christmas, and I'll keep my Christmas humour to the last. So A Merry Christmas, uncle!"

"Good afternoon!" said Scrooge.

"And A Happy New Year!"

"Good afternoon!" said Scrooge.

His nephew left the room without an angry word, notwithstanding. He stopped at the outer door to bestow the greetings of the season on the clerk, who, cold as he was, was warmer than Scrooge; for he returned them cordially.

"There's another fellow," muttered Scrooge; who overheard him: "my clerk, with fifteen shillings a week, and a wife and family, talking about a merry Christmas. I'll retire to Bedlam."

The clerk, in letting Scrooge's nephew out, had let two other people in. They were portly gentlemen, pleasant to behold, and now stood, with their hats off, in Scrooge's office.

"Scrooge and Marley's, I believe," said one of the gentlemen, referring to his list. "Have I the pleasure of addressing Mr Scrooge, or Mr Marley?"

"Mr Marley has been dead these seven years," Scrooge replied. "He died seven years ago, this very night."

"We have no doubt his liberality is well represented by his surviving partner," said the gentleman.

It certainly was; for they had been two kindred spirits. At

the ominous word "liberality," Scrooge frowned.

"At this festive season of the year, Mr Scrooge," said the gentleman, taking up a pen, "it is more than usually desirable that we should make some slight provision for the Poor and destitute, who suffer greatly at the present time."

"Are there no prisons?" asked Scrooge.

"Plenty of prisons," said the gentleman, laying down the pen again.

"And the Union workhouses?" demanded Scrooge. "Are they still in operation?"

"They are. Still," returned the gentleman, "I wish I could say they were not."

"The Treadmill and the Poor Law are in full vigour, then?" said Scrooge.

"Both very busy, sir."

"Oh! I was afraid, from what you said at first, that something had occurred to stop them in their useful course," said Scrooge. "I'm very glad to hear it."

"Under the impression that they scarcely furnish Christian cheer of mind or body to the multitude," returned the gentleman, "a few of us are endeavouring to raise a fund to buy the Poor some meat and drink, and means of warmth. We choose this time because it is a time, of all others, when Want is keenly felt, and Abundance rejoices. What shall I put you down for?"

"Nothing!" Scrooge replied.

"You wish to be anonymous?"

"I wish to be left alone," said Scrooge. "I don't make merry myself at Christmas and I can't afford to make idle people merry. I help to support the establishments I have mentioned – they cost enough; and those who are badly off must go there."

"Many can't go there; and many would rather die."

"If they would rather die," said Scrooge, "they had

180

better do it, and decrease the surplus population. Good afternoon, gentlemen!"

Seeing clearly that it would be useless to pursue their point, the gentlemen withdrew. Scrooge resumed his labours with an improved opinion of himself, and in a more facetious temper than was usual with him.

Meanwhile the fog and darkness thickened so, that people ran about with flaring links, proffering their services to go before horses in carriages, and conduct them on their way.

The ancient tower of a church, whose gruff old bell was always peeping slily down at Scrooge out of a gothic window in the wall, became invisible, and struck the hours and quarters in the clouds, with tremulous vibrations afterwards as if its teeth were chattering in its frozen head up there.

Foggier yet, and colder. Piercing, searching, biting cold. If the good Saint Dunstan had but nipped the Evil Spirit's nose with a touch of such weather as that, instead of using his familiar weapons, then indeed he would have roared to lusty purpose.

The owner of one scant young nose, gnawed and mumbled by the hungry cold as bones are gnawed by dogs, stooped down at Scrooge's keyhole to regale him with a Christmas carol: but at the first sound of

> "God bless you, merry gentleman!
> May nothing you dismay!"

Scrooge seized the ruler with such energy of action, that the singer fled in terror, leaving the keyhole to the fog and even more congenial frost.

At length the hour of shutting up the counting-house arrived. With an ill-will Scrooge dismounted from his stool, and admitted the fact to the expectant clerk, who instantly snuffed his candle out, and put on his hat.

"You'll want all day tomorrow, I suppose?" said Scrooge.

"If quite convenient, sir."

"It's not convenient," said Scrooge, "and it's not fair. If I was to stop half-a-crown for it, you'd think yourself ill-used, I'll be bound?"

The clerk smiled faintly.

"And yet," said Scrooge, "you don't think *me* ill-used, when I pay a day's wages for no work."

The clerk observed that it was once a year.

"A poor excuse for picking a man's pocket every twenty-fifth of December!" said Scrooge, buttoning his great-coat to the chin. "But I suppose you must have the whole day. Be here all the earlier next morning."

The clerk promised that he would; and Scrooge walked out with a growl. The office was closed in a twinkling, and the clerk, with the long ends of his white comforter dangling below his waist (for he boasted no great-coat), went down a slide on Cornhill, at the end of a lane of boys, twenty times, in honour of its being Christmas Eve.

## Marley's Ghost

Scrooge took his melancholy dinner in his usual melancholy tavern; and having read all the newspapers, and beguiled the rest of the evening with his banker's-book, went home to bed. He lived in chambers which had once belonged to his deceased partner. They were a gloomy suite of rooms, old enough now, and dreary enough, for nobody lived here but Scrooge, the other rooms being all let out as offices. The yard was so dark that even Scrooge, who knew its every stone, was fain to grope with his hands.

Now, it is a fact, that there was nothing at all particular about the knocker on the door, except that it was very

large. It is also a fact, that Scrooge had seen it, night and morning, during his whole residence in that place. Let it also be borne in mind that Scrooge had not bestowed one thought on Marley, since his last mention of his seven-years' dead partner that afternoon. And then let any man explain to me, if he can, how it happened that Scrooge, having his key in the lock of the door, saw in the knocker, without its undergoing any intermediate process of change – not a knocker, but Marley's face.

Marley's face. It was not in impenetrable shadow as the other objects in the yard were, but had a dismal light about it, like a bad lobster in a dark cellar. It was not angry or ferocious, but looked at Scrooge as Marley used to look: with ghostly spectacles turned up on its ghostly forehead. The hair was curiously stirred, as if by breath or hot air; and, though the eyes were wide open, they were perfectly motionless. That, and its livid colour, made it horrible.

As Scrooge looked fixedly at this phenomenon, it was a knocker again.

To say that he was not startled, or that his blood was not conscious of a terrible sensation, would be untrue. But he put his hand upon the key he had relinquished, turned it sturdily, walked in, and lighted his candle.

He *did* pause, with a moment's irresolution, before he shut the door; and he *did* look cautiously behind it first, as if he half expected to be terrified with the sight of Marley's pigtail sticking out into the hall. But there was nothing on the back of the door, except the screws and nuts that held the knocker on, so he said, "Pooh, pooh!" and closed it with a bang.

The sound resounded through the house like thunder. Every room above, and every cask in the wine-merchant's cellars below, appeared to have a separate peal of echoes of its own. Scrooge was not a man to be frightened by echoes. He fastened the door, and walked across the hall, and up the stairs; slowly too: trimming his candle as he went.

Before he shut his heavy door, he walked through his rooms to see that all was right.

Sitting-room, bed-room, lumber-room. All as they should be. Nobody under the table, nobody under the sofa; a small fire in the grate; spoon and basin ready; and the little saucepan of gruel upon the hob. Nobody under the bed; nobody in the closet; nobody in his dressing-gown, which was hanging up in a suspicious attitude against the wall.

Quite satisfied, he closed the door, and locked himself in; double-locked himself in, which was not his custom. Thus secured against surprise, he took off his cravat; put on his dressing-gown and slippers, and his nightcap; and sat down before the fire to take his gruel.

As he threw his head back in the chair, his glance happened to rest upon a bell, a disused bell, that hung in the room, and communicated for some purpose now forgotten with a chamber in the highest storey of the building. It was with great astonishment, and with a strange, inexplicable dread, that as he looked, he saw this bell begin to swing. It swung so softly in the outset that it scarcely made a sound; but soon it rang out loudly, and so did every bell in the house.

This might have lasted half a minute, or a minute, but it seemed an hour. The bells ceased as they had begun, together. They were succeeded by a clanking noise, deep down below; as if some person were dragging a heavy chain over the casks in the wine-merchant's cellar. Scrooge then remembered to have heard that ghosts in haunted houses were described as dragging chains.

The cellar-door flew open with a booming sound, and then he heard the noise much louder, on the floors below; then coming up the stairs; then coming straight towards his door.

"It's humbug still!" said Scrooge. "I won't believe it."

His colour changed though, when, without a pause, it came on through the heavy door, and passed into the room before his eyes.

The same face: the very same. Marley in his pigtail, usual waistcoat, tights, and boots; the tassels on the latter bristling, like his pigtail, and his coat-skirts, and the hair upon his head. The chain he drew was clasped about his middle. It was long, and wound about him like a tail; and it was made (for Scrooge observed it closely) of cash-boxes, keys, padlocks, ledgers, deeds, and heavy purses wrought in steel. His body was transparent; so that Scrooge, observing him, and looking through his waistcoat, could see the two buttons on his coat behind.

Scrooge had often heard it said that Marley had no bowels, but he had never believed it until now.

No, nor did he believe it even now. Though he looked the phantom through and through, and saw it standing before him; though he felt the chilling influence of its death-cold eyes, he was still incredulous, and fought against his senses.

"How now!" said Scrooge, caustic and cold as ever. "What do you want with me?"

"Much!" – Marley's voice, no doubt about it.

"Who are you?"

"Ask me who I *was*."

"Who *were* you then?" said Scrooge, raising his voice.

"In life I was your partner, Jacob Marley."

"You don't believe in me," observed the Ghost.

"I don't," said Scrooge.

"What evidence would you have of my reality beyond that of your senses?"

"I don't know," said Scrooge.

"Why do you doubt your senses?"

186

"Because," said Scrooge, "a little thing affects them. A slight disorder of the stomach makes them cheats. You may be an indigested bit of beef, a blot of mustard, a crumb of cheese, a fragment of an underdone potato. There's more of gravy than of grave about you, whatever you are!"

Scrooge was not much in the habit of cracking jokes, nor did he feel, in his heart, by any means waggish then. The truth is, that he tried to be smart, as a means of distracting his own attention, and keeping down his terror; for the spectre's voice disturbed the very marrow in his bones.

"You see this toothpick?" said Scrooge, returning quickly to the charge, for the reason just assigned; and wishing; though it were only for a second, to divert the vision's stony gaze from himself.

"I do," replied the Ghost.

"Well!" returned Scrooge, "I have but to swallow this, and be for the rest of my days persecuted by a legion of goblins, all of my own creation. Humbug, I tell you! humbug!"

At this the spirit raised a frightful cry, and shook its chain with such a dismal and appalling noise, that Scrooge held on tight to his chair, to save himself from falling in a swoon. But how much greater was his horror, when the phantom taking off a bandage from round its head, as if it were too warm to wear in-doors, dropped its lower jaw down upon its breast!

Scrooge fell upon his knees, and clasped his hands before his face.

"Mercy!" he said. "Dreadful apparition, why do you trouble me?"

"Man of the worldly mind!" replied the Ghost, "do you believe in me or not?"

"I do," said Scrooge. "I must. But why do spirits walk the earth, and why do they come to me?"

"It is required of every man," the Ghost returned, "that the spirit within him should walk among his fellow-men, and travel far and wide; and if that spirit goes not forth in life, it is condemned to do so after death. It is doomed to wander through the world and witness what it cannot share, but might have shared on earth, and turned to happiness!"

Again the spectre raised a cry, and shook its chain and wrung its shadowy hands.

"You are fettered," said Scrooge, trembling. "Tell me why?"

"I wear the chain I forged in life," replied the Ghost. "I made it link by link, and yard by yard; I girded it on of my own free will, and of my own free will I wore it. Is its pattern strange to you?"

Scrooge trembled more and more.

"Or would you know," pursued the Ghost, "the weight and length of the strong coil you bear yourself? It was full as heavy and as long as this, seven Christmas Eves ago. You have laboured on it since. It is a ponderous chain!"

Scrooge glanced about him on the floor, in the expectation of finding himself surrounded by some fifty or sixty fathoms of iron cable: but he could see nothing.

"Jacob," he said, imploringly. "Old Jacob Marley, tell me more. Speak comfort to me, Jacob!"

"I have none to give," the Ghost replied. "It comes from other regions, Ebenezer Scrooge, and is conveyed by other ministers, to other kinds of men. Nor can I tell you what I would. A very little more is all permitted to me. I cannot rest, I cannot stay, I cannot linger anywhere. My spirit never walked beyond our counting-house – mark me! – in life my spirit never roved beyond the narrow limits of our money-changing hole; and weary journeys lie before me!"

"But you were always a good man of business, Jacob,"

faltered Scrooge.

"Business!" cried the Ghost, wringing its hands again. "Mankind was my business. The common welfare was my business; charity, mercy, forbearance, and benevolence, were all my business. The dealings of my trade were but a drop of water in the comprehensive ocean of my business!"

It held up its chain at arm's length, as if that were the cause of all its unavailing grief, and flung it heavily upon the ground again.

"At this time of the rolling year," the spectre said, "I suffer most. Why did I walk through crowds of fellow-beings with my eyes turned down, and never raise them to that blessed Star which led the Wise Men to a poor abode! Were there no poor homes to which its light would have conducted *me*!"

Scrooge was very much dismayed to hear the spectre going on at this rate, and began to quake exceedingly.

"Hear me!" cried the Ghost. "My time is nearly gone."

"I will," said Scrooge. "But don't be hard upon me! Don't be flowery, Jacob! Pray!"

"How it is that I appear before you in a shape that you can see, I may not tell. I have sat invisible beside you many and many a day."

It was not an agreeable idea. Scrooge shivered, and wiped the perspiration from his brow.

"That is no light part of my penance," pursued the Ghost. "I am here tonight to warn you, that you have yet a chance and hope of escaping my fate. A chance and hope of my procuring, Ebenezer."

"You were always a good friend to me," said Scrooge. "Thank'ee!"

"You will be haunted," resumed the Ghost, "by Three Spirits."

Scrooge's countenance fell almost as low as the Ghost's

had done.

"Is that the chance and hope you mentioned, Jacob?" he demanded, in a faltering voice.

"It is."

"I – I think I'd rather not," said Scrooge.

"Without their visits," said the Ghost, "you cannot hope to shun the path I tread. Expect the first tomorrow, when the bell tolls One."

"Couldn't I take 'em all at once, and have it over, Jacob?" hinted Scrooge.

"Expect the second on the next night at the same hour. The third upon the next night when the last stroke of Twelve has ceased to vibrate. Look to see me no more."

When it had said these words, the spectre took its wrapper from the table, and bound it round its head, as before. Scrooge knew this, by the smart sound its teeth made, when the jaws were brought together by the bandage. He ventured to raise his eyes again, and found his supernatural visitor, its chain wound over its arm, walking backwards from him. At every step it took the window raised itself a little, so that when the spectre reached it, it was wide open, and the apparition floated out upon the bleak, dark night.

Scrooge followed to the window. He looked out.

The air was filled with phantoms, wandering hither and thither in restless haste, and moaning as they went. Every one of them wore chains like Marley's Ghost. Many had been personally known to Scrooge in their lives. He had been quite familiar with one old ghost, in a white waistcoat, with a monstrous iron safe attached to its ankle.

Whether these creatures faded into mist, or mist enshrouded them, he could not tell. But they and their spirit voices faded together; and the night became as it had been when he walked home.

Scrooge closed the window, and examined the door by

which the Ghost had entered. It was double-locked, as he had locked it with his own hands, and the bolts were undisturbed. He tried to say, "Humbug!" but stopped at the first syllable. And being, from the emotion he had undergone, much in need of repose; went straight to bed, without undressing, and fell asleep upon the instant.

## The First Of The Three Spirits

When Scrooge awoke, it was so dark that, looking out of bed, he could scarcely distinguish the transparent window from the opaque walls of his chamber. He was endeavouring to pierce the darkness with his ferret eyes, when the chimes of a neighbouring church struck the four quarters. So he listened for the hour.

To his great astonishment the heavy bell went on from six to seven, and from seven to eight, and regularly up to twelve; then stopped. Twelve! It was past two when he went to bed. The clock was wrong.

"Why, it isn't possible," said Scrooge, "that I can have slept through a whole day and far into another night. It isn't possible that anything has happened to the sun, and this is twelve at noon!"

The idea being an alarming one, he scrambled out of bed, and groped his way to the window. All he could make out was, that it was still very foggy and extremely cold, and that there was no noise of people running to and fro, and making a great stir, as there unquestionably would have been if night had beaten off bright day, and taken possession of the world.

Scrooge went to bed again, and thought, and thought, and thought it over and over and over, and could make nothing of it.

Marley's Ghost bothered him exceedingly. Every time he resolved within himself, that it was all a dream, his mind flew back again, to its first position, and presented the same problem to be worked all through. "Was it a dream or not?"

Scrooge lay in this state until the chime had gone three quarters more, when he remembered, on a sudden, that the Ghost had warned him of a visitation when the bell tolled one. He resolved to lie awake until the hour was passed; and, considering that he could no more go to sleep than go to Heaven, this was perhaps the wisest resolution in his power.

The quarter was so long, that he was more than once convinced he must have sunk into a doze unconsciously, and missed the clock. At length it broke upon his listening ear.

"Ding, dong!"

"A quarter past," said Scrooge, counting.

"Ding, dong!"

"Half-past!" said Scrooge.

"Ding, dong!"

"A quarter to it," said Scrooge.

"Ding, dong!"

"The hour itself," said Scrooge, triumphantly, "and nothing else!"

He spoke before the hour bell sounded, which it now did with a deep, dull, hollow, melancholy ONE. Light flashed up in the room upon the instant, and the curtains of his bed were drawn.

The curtains of his bed were drawn aside, I tell you, by a hand; and Scrooge, starting up into a half-recumbent attitude, found himself face to face with the unearthly visitor who drew them: as close to it as I am now to you.

It was a strange figure – like a child: yet not so like a child as like an old man. Its hair, which hung about its neck and down its back, was white as if with age; and yet the face had not a wrinkle in it, and the tenderest bloom was on the skin. The arms were very long and muscular; the hands the

193

same, as if its hold were of uncommon strength. Its legs and feet, most delicately formed, were, like those upper members, bare. It wore a tunic of the purest white; and round its waist was bound a lustrous belt, the sheen of which was beautiful. It held a branch of fresh green holly in its hand; and, in singular contradiction of that wintry emblem, had its dress trimmed with summer flowers. But the strangest thing about it was, that from the crown of its head there sprung a bright clear jet of light, by which all this was visible.

"Are you the Spirit, sir, whose coming was foretold to me?" asked Scrooge.

"I am!" The voice was soft and gentle.

"Who, and what are you?" Scrooge demanded.

"I am the Ghost of Christmas Past."

It put out its strong hand as it spoke, and clasped him gently by the arm.

"Rise! and walk with me!"

It would have been in vain for Scrooge to plead that the weather and the hour were not adapted to pedestrian purposes; that the bed was warm, and the thermometer a long way below freezing; that he was clad but lightly in his slippers, dressing-gown, and nightcap; and that he had a cold upon him at that time. The grasp, though gentle as a woman's hand, was not to be resisted. He rose: but finding that the Spirit made towards the window, clasped his robe in supplication.

"I am a mortal," Scrooge remonstrated, "and liable to fall."

"Bear but a touch of my hand *there*," said the Spirit, laying it upon his heart, "and you shall be upheld in more than this!"

As the words were spoken, they passed through the wall, and stood upon an open country road, with fields on either hand. The city had entirely vanished. The darkness

and the mist had vanished with it, for it was a clear, cold, winter day, with snow upon the ground.

"Good Heaven!" said Scrooge, clasping his hands together, as he looked about him. "I was bred in this place. I was a boy here!"

The Spirit gazed upon him mildly. "Your lip is trembling," said the Ghost.

Scrooge muttered, with an unusual catching in his voice, and begged the Ghost to lead him where he would.

"You recollect the way?" inquired the Spirit.

"Remember it!" cried Scrooge with fervour; "I could walk it blindfold."

They walked along the road, Scrooge recognizing every gate, and post, and tree; until a little market-town appeared in the distance, with its bridge, its church, and winding river. Some shaggy ponies now were seen trotting towards them with boys upon their backs, who called to other boys in country gigs and carts. All these boys were in great spirits, and shouted to each other and as they came, Scrooge knew and named them every one. Why was he filled with gladness when he heard them give each other Merry Christmas, as they parted at cross-roads and by-ways, for their several homes! What was merry Christmas to Scrooge? What good had it ever done to him?

"The school is not quite deserted," said the Ghost. "A solitary child, neglected by his friends, is left there still."

Scrooge said he knew it. And he sobbed.

They left the high-road, by a well-remembered lane, and soon approached a mansion of dull red brick. It was a large house, but one of broken fortunes; for the spacious offices were little used, their walls were damp and mossy, their windows broken, and their gates decayed. Fowls clucked and strutted in the stables; and the coach-houses and sheds were over-run with grass. Nor was it more retentive of its ancient state, within; for entering the dreary hall, and glancing through the open doors of many rooms, they found them poorly furnished, cold, and vast.

They went, the Ghost and Scrooge, across the hall, to a door at the back of the house. It disclosed a long, bare, melancholy room, made barer still by lines of forms and desks. At one of these a lonely boy was reading near a feeble fire; and Scrooge sat down upon a form, and wept to see his poor forgotten self as he used to be.

Not a latent echo in the house, not a squeak and scuffle from the mice behind the panelling, not a drip from the half-thawed water-spout in the dull yard behind, not a sigh among the leafless boughs of one despondent poplar, not the idle swinging of an empty store-house door, no, not a clicking in the fire, but fell upon the heart of Scrooge with a softening influence, and gave a freer passage to his tears.

"I wish," Scrooge muttered, putting his hand in his pocket, and looking about him, after drying his eyes with his cuff: "but it's too late now."

"What is the matter?" asked the Spirit.

"Nothing," said Scrooge. "Nothing. There was a boy singing a Christmas Carol at my door last night. I should like to have given him something: that's all."

The Ghost smiled thoughtfully, and waved its hand: saying as it did so, "Let us see another Christmas!"

Scrooge's former self grew larger at the words, and the room became a little darker and more dirty. The panels shrunk, the windows cracked; fragments of plaster fell out of the ceiling, but how all this was brought about, Scrooge knew no more than you do. He only knew that it was quite correct; that everything had happened so; that there he was, alone again, when all the other boys had gone home for the jolly holidays.

He was not reading now, but walking up and down despairingly. Scrooge looked at the Ghost, and with a

197

mournful shaking of his head, glanced anxiously towards the door.

It opened; and a little girl, much younger than the boy, came darting in, and putting her arms about his neck, and often kissing him, addressed him as, "Dear, dear brother."

"I have come to bring you home, dear brother!" said the child, clapping her tiny hands, and bending down to laugh.

"Home, little Fan?" returned the boy.

"Yes!" said the child, brimful of glee. "Home, for good and all. Home, for ever and ever. Father is so much kinder than he used to be, that home's like Heaven! And you're to be a man!" said the child, opening her eyes, "and are never to come back here; but first, we're to be together all the Christmas long, and have the merriest time in all the world."

Then she began to drag him, in her childish eagerness, towards the door; and he, nothing loth to go, accompanied her.

"Always a delicate creature, whom a breath might have withered," said the Ghost. "But she had a large heart!"

"So she had," cried Scrooge.

"She died a woman," said the Ghost, "and had, as I think, children."

"One child," Scrooge returned.

"True," said the Ghost. "Your nephew!"

Scrooge seemed uneasy in his mind; and answered briefly, "Yes."

Although they had but that moment left the school behind them, they were now in the busy thoroughfares of a city. It was made plain enough, by the dressing of the shops, that here too it was Christmas time again; but it was evening, and the streets were lighted up.

The Ghost stopped at a certain warehouse door, and asked Scrooge if he knew it.

"Know it!" said Scrooge. "Was I not apprenticed here!"

They went in. At sight of an old gentleman in a Welsh wig, sitting behind a high desk, Scrooge cried in great excitement: "Why, it's old Fezziwig! Bless his heart; it's Fezziwig alive again!"

Old Fezziwig laid down his pen, and looked up at the clock, which pointed to the hour of seven. He rubbed his hands; adjusted his capacious waistcoat; laughed all over himself and called out in a comfortable, oily, rich, fat, jovial voice: "Yo ho, there! Ebenezer! Dick!"

Scrooge's former self, now grown a young man, came briskly in, accompanied by his fellow-'prentice.

"Dick Wilkins, to be sure!" said Scrooge to the Ghost. "Bless me, yes. There he is. He was very much attached to me, was Dick. Poor Dick! Dear, dear!"

"Yo ho, my boys!" said Fezziwig. "No more work tonight. Christmas Eve, Dick. Christmas, Ebenezer! Let's have the shutters up," cried old Fezziwig, with a sharp clap of his hands.

"Hilli-ho!" he cried, skipping down from the high desk, with wonderful agility. "Clear away, my lads, and let's have lots of room here!"

It was done in a minute. Every movable was packed off, as if it were dismissed from public life for evermore; the floor was swept and watered, the lamps were trimmed, fuel was heaped upon the fire; and the warehouse was as snug, and warm, and dry, and bright a ball-room, as you would desire to see upon a winter's night.

In came a fiddler with a music-book, and went up to the lofty desk, and made an orchestra of it, and tuned like fifty stomach-aches. In came Mrs Fezziwig, one vast substantial smile. In came the three Miss Fezziwigs, beaming and lovable. In came the six young followers whose hearts they broke. In came all the young men and women employed in the business. In came the housemaid, with her cousin, the baker. In they all came, one after another.

Away they all went, twenty couples at once; hands half round and back again the other way; down the middle and up again; round and round in various stages of affectionate grouping; old top couple always turning up in the wrong place; new top couple starting off again, as soon as they got there; all top couples at last, and not a bottom one to help them! When this result was brought about, old Fezziwig, clapping his hands to stop the dance, cried out, "Well done!" and the fiddler plunged his hot face into a pot of porter, especially provided for that purpose. But scorning rest, upon his reappearance, he instantly began again, though there were no dancers yet, as if the other fiddler had been carried home, exhausted, on a shutter, and he were a bran-new man resolved to beat him out of sight, or perish.

When the clock struck eleven, this domestic ball broke up. Mr and Mrs Fezziwig took their stations, one on either side of the door, and, shaking hands with every person individually as he or she went out, wished him or her a Merry Christmas.

During the whole of this time, Scrooge had acted like a man out of his wits. His heart and soul were in the scene, and with his former self. He corroborated everything, remembered everything, enjoyed everything, and underwent the strangest agitation.

"A small matter," said the Ghost, "to make these silly folks so full of gratitude."

"Small!" echoed Scrooge.

The Spirit signed to him to listen to the two apprentices, who were pouring out their hearts in praise of Fezziwig: and when he had done so, said,

"Why! Is it not? He has spent but a few pounds of your mortal money: three or four perhaps. Is that so much that he deserves this praise?

"It isn't that," said Scrooge, heated by the remark, and

speaking unconsciously like his former, not his latter, self. "It isn't that, Spirit. He has the power to render us happy or unhappy; to make our service light or burdensome; a pleasure or a toil. Say that his power lies in words and looks; in things so slight and insignificant that it is impossible to add and count 'em up: what then? The happiness he gives, is quite as great as if it cost a fortune."

He felt the Spirit's glance, and stopped.

"What is the matter?" asked the Ghost.

"Nothing particular," said Scrooge. "I should like to be able to say a word or two to my clerk just now. That's all."

His former self turned down the lamps as he gave utterance to the wish; and Scrooge and the Ghost again stood side by side in the open air.

"My time grows short," observed the Spirit. "Quick!"

This was not addressed to Scrooge, or to any one whom he could see, but it produced an immediate effect. For again Scrooge saw himself. He was older now; a man in the prime of life. His face had not the harsh and rigid lines of later years; but it had begun to wear the signs of care and avarice. There was an eager, greedy, restless motion in the eye, which showed the passion that had taken root, and where the shadow of the growing tree would fall.

"Spirit!" said Scrooge, "show me no more! Conduct me home. Why do you delight to torture me?"

Scrooge was conscious of being exhausted, and overcome by an irresistible drowsiness; and, further, of being in his own bedroom. He had barely time to reel to bed, before he sank into a heavy sleep.

## The Second Of The Three Spirits

Awaking in the middle of a prodigiously tough snore, and sitting up in bed to get his thoughts together, Scrooge had

no occasion to be told that the bell was again upon the stroke of One. But finding that he turned uncomfortably cold when he began to wonder which of his curtains this new spectre would draw back, he put them every one aside with his own hands, and lying down again, established a sharp look-out all round the bed. For he wished to challenge the Spirit on the moment of its appearance, and did not wish to be taken by surprise, and made nervous.

Now, being prepared for almost anything, he was not by any means prepared for nothing; and, consequently, when the Bell struck One, and no shape appeared, he was taken with a violent fit of trembling. Five minutes, ten minutes, a quarter of an hour went by, yet nothing came. All this time, he lay upon his bed, the very core and centre of a blaze of ruddy light, which streamed upon it when the clock proclaimed the hour; and which, being only light, was more alarming than a dozen ghosts, as he was powerless to make out what it meant, or would be at; and was sometimes apprehensive that he might be at that very moment an interesting case of spontaneous combustion, without having the consolation of knowing it. At last, however, he began to think that the source and secret of this ghostly light might be in the adjoining room, from whence, on further tracing it, it seemed to shine. This idea taking full possession of his mind, he got up softly and shuffled in his slippers to the door.

The moment Scrooge's hand was on the lock, a strange voice called him by his name, and bade him enter. He obeyed.

It was his own room. There was no doubt about that. But it had undergone a surprising transformation. The walls and ceiling were so hung with living green, that it looked a perfect grove; from every part of which, bright gleaming berries glistened. The crisp leaves of holly, mistletoe, and ivy reflected back the light, as if so many little mirrors had been scattered there. Heaped up on the floor, to form a kind of throne, were turkeys, geese, game, poultry, long wreaths of sausages, mince-pies, plum-puddings, barrels of oysters, red-hot chestnuts, cherry-cheeked apples, juicy oranges, luscious pears, immense twelfth-cakes, and seething bowls of punch, that made the chamber dim with their delicious steam. In easy state upon this couch, there sat a jolly Giant, glorious to see; who bore a glowing torch.

"Come in!" exclaimed the Ghost. "Come in! and know me better, man!"

Scrooge entered timidly, and hung his head before this Spirit. He was not the dogged Scrooge he had been.

"I am the Ghost of Christmas Present," said the Spirit. "Look upon me!"

Scrooge reverently did so. It was clothed in one simple green robe, or mantle, bordered with white fur. This garment hung so loosely on the figure, that its capacious breast was bare. Its feet, observable beneath the ample folds of the garment, were also bare; and on its head it wore no other covering than a holly wreath, set here and there with shining icicles. Its dark brown curls were long and free; free as its genial face, its sparkling eye, its open hand, its cheery voice, its unconstrained demeanour, and its joyful air.

The Ghost of Christmas Present rose.

"Spirit," said Scrooge submissively, "conduct me where you will."

"Touch my robe!"

Scrooge did as he was told, and held it fast.

Holly, mistletoe, red berries, ivy, turkeys, geese, game, poultry, sausages, oysters, pies, puddings, fruit, and punch, all vanished instantly. So did the room and the hour of night. They were stood in the city streets on Christmas morning, where (for the weather was severe) the people made a rough, but brisk and not unpleasant kind of music, in scraping the snow from the pavement in front of their dwellings.

But soon the steeples called good people all, to church and chapel, and away they came, flocking through the streets in their best clothes, and with their gayest faces. And at the same time there emerged from scores of bye-streets, lanes, and nameless turnings, innumerable people, carrying their dinners to the bakers' shops. The sight of these poor revellers appeared to interest the Spirit very much, for he stood with Scrooge beside him in a baker's doorway, and taking off the covers as their bearers passed, sprinkled incense on their dinners from his torch. And it was a very uncommon kind of torch, for once or twice when there were angry words between some dinner-carriers who had jostled each other, he shed a few drops of water on them from it, and their good humour was restored directly. For they said, it was a shame to quarrel upon Christmas Day. And so it was! God love it, so it was!

They went on, invisible, as they had been before, into the suburbs of the town. It was a remarkable quality of the Ghost (which Scrooge had observed at the baker's), that notwithstanding his gigantic size, he could accommodate himself to any place with ease; and that he stood beneath a low roof quite as gracefully and like a supernatural creature, as it was possible he could have done in any lofty hall.

The spirit led him straight to the home of his clerk, and on the threshold of the door the Spirit smiled, and stopped to bless Bob Cratchit's dwelling with the sprinkling of his torch. Think of that! Bob had but fifteen 'Bob' a-week himself; and yet the Ghost of Christmas Present blessed his four-roomed house!

Then up rose Mrs Cratchit, Cratchit's wife, dressed out

but poorly in a twice-turned gown, but brave in ribbons, which are cheap and make a goodly show for sixpence; and she laid the cloth, assisted by Belinda Cratchit, second of her daughters, also brave in ribbons; while Master Peter Cratchit plunged a fork into the saucepan of potatoes. And now two smaller Cratchits, boy and girl, came tearing in; and basking in luxurious thoughts of sage and onion, these young Cratchits danced about the table, and exalted Master Peter Cratchit to the skies, while he blew the fire, until the slow potatoes bubbling up, knocked loudly at the saucepan-lid to be let out and peeled.

"What has ever got your precious father then?" said Mrs Cratchit. "And your brother, Tiny Tim! And Martha warn't as late last Christmas Day by half-an-hour."

"Here's Martha, mother!" said a girl, appearing as she spoke.

"Why, bless your heart alive, my dear, how late you are!" said Mrs Cratchit, kissing her a dozen times, and taking off her shawl and bonnet for her with officious zeal.

"We'd a deal of work to finish up last night," replied the girl, "and had to clear away this morning, mother!"

"Well! Never mind so long as you are come," said Mrs Cratchit. "Sit ye down before the fire, my dear, and have a warm, Lord bless ye!"

"No, no! There's father coming," cried the two young Cratchits, who were everywhere at once. "Hide, Martha, hide!"

So Martha hid herself, and in came little Bob, the father, with at least three feet of comforter exclusive of the fringe, hanging down before him; and his threadbare clothes darned up and brushed, to look seasonable; and Tiny Tim upon his shoulder. Alas for Tiny Tim, he bore a little crutch, and had his limbs supported by an iron frame!

"Why, where's our Martha?" cried Bob Cratchit, looking round.

"Not coming," said Mrs Cratchit.

"Not coming!" said Bob, with a sudden declension in his high spirits. "Not coming upon Christmas Day!"

Martha didn't like to see him disappointed, if it were only in joke; so she came out prematurely from behind the closet door, and ran into his arms, while the two young Cratchits hustled Tiny Tim, and bore him off into the wash-house, that he might hear the pudding singing in the copper.

"And how did little Tim behave?" asked Mrs Cratchit, when she had rallied Bob on his credulity, and Bob had hugged his daughter to his heart's content.

"As good as gold," said Bob, "and better. Somehow he gets thoughtful, sitting by himself so much, and thinks the strangest things you ever heard. He told me, coming home, that he hoped the people saw him in the church, because he was a cripple, and it might be pleasant to them to remember upon Christmas Day, who made lame beggars walk, and blind men see."

Bob's voice was tremulous when he told them this, and trembled more when he said that Tiny Tim was growing strong and hearty.

His active little crutch was heard upon the floor, and back came Tiny Tim before another word was spoken, escorted by his brother and sister to his stool before the fire; and while Bob compounded some hot mixture in a jug with gin and lemons, and stirred it round and round and put it on the hob to simmer; Master Peter, and the two ubiquitous young Cratchits went to fetch the goose, with which they soon returned in high procession.

Such a bustle ensued that you might have thought a goose the rarest of all birds. Mrs Cratchit made the gravy (ready beforehand in a little saucepan) hissing hot; Master Peter mashed the potatoes with incredible vigour; Miss Belinda sweetened up the apple-sauce; Martha dusted the hot plates; Bob took Tiny Tim beside him in a tiny corner at the table; the two young Cratchits set chairs for everybody, not forgetting themselves, and mounting guard upon their posts, crammed spoons into their mouths. At last the dishes were set on, and grace was said. It was succeeded by a breathless pause, as Mrs Cratchit, looking slowly all along the carving-knife, prepared to plunge it in the breast; but when she did, and when the long expected gush of stuffing issued forth, one murmur of delight arose all round the board, and even Tiny Tim, excited by the two young Cratchits, beat on the table with the handle of his knife, and feebly cried "Hurrah!"

At last the dinner was all done, the cloth was cleared, the hearth swept, and the fire made up. The compound in the jug being tasted, and considered perfect, apples and oranges were put upon the table, and a shovel-full of chestnuts on the fire. Then all the Cratchit family drew round the hearth, and at Bob Cratchit's elbow stood the family display of glass: two tumblers, and a custard-cup without a handle.

These held the hot stuff from the jug. Bob served it out with beaming looks, while the chestnuts on the fire sputtered and cracked noisily. Then Bob proposed: "A Merry Christmas to us all, my dears. God bless us!"

Which all the family re-echoed.

"God bless us every one!" said Tiny Tim, last of all, very close to his father's side upon his little stool.

"Spirit," said Scrooge, with an interest he had never felt before, "tell me if Tiny Tim will live."

"I see a vacant seat," replied the Ghost, "in the poor chimney-corner, and a crutch without an owner, carefully preserved. If these shadows remain unaltered by the Future, the child will die."

"No, no," said Scrooge. "Oh, no, kind Spirit! say he will be spared."

"If he be like to die, he had better do it, and decrease the surplus population," returned the Ghost.

Scrooge hung his head to hear his own words quoted by the Spirit, and was overcome with penitence and grief.

It was a great surprise to Scrooge to hear a hearty laugh. It was a much greater surprise to Scrooge to recognize it as his own nephew's, and to find himself in a bright, dry, gleaming room, with the Spirit standing smiling by his side, and looking at that same nephew with approving affability!

"Ha, ha!" laughed Scrooge's nephew. "Ha, ha, ha!"

If you should happen, by any unlikely chance, to know a man more blest in a laugh than Scrooge's nephew, all I can say is, I should like to know him too. Introduce him to me, and I'll cultivate his acquaintance.

It is a fair, even-handed, noble adjustment of things, that while there is infection in disease and sorrow, there is nothing in the world so irresistibly contagious as laughter and good-humour. When Scrooge's nephew laughed in this way: holding his sides, rolling his head, and twisting his face into the most extravagant contortions: Scrooge's niece, by marriage, laughed as heartily as he. And their assembled friends being not a bit behindhand, roared out lustily.

"Ha, ha! Ha, ha, ha, ha" laughed the guests.

"He said that Christmas was a humbug, as I live!" cried Scrooge's nephew. "He believed it too!"

"More shame for him, Fred!" said Scrooge's niece, indignantly.

"He's a comical old fellow," said Scrooge's nephew, "that's the truth: and not so pleasant as he might be. However, his offences carry their own punishment, and I have nothing to say against him."

"I'm sure he is very rich, Fred," hinted Scrooge's niece. "At least you always tell *me* so."

"What of that, my dear!" said Scrooge's nephew. "His

wealth is of no use to him. He don't do any good with it. He don't make himself comfortable with it. He hasn't the satisfaction of thinking – ha, ha, ha! – that he is ever going to benefit US with it."

"I have no patience with him," observed Scrooge's niece. Scrooge's niece's sisters, and all the other ladies, expressed the same opinion.

"Oh, I have!" said Scrooge's nephew. "I am sorry for him; I couldn't be angry with him if I tried. Who suffers by his ill whims! Himself, always."

After a while everyone played at forfeits; for it is good to be children sometimes, and never better than at Christmas. There might have been twenty people there, young and old, but they all played, and so did Scrooge.

The Ghost was greatly pleased to find him in this mood, and looked upon him with such favour, that he begged like a boy to be allowed to stay until the guests departed. But this the Spirit said could not be done.

"My life upon this globe, is very brief. It ends tonight."

"Tonight!" cried Scrooge.

"Tonight at midnight. Hark! The time is drawing near."

The bell struck twelve.

Scrooge looked about him for the Ghost, and saw it not. As the last stroke ceased to vibrate, he remembered the prediction of old Jacob Marley, and lifting up his eyes, beheld a solemn Phantom, draped and hooded, coming, like a mist towards him.

## The Last Of The Spirits

The Phantom slowly, gravely, silently approached. When it came near him, Scrooge bent down upon his knee; for in the very air through which this Spirit moved it seemed to scatter gloom and mystery.

It was shrouded in a deep black garment, which concealed its head, its face, its form, and left nothing of it visible save one outstretched hand. But for this it would have been difficult to detach its figure from the night, and separate it from the darkness by which it was surrounded.

He felt that it was tall and stately when it came beside him, and that its mysterious presence filled him with a solemn dread.

"I am in the presence of the Ghost of Christmas Yet To Come?" said Scrooge.

The Spirit answered not, but pointed onward with its hand.

"Ghost of the Future!" he exclaimed, "I fear you more than any spectre I have seen. But as I know your purpose is to do me good, and as I hope to live to be another man from what I was, I am prepared to bear you company, and do it with a thankful heart. Will you not speak to me?"

It give him no reply. The hand was pointed straight before him.

"Lead on!" said Scrooge. "Lead on! The night is waning fast, and it is precious time to me, I know. Lead on, Spirit!"

The Phantom moved away as it had come towards him. Scrooge followed in the shadow of its dress, which bore him up, he thought, and carried him along.

They scarcely seemed to enter the city; for the city rather seemed to spring up about them, and encompass them of its own act. But there they were, in the heart of it; amongst the merchants, who hurried up and down, and chinked the money in their pockets, and conversed in groups, and looked at their watches, and trifled thoughtfully with their great gold seals; and so forth, as Scrooge had seen them often.

The Spirit stopped beside one little knot of business men. Observing that the hand was pointed to them, Scrooge advanced to listen to their talk.

214

"No," said a great fat man with a monstrous chin. "I don't know much about it, either way. I only know he's dead."

"When did he die?" inquired another.

"Last night, I believe."

"Why, what was the matter with him?" asked a third, taking a vast quantity of snuff out of a very large snuff-box. "I thought he'd never die."

"God knows," said the first, with a yawn.

"What has he done with his money?" asked a red-faced gentleman.

"I haven't heard," said the man with the large chin, yawning again. "Left it to his company, perhaps. He hasn't left it to *me*. That's all I know."

This pleasantry was received with a general laugh.

"It's likely to be a very cheap funeral," said the same speaker; "for upon my life I don't know of anybody to go to it. Suppose we make up a party and volunteer?"

"I don't mind going if a lunch is provided," observed the other gentleman.

Another laugh.

Scrooge knew the men, and looked towards the Spirit for an explanation.

The Phantom glided on into a street. Its finger pointed to two persons meeting. Scrooge listened again, thinking that the explanation might lie here.

He knew these men, also, perfectly. They were men of business: very wealthy, and of great importance. He had made a point always of standing well in their esteem: in a business point of view, that is; strictly in a business point of view.

"How are you?" said one.

"How are you?" returned the other.

"Well!" said the first. "Old Scratch has got his own at last, hey?"

"So I am told," returned the second. "Cold, isn't it?"

Scrooge was at first inclined to be surprised that the Spirit should attach importance to conversations apparently so trivial; but feeling assured that they must have some hidden purpose, he set himself to consider what it was likely to be. They could scarcely be supposed to have any bearing on the death of Jacob, his old partner, for that was Past, and this Ghost's province was the Future. Nor could he think of anyone immediately connected with himself, to whom he could apply them. But nothing doubting that to whomsoever they applied they had some latent moral for his own improvement, he resolved to treasure up every word he heard, and everything he saw; and especially to observe the shadow of himself when it appeared. For he had an expectation that the conduct of his future self would give him the clue he missed, and would render the solution of these riddles easy.

He looked about in that very place for his own image; but another man stood in his accustomed corner, and though the clock pointed to his usual time of day for being there, he saw no likeness of himself among the multitudes that poured in through the Porch. It gave him little surprise, however, for he had been revolving in his mind a change of life, and thought and hoped he saw his new-born resolutions carried out in this.

Quiet and dark, beside him stood the Phantom, with its outstretched hand. When he roused himself from his thoughtful quest, he fancied from the turn of the hand, and its situation in reference to himself, that the Unseen Eyes were looking at him keenly. It made him shudder, and feel very cold.

"Spirit!" said Scrooge, shuddering from head to foot. "I see, I see. The case of this unhappy man might be my own. Merciful Heaven, what is this!"

He recoiled in terror, for the scene had changed, and

now he almost touched a bed: a bare, uncurtained bed: on which, beneath a ragged sheet, there lay a something covered up, which, though it was dumb, announced itself in awful language.

The room was very dark, too dark to be observed with any accuracy, though Scrooge glanced round it in obedience to a secret impulse, anxious to know what kind of room it was. A pale light, rising in the outer air, fell straight upon the bed; and on it, plundered and bereft, unwatched, unwept, uncared for, was the body.

Scrooge glanced towards the Phantom. Its steady hand was pointed to the head. The cover was so carelessly adjusted that the slightest raising of it, the motion of a finger upon Scrooge's part, would have disclosed the face, he thought of it, felt how easy it would be to do, and longed to do it; but had no more power to withdraw the veil than to dismiss the spectre at his side.

Still the Ghost pointed with an unmoved finger to the head.

"I understand you," Scrooge returned, "and I would do it, if I could. But I have not the power, Spirit. I have not the power."

Again it seemed to look upon him.

"If there is any person in the town, who feels emotion caused by this man's death," said Scrooge quite agonized, "show that person to me, Spirit, I beseech you!"

The Phantom spread its dark robe before him for a moment, like a wing, and withdrawing it, revealed a room by daylight, where a mother and her children were.

She was expecting someone, and with anxious eagerness; for she walked up and down the room.

At length the long-expected knock was heard. She hurried to the door, and met her husband; a man whose face was careworn and depressed, though he was young.

"Is it good?" she said, "or bad?" – to help him.

217

"Bad," he answered.

"We are quite ruined?"

"No. There is hope yet, Caroline."

"If *he* relents," she said, amazed, "there is! Nothing is past hope, if such a miracle has happened."

"He is past relenting," said her husband. "He is dead."

She was a mild and patient creature if her face spoke truth; but she was thankful in her soul to hear it, and she said so, with clasped hands. She prayed forgiveness the next moment, and was sorry; but the first was the emotion of her heart.

"To whom will our debt be transferred?"

"I don't know. But before that time we shall be ready with the money; and even though we were not, it woud be a bad fortune indeed to find so merciless a creditor in his successor. We may sleep tonight with light hearts, Caroline!"

Yes. Soften it as they would, their hearts were lighter. The children's faces, hushed and clustered round to hear what they so little understood, were brighter; and it was a happier house for this man's death! The only emotion that the Ghost could show him, caused by the event was one of pleasure.

"Let me see some tenderness connected with a death," said Scrooge; "or that dark chamber, Spirit, which we left just now, will be for ever present to me."

The Ghost conducted him through several streets familiar to his feet; and as they went along, Scrooge looked here and there to find himself, but nowhere was he to be seen. They entered Poor Bob Cratchit's house; the dwelling he had visited before; and found the mother and the children seated round the fire.

They were quiet. Very quiet. The noisy little Cratchits were as still as statues in one corner, and sat looking up at

Peter, who had a book before him. The mother and her daughters were engaged in sewing. But surely they were very quiet!

"'And He took a child, and set him in the midst of them.'"

Where had Scrooge heard those words? He had not dreamed them. The boy must have read them out, as he and the Spirit crossed the threshold. Why did he not go on?

The mother laid her work upon the table, and put her hand up to her face.

"The colour hurts my eyes," she said.

The colour? Ah, poor Tiny Tim!

"They're better now again," said Cratchit's wife. "It makes them weak by candle-light; and I wouldn't show weak eyes to your father when he comes home, for the world. It must be near his time."

"Past it rather," Peter answered, shutting up his book. "But I think he has walked a little slower than he used, these few last evenings, mother."

They were very quiet again. At last she said, and in a steady, cheerful voice, that only faltered once:

"I have known him walk with – I have known him walk with Tiny Tim upon his shoulder, very fast indeed."

"And so have I," cried Peter. "Often."

"And so have I," exclaimed another. So had all.

"There is your father at the door!" said Mrs Cratchit.

She hurried out to meet him; and little Bob in his comforter – he had need of it, poor fellow – came in. His tea was ready for him on the hob, and they all tried who should help him to it most. Then the two young Cratchits got upon his knees and laid, each child a little cheek, against his face, as if they said, "Don't mind it, father. Don't be grieved!"

He broke down all at once. He couldn't help it. He left the room, and went upstairs into the room above, which was lighted cheerfully, and hung with Christmas. There was a chair set close beside the child, and there were signs of someone having been there, lately. Poor Bob sat down in it, and when he had thought a little and composed himself, he kissed the little face. He was reconciled to what had happened, and went down again quite happy.

They drew about the fire, and talked; the girls and mother working still. Bob told them of the extraordinary kindness of Mr Scrooge's nephew, whom he had scarcely seen but once, and who, meeting him in the street that day, and seeing that he looked a little – "just a little down you know," said Bob, inquired what had happened to distress him. "On which," said Bob, "for he is the pleasantest-spoken gentleman you ever heard, I told him. 'I am heartily sorry for it, Mr Cratchit,' he said, 'and heartily sorry for your good wife. If I can be of service to you in any way,' he said, giving me his card, 'that's where I live. Pray come to me.'

"Now, it wasn't," cried Bob, "for the sake of anything he might be able to do for us, so much as for his kind way, that this was quite delightful. It really seemed as if he had known our Tiny Tim, and felt with us."

"I'm sure he's a good soul!" said Mrs Cratchit.

"You would be surer of it, my dear," returned Bob, "if you saw and spoke to him. I shouldn't be at all surprised – mark what I say! – if he got Peter a better situation."

"Only hear that, Peter," said Mrs Cratchit.

"And then," cried one of the girls, "Peter will be keeping company with someone, and setting up for himself."

"Get along with you!" retorted Peter, grinning.

"It's just as likely as not," said Bob, "one of these days; though there's plenty of time for that, my dear. But, however and whenever we part from one another, I am sure we shall none of us forget poor Tiny Tim – shall we – or the first parting that there was among us?"

"Never, father!" cried they all.

"And I know," said Bob, "I know, my dears, that when we recollect how patient and how mild he was; although he was a little, little child; we shall not quarrel easily among ourselves, and forget poor Tiny Tim in doing it."

"No, never, father!" they all cried again.

"I am very happy," said little Bob, "I am very happy!"

Mrs Cratchit kissed him, his daughters kissed him, the two young Cratchits kissed him, and Peter and himself shook hands. Spirit of Tiny Tim, thy childish essence was from God!

"Spectre," said Scrooge, "something informs me that our parting moment is at hand. I know it, but I know not how. Tell me what man that was whom we saw lying dead?"

The Ghost of Christmas Yet To Come conveyed him, as before – though at a different time, he thought, into the resorts of business men, but showed him not himself. Indeed, the Spirit did not stay for anything, but went straight on, as to the end just now desired, until besought by Scrooge to tarry for a moment.

"This court," said Scrooge, "through which we hurry now, is where my place of occupation is, and has been for a length of time. I see the house. Let me behold what I shall be, in days to come!"

The Spirit stopped; the hand was pointed elsewhere.

"The house is yonder," Scrooge exclaimed. "Why do you point away?"

The inexorable finger underwent no change.

Scrooge hastened to the window of his office, and looked in. It was an office still, but not his. The furniture was not the same, and the figure in the chair was not himself. The Phantom pointed as before.

He joined it once again, and wondering why and whither he had gone, accompanied it until they reached an

iron gate. He paused to look round before entering.

A churchyard. Here, then, the wretched man whose name he had now to learn, lay underneath the ground. It was a worthy place. Walled in by houses; overrun by grass and weeds, the growth of vegetation's death, not life; choked up with too much burying; fat with repleted appetite. A worthy place!

The Spirit stood among the graves, and pointed down to One. Scrooge advanced towards it, trembling.

"Before I draw nearer to that stone to which you point," said Scrooge, "answer me one question. Are these the shadows of the things that Will be, or are they shadows of things that May be, only?"

Still the Ghost pointed downward to the grave by which it stood.

"Men's courses will foreshadow certain ends, to which, if persevered in, they must lead," said Scrooge. "But if the courses be departed from, the ends will change. Say it is thus with what you show me!"

The Spirit was immovable as ever.

Scrooge crept towards it, trembling as he went; and following the finger, read upon the stone of the neglected grave his own name, EBENEZER SCROOGE.

"Am *I* that man who lay upon the bed?" he cried, upon his knees.

The finger pointed from the grave to him, and back again.

"No, Spirit! Oh, no, no!"

The finger still was there.

"Spirit!" he cried, tight clutching at its robe, "hear me! I am not the man I was. Why show me this, if I am past all hope?"

For the first time the hand appeared to shake.

"Good Spirit," he pursued, as down upon the ground he fell before it: "Your nature intercedes for me, and pities me. Assure me that I yet may change these shadows you have shown me, by an altered life!"

The kind hand trembled.

"I will honour Christmas in my heart, and try to keep it all the year. I will live in the Past, the Present, and the Future. The Spirits of all Three shall strive within me. I will not shut out the lessons that they teach. Oh, tell me I may sponge away the writing on this stone!"

In his agony, he caught the spectral hand. It sought to free itself, but he was strong in his entreaty, and detained it. The Spirit, stronger yet, repulsed him.

Holding up his hands in a last prayer to have his fate reversed, he saw an alteration in the Phantom's hood and dress. It shrunk, collapsed, and dwindled down into a bedpost.

## The End Of It

Yes! and the bedpost was his own. The bed was his own, the room was his own. Best and happiest of all, the Time before him was his own, to make amends in!

"I will live in the Past, the Present, and the Future!" Scrooge repeated, as he scrambled out of bed. "The Spirits of all Three shall strive within me. Oh Jacob Marley! Heaven, and the Christmas Time be praised for this! I say it on my knees, old Jacob, on my knees!"

He was checked in his transports by the churches ringing out the lustiest peals he had ever heard. Clash, clang, hammer; ding, dong, bell.

Running to the window, he opened it, and put out his head. No fog, no mist; clear, bright, jovial, stirring, cold; golden sunlight; Heavenly sky; sweet fresh air; merry bells. Oh, glorious!

"What's today?" cried Scrooge, calling downward to a boy in Sunday clothes.

"Today!" replied the boy. "Why, CHRISTMAS DAY."

225

"It's Christmas Day!" said Scrooge to himself. "I haven't missed it. The Spirits have done it all in one night. They can do anything they like. Of course they can. Of course they can. Hallo, my fine fellow!"

"Hallo!" returned the boy.

"Do you know the Poulterer's, in the next street but one, at the corner?" Scrooge inquired.

"I should hope I did," replied the lad.

"Do you know whether they've sold the prize Turkey that was hanging up there?"

"It's hanging there now," replied the boy.

"Is it?" said Scrooge. "Go and buy it, and tell 'em to bring it here, that I may give them the direction where to take it. Come back with the man, and I'll give you a shilling. Come back with him in less than five minutes and I'll give you half-a-crown!"

The boy was off like a shot.

"I'll send it to Bob Cratchit's!" whispered Scrooge. "He sha'n't know who sends it."

The chuckle with which he said this, and the chuckle with which he paid for the Turkey, and the chuckle with which he recompensed the boy, were only to be exceeded by the chuckle with which he sat down breathless in his chair again, and chuckled till he cried.

He dressed himself "all in his best", and at last got out into the streets.

He had not gone far, when coming on towards him he beheld the portly gentleman, who had walked into his counting-house the day before, and said, "Scrooge and Marley's, I believe?" It sent a pang across his heart to think how this old gentleman would look upon him when they met; but he knew what path lay straight before him, and he took it.

"My dear sir," said Scrooge, quickening his pace, and taking the old gentleman by both his hands. "How do you

226

do? I hope you succeeded yesterday. It was very kind of you. A Merry Christmas to you, sir!"

"Mr Scrooge?"

"Yes," said Scrooge. "That is my name, and I fear it may not be pleasant to you. Allow me to ask your pardon. And will you have the goodness" – here Scrooge whispered in his.

"Lord bless me!" cried the gentleman, as if his breath were taken away. "My dear Mr Scrooge, are you serious?"

"If you please," said Scrooge. "Not a farthing less. A great many back-payments are included in it, I assure you. Will you do me that favour?"

"I will!" cried the old gentleman. And it was clear he meant to do it.

"Thank'ee," said Scrooge. "I am much obliged to you. I thank you fifty times. Bless you!"

He went to church, and walked about the streets, and watched the people hurrying to and fro, and patted children on the head, and questioned beggars, and looked down into the kitchens of houses, and up to the windows, and found that everything could yield him pleasure. He had never dreamed that any walk – that anything – could give him so much happiness. In the afternoon he turned his steps towards his nephew's house.

He passed the door a dozen times, before he had the courage to go up and knock. But he made a dash, and did it. "Is your master at home, my dear?" said Scrooge to the girl. Nice girl! Very.

"Yes, sir."

"Where is he, my love?" said Scrooge.

"He's in the dining-room, sir, along with mistress. I'll show you upstairs, if you please."

"Thank'ee. He knows me," said Scrooge, with his hand already on the dining-room lock. "I'll go in here, my dear."

"Why bless my soul!" cried Fred, "what's that?"

"It's I. Your uncle Scrooge. I have come to dinner. Will you let me in, Fred?"

Let him in! It is a mercy he didn't shake his arm off. He was at home in five minutes. Nothing could be heartier. Wonderful party, wonderful games, wonderful unanimity, won-der-ful happiness!

But he was early at the office next morning. Oh, he was early there. If he could only be there first, and catch Bob Cratchit coming late! That was the thing he had set his heart upon.

And he did it; yes, he did! The clock struck nine. No Bob. A quarter past. No Bob. He was full eighteen minutes and a half behind his time. Scrooge sat with his door wide open, that he might see him come into the Tank.

His hat was off, before he opened the door; his comforter too. He was on his stool in a jiffy; driving away with his pen, as if he were trying to overtake nine o'clock.

"Hallo!" growled Scrooge, in his accustomed voice, as near as he could feign it. "What do you mean by coming here at this time of day?"

"I am very sorry, sir," said Bob. "I *am* behind my time."

"You are?" repeated Scrooge. "Yes. I think you are. Step this way, sir, if you please."

"It's only once a year, sir," pleaded Bob, appearing from the Tank. "It shall not be repeated."

"Now, I'll tell you what, my friend," said Scrooge, "I am not going to stand this sort of thing any longer. And therefore," he continued, leaping from his stool, and giving Bob such a dig in the waistcoat that he staggered back into the Tank again; "and therefore I am about to raise your salary!"

Bob trembled, and got a little nearer to the ruler. He had a momentary idea of knocking Scrooge down with it, holding him, and calling for help.

228

"A merry Christmas, Bob!" said Scrooge, with an earnestness that could not be mistaken, as he clapped him on the back. "A merrier Christmas, Bob, my good fellow, than I have given you for many a year! I'll raise your salary, and endeavour to assist your struggling family, and we will discuss your affairs this very afternoon, over a Christmas bowl of smoking bishop, Bob! Make up the fires, and buy another coal-scuttle before you dot another i, Bob Cratchit!"

Scrooge was better than his word. He did it all, and infinitely more; and to Tiny Tim, who did NOT die, he was a second father. He became as good a friend, as good a master, and as good a man, as the good old city knew, or any other good old city, town, or borough, in the good old world. Some people laughed to see the alteration in him, but he let them laugh, and little heeded them; for he was wise enough to know that nothing ever happened on this globe, for good, at which some people did not have their fill of laughter in the outset; and knowing that such as these would be blind anyway, he thought it quite as well that they should wrinkle up their eyes in grins, as have the malady in less attractive forms. His own heart laughed; and that was quite enough for him.

He had no further intercourse with Spirits, and it was always said of him, that he knew how to keep Christmas well, if any man alive possessed the knowledge. May that be truly said of us, and all of us!

# The
# Old Curiosity
# Shop

## At the Shop

The place was one of those receptacles for old and curious things which seem to crouch in odd corners of this town and to hide their musty treasures from the public eye in jealousy and distrust. There were suits of mail standing like ghosts in armour here and there, fantastic carvings brought from monkish cloisters, rusty weapons of various kinds, distorted figures in china and wood and iron and ivory: tapestry and strange furniture that might have been designed in dreams. The haggard aspect of the little old man was wonderfully suited to the place; he might have groped among old churches and tombs and deserted houses and gathered all the spoils with his own hands. There was nothing in the whole collection but was in keeping with himself; nothing that looked older or more worn than he.

The door opened, a child entered and addressed him as grandfather.

"Why, bless thee, child," said the old man, patting her on the head, "you've been a long time. What if thou missed thy way? What if I had lost thee, Nell."

"I would have found my way back to you, grandfather," said the child boldly; "never fear".

There was a knock at the door and Nell, bursting into a hearty laugh, said it was no doubt dear old Kit come back at last.

Kit was a shock-headed shambling awkward lad with an uncommonly wide mouth, very red cheeks, a turned-up nose, and the most comical expression of face. He was the comedy of the child's life.

"A long way, wasn't it, Kit?" said the little old man.

"Why then, it was a goodish stretch, master," returned Kit.

"Did you find the house easily?"

"Why then, not over and above easy, master," said Kit.

"Of course you have come back hungry?"

"Why then, I do consider myself rather so, master," was the answer.

He carried a large slice of bread and meat and a mug of beer into a corner, and applied himself to disposing of them with great voracity

"Ah!" said the old man, with a sigh. "Come hither, Nell."

The little girl hastened from her seat, and put her arm about his neck.

"Do I love thee, Nell?" said he. "Say – do I love thee, Nell, or no?"

"Indeed, indeed you do," replied the child with great earnestness, "Kit knows you do."

"She is poor now," said the old man, patting the child's cheek, "but I say again that the time is coming when she shall be rich. It has been a long time coming, but it must come at last; a very long time, but it surely must come. It has come to other men who do nothing but waste and riot. When *will* it come to me!"

"I am very happy as I am, grandfather," said the child.

"Tush, tush!" returned the old man, "thou dost not know – how shouldst thou!" Then he muttered between his teeth. And still holding the child between his knees he appeared to be insensible to everything around him.

The child soon occupied herself in preparations for giving Kit a writing lesson, of which it seemed he had a couple every week, and one regularly on that evening, to the great mirth and enjoyment both of himself and his instructress.

The lesson was given – evening passed and night came on – the old man grew restless and impatient – he quitted the house secretly – and the child was left alone within its gloomy walls.

232

# Enter Mr Quilp

Mr Quilp could scarcely be said to be of any particular trade or calling, though his pursuits were diversified and his occupations numerous. He collected the rents of whole colonies of filthy streets and alleys by the waterside, advanced money to the seamen and petty officers of merchant vessels, had a share in the ventures of divers mates of East Indiamen, and smoked his smuggled cigars under the very nose of the Custom House. On the Surrey side of the river was a small rat-infested dreary yard called 'Quilp's Wharf', in which were a little wooden counting-house burrowing all awry in the dust as if it had fallen from the clouds and ploughed into the ground; a few fragments of rusty anchors; several large iron rings; some piles of rotten wood; and two or three heaps of old sheet copper, crumpled, cracked, and battered. On Quilp's Wharf, Daniel Quilp was a ship-breaker, yet to judge from these appearances he must either have been a ship-breaker on a very small scale, or have broken his ships up very small indeed.

It was flood tide when Daniel Quilp sat himself down in the boat to cross to the opposite shore.

Arrived at his destination, the first object that presented itself to his view was a pair of very imperfectly shod feet elevated in the air with the soles upwards, which remarkable appearance was referable to a boy, who being of an eccentric spirit and having a natural taste for tumbling was now standing on his head and contemplating the aspect of the river under these uncommon circumstances. He was speedily brought on his heels by the sound of his master's voice, and as soon as his head was in its right position, Mr Quilp, to speak expressively in the absence of a better verb, 'punched it' for him.

"Come, you let me alone," said the boy, parrying Quilp's hand with both his elbows alternately. "You'll get

233

something you won't like if you don't, and so I tell you."

"You dog," snarled Quilp, "I'll beat you with an iron rod, I'll scratch you with a rusty nail, I'll pinch your eyes, if you talk to me – I will. Now, open the counting-house."

The boy sulkily complied, muttering at first, but desisting when he looked round and saw that Quilp was following him with a steady look.

It was a dirty little box, this counting-house, with nothing in it but an old rickety desk and two stools, a hat-peg, an ancient almanac, an inkstand with no ink and the stump of one pen, and an eight-day clock which hadn't gone for eighteen years at least and of which the minute-hand had been twisted off for a tooth-pick. Daniel Quilp pulled his hat over his brows, climbed on to the desk (which had a flat top), and stretching his short length upon it (for Quilp was a dwarf) went to sleep with the ease of an old practitioner.

He had not been asleep a quarter of an hour when the boy opened the door and thrust in his head. Quilp was a light sleeper and started up directly.

"Here's somebody for you," said the boy.

"Who?"

"I don't know."

"Ask!" said Quilp, seizing a piece of wood and throwing it at him with such dexterity that it was well the boy disappeared before it reached the spot on which he had stood. "Ask, you dog."

Not caring to venture within range of such missiles again, the boy discreetly sent in his stead the first cause of the interruption, who now presented herself at the door.

"What, Nelly!" cried Quilp.

"Yes," said the child, hesitating whether to enter or retreat, for the dwarf just roused, with his dishevelled hair hanging all about him and a yellow handkerchief over his head, was something fearful to behold; "it's only me, sir."

"Well. Now, come in and shut the door. What's your message, Nelly?"

The child handed him a letter; Mr Quilp, without changing his position further than to turn over a little more on his side and rest his chin on his hand, proceeded to make himself acquainted with its contents.

"Hallo here!" he said at length, in a voice, and with a suddenness, which made the child start as though a gun had been fired off at her ear. "Nelly!"

"Yes, sir."

"Do you know what's inside this letter, Nell?"

"No, sir!"

"Are you sure, quite sure, quite certain, upon your soul?"

"Quite sure, sir."

"Do you wish you may die if you do know, hey?" said the dwarf.

"Indeed I don't know," returned the child.

"Well!" muttered Quilp, as he marked her earnest look. "I believe you. Humph! Gone already? Gone in four-and-twenty hours! What the devil has he done with it, that's the mystery!"

This reflection set him scratching his head and biting his nails once more. While he was thus employed his features gradually relaxed into what was with him a cheerful smile, but which in any other man would have been a ghastly grin of pain.

"Are you tired, Nelly?"

"No, sir. I'm in a hurry to get back, for he will be anxious while I am away."

"There's no hurry, little Nell, no hurry at all," said Quilp.

"I must go back," said the child. "He told me to return directly I had the answer."

The child, overpowered by the weight of her sorrows and anxieties burst into a passion of tears.

"Well," he said, "here's the note. It's only to say that I shall see him tomorrow or maybe next day, and that I couldn't do that little business for him this morning. Goodbye, Nelly."

Nelly, shedding tears, departed.

## Nell's Troubles

It was not the monotonous day unchequered by variety and uncheered by pleasant companionship, it was not the dark dreary evenings or the long solitary nights, it was not the absence of every slight and easy pleasure for which young hearts beat high, or the knowing nothing of childhood but its weakness and its easily wounded spirit, that had wrung such tears from Nell. To see her grandfather struck down beneath the pressure of some hidden grief, to mark his wavering and unsettled state, to be agitated at times with a dreadful fear that his mind was wandering, and to trace in his words and looks the dawning of despondent madness; to watch and wait and listen for confirmation of these things day after day, and to feel and know that, come what might, they were alone in the world with no one to help or advise or care about them – these were causes of depression and anxiety that might have sat heavily on an older breast with many influences at work to cheer and gladden it, but how heavily on the mind of a young child to whom they were ever present.

And yet, to the old man's vision, Nell was still the same; there was the same smile for him, the same earnest words, the same merry laugh, the same love and care that sinking deep into his soul seemed to have been present to him through his whole life.

One night, the third after Nelly's interview with Mr Quilp, the old man, who had been weak and ill all day, said he would not leave home that night. The child's eyes sparkled at the intelligence, but her joy subsided when they reverted to his worn and sickly face.

"Two days," he said, "two whole, clear days have passed, and there is no reply. What *did* he tell thee, Nell?"

"Exactly what I told you, dear grandfather, indeed."

"True," said the old man, faintly. "Yes. But tell me again, Nell. My head fails me. What was it that he told thee? Nothing more than that he would see me tomorrow or next day? That was in the note."

"Nothing more," said the child. "Shall I go to him again tomorrow, dear grandfather? Very early? I will be there and back before breakfast."

The old man shook his head, and sighing mournfully, drew her towards him.

"'Twould be of no use, my dear, no earthly use. But if he deserts me, Nell, at this moment – if he deserts me now, when I should, with his assistance, be recompensed for all the time and money I have lost, and all the agony of mind I have undergone, which makes me what you see, I am ruined, and – worse, far worse that that – have ruined thee, for whom I ventured all. If we are beggars –!"

"What if we are?" said the child boldly. "Let us be beggars, and be happy."

"Beggars – and happy!" said the old man. "Poor child!"

"Dear grandfather," cried the girl, with an energy which shone in her flushed face, trembling voice, and impassioned gesture, "I am not a child in that I think, but even if I am, oh hear me pray that we may beg, or work in open roads or fields, to earn a scanty living, rather than live as we do now."

The child's voice was lost in sobs as she dropped upon the old man's neck; not did she weep alone.

These were not words for other ears, nor was it a scene for other eyes. And yet other ears and eyes were there and greedily taking in all that passed, and moreover they were the ears and eyes of no less a person than Mr Daniel Quilp, who, having entered unseen when the child first placed herself at the old man's side, refrained – actuated, no doubt, by motives of the purest delicacy – from interrupting the conversation, and stood looking on with his accustomed grin.

The old man at length chanced to see him, to his unbounded astonishment.

Nell looked at the old man, who nodded to her to retire, and kissed her cheek.

The dwarf said never a word, but watched his companion as he paced restlessly up and down the room, and presently returned to his seat. Here he remained, with his head bowed upon his breast for some time, and then suddenly raising it, said, "Once, and once for all, have you brought me any money?"

"No!" replied Quilp.

"Then," said the old man, clenching his hands desperately, and looking upward, "the child and I are lost!"

"Neighbour," said Quilp, glancing sternly at him, "let me be plain with you. You have no secret from me now."

The old man looked up, trembling.

"You are surprised," said Quilp. "Well, perhaps that's natural. You have no secret from me now, I say; no, not one. For now I know that all those sums of money, that all those loans, advances, and supplies that you have had from me, have found their way to – shall I say the word?"

"Aye!" replied the old man, "say it, if you will."

"To the gaming-table," rejoined Quilp, "your nightly haunt. This was the precious scheme to make your fortune, was it; this was the secret certain source of wealth in which I was to have sunk my money (if I had been the fool you took me for); this was your inexhaustible mine of gold, your El Dorado, eh?"

"Yes," cried the old man, turning upon him with gleaming eyes, "it was. It is. It will be till I die."

"That I should have been blinded," said Quilp, looking contemptuously at him, "by a mere shallow gambler!"

"I am no gambler," cried the old man fiercely. "I call Heaven to witness that I never played for gain of mine, or love of play; that at every piece I staked, I whispered to myself that orphan's name and called on Heaven to bless the venture, which it never did."

"I thought," sneered the dwarf, "that if a man played long enough he was sure to win at last, or at the worst not to come off a loser."

"And so he is," cried the old man, suddenly rousing himself from his state of despondency. "I have no resource but you, give me some help, let me try this one last hope. Help me for her sake I implore you – not for mine, for hers!"

"I'm sorry, I've got an appointment in the city," said Quilp, looking at his watch with perfect self-possession, "or I should have been very glad to have spent half an hour with you while you composed yourself – very glad."

"I was so deceived by your miserly way, the reputation you had among those who knew you of being rich, and your repeated assurances that you would make of my advances treble and quadruple the interest you paid me, that I'd have advanced you even now what you want, on your simple note of hand, though I had been led to suspect something wrong, if I hadn't unexpectedly become acquainted with your secret way of life," said Quilp.

"Who is it," retorted the old man desperately, "that notwithstanding all my caution, told you? Come. Let me know the name – the person."

The crafty dwarf, stopped short in his answer and said, "Now, who do you think?"

"It was Kit, it must have been the boy; he played the spy," said the old man.

"How came you to think of him?" said the dwarf in a

tone of great commiseration. "Yes, it was Kit. Poor Kit!"

So saying, he nodded in a friendly manner, and took his leave, still chuckling as he went.

## Poor Kit

Daniel Quilp neither entered nor left the old man's house, unobserved. In the shadow of an archway nearly opposite, there lingered one who having taken up his position when the twilight first came on, scarcely changed his attitude for the hour together.

At length he gave the matter up as hopeless for that night, and suddenly breaking into a run as though to force himself away, scampered off at his utmost speed, nor once ventured to look behind him lest he should be tempted back again.

This mysterious individual dashed on through a great many alleys and making for a small house from the window of which a light was shining, lifted the latch of the door and passed in.

"Bless us!" cried a woman, turning sharply round, "who's that? Oh! It's you, Kit!"

"Yes, mother, it's me."

"Why, how tired you look, my dear!"

"Old master an't gone out tonight," said Kit. "Worse luck."

"You should say better luck, I think," returned his mother, "because Miss Nelly won't have been left alone."

"Ah!" said Kit, "I forgot that. I said worse luck, because I've been watching ever since eight o'clock, and seen nothing of her."

"I wonder what she'd say," cried his mother, stopping in her work and looking round, "if she knew that every night, when she – poor thing – is sitting alone at that window, you are watching in the open street for fear any harm should come to her, and that you never leave the place or come home to your bed though you're ever so tired, till such time as you think she's safe in hers."

"Never mind what she'd say," replied Kit, with something like a blush on his uncouth face; "she'll never know nothing, and consequently, she'll never say nothing."

"Some people would say that you'd fallen in love with her, I know they would."

To this, Kit replied by bashfully bidding his mother, "Get out."

"Speaking seriously though, Kit," said his mother, taking up the theme afresh, after a time, "it's a cruel thing to keep the dear child shut up there. I don't wonder that the old gentleman wants to keep it from you."

"He don't think it's cruel, bless you," said Kit, "and don't mean it to be so, or he wouldn't do it — I do consider, mother, that he wouldn't do it for all the gold and silver in the world. No, no, that he wouldn't. I know him better than that."

"Then what does he do it for, and why does he keep it so close from you?" said Mrs Nubbles.

"That I don't know," returned her son. "If he hadn't tried to keep it so close though, I should never have found it out, for it was his getting me away at night and sending me off so much earlier than he used to, that first made me curious to know what was going on. Hark! what's that?"

"It's only somebody outside."

"It's somebody crossing over here," said Kit, standing up to listen, "and coming very fast too. He can't have gone out after I left, and the house caught fire, mother!"

The footsteps drew nearer, the door was opened with a hasty hand, and the child herself, pale and breathless, and hastily wrapped in a few disordered garments, hurried into the room.

"Miss Nelly! What is the matter!" cried mother and son together.

"I must not stay a moment," she returned, "grandfather has been taken very ill, I found him in a fit upon the floor –"

"I'll run for a doctor," said Kit, seizing his brimless hat. "I'll be there directly, I'll –"

"No, no," cried Nell, "there is one there, you're not wanted, you – you – must never come near us any more!"

"What!" roared Kit.

"Never again," said the child. "Don't ask me why, for I don't know. Pray don't ask me why, pray don't be sorry, pray don't be vexed with me, I have nothing to do with it indeed! He complains and raves of you. I don't know what you have done, but I hope it's nothing very bad."

The unfortunate Kit looked at his young mistress harder and harder, and with eyes growing wider and wider, but was perfectly motionless and silent.

"I have brought his money for the week," said the child, looking to the woman and laying it on the table, "and – and – a little more, for Kit was always good and kind to me. It grieves me very much to part with him like this, but there is no help. It must be done. Good night!"

With the tears streaming down her face, and her slight figure trembling with the agitation of the scene she had left, the shock she had received, the errand she had just discharged, and a thousand painful and affectionate feelings, the child hastened to the door, and disappeared as rapidly as she had come.

The poor woman, who had no cause to doubt her son, but every reason for relying on his honesty and truth, was staggered by his not having advanced one word in his defence.

Kit, insensible to all the din and tumult, remained in a state of utter stupefaction.

## Escape

Next morning the old man was in a raging fever accompanied with delirium, and sinking under the influence of this disorder he lay for many weeks in imminent peril of his life.

The child was more alone than she had ever been before.

The house was no longer theirs. Even the sick chamber seemed to be retained on the uncertain tenure of Mr Quilp's favour. The old man's illness had not lasted many days when Quilp took formal possession of the premises and all upon them, in virtue of certain legal powers to that effect, which few understood and none presumed to call in question. This important step secured, with the assistance of a man of law whom he brought with him for the purpose, the dwarf proceeded to establish himself and his assistant, Brass, in the house.

Brass was an attorney of no very good repute in the city of London. Dust and cobwebs were among the most prominent decorations of the office of Mr Sampson Brass.

His clerk, assistant, housekeeper, secretary, confidential plotter, adviser, intriguer, and bill of cost increaser was Miss Brass – a kind of amazon at common law.

Miss Sally Brass was a lady of thirty-five or thereabouts, of a gaunt and bony figure, and a resolute bearing, which if it repressed the softer emotions of love, and kept admirers at a distance, certainly inspired a feeling akin to awe in the breasts of those male strangers who had the happiness to approach her.

## The Adventurers Depart

Thursday arrived, and there was no alteration in the old man. But a change came upon him that evening as he and the child sat silently together.

He shed tears – tears that it lightened her aching heart to see – and making as though he would fall upon his knees, besought her to forgive him.

"Forgive you – what?" said Nell, interposing to prevent his purpose. "Oh grandfather, what should *I* forgive?"

"All that is past, all that has come upon thee, Nell," returned the old man.

"Do not talk so," said the child. "Pray do not. Let us speak of something else."

"Yes, yes, we will," he rejoined. "And it shall be of what we talked of long ago – many months – months is it, or weeks, or days? Which is it, Nell?"

"I do not understand you," said the child.

"It has come back upon me today, it has all come back since we have been sitting here. I bless thee for it, Nell!"

"For what, dear grandfather?"

"For what you said when we were first made beggars, Nell. Let us speak softly. Hush! for if they knew our purpose downstairs, they would cry that I was mad and take thee from me. We will not stop here another day. We will go far away from here."

"Yes, let us go," said the child earnestly. "Let us be gone from this place, and never turn back or think of it again. Let us wander barefoot through the world, rather than linger here."

"We will," answered the old man, "we will travel afoot through fields and woods, and by the side of rivers, and trust ourselves to God in the places where He dwells."

"We will be happy," cried the child. "We never can be here."

"No, we never can again – never again – that's truly said," rejoined the old man. "Let us steal away tomorrow morning – early and softly, that we may not be seen or heard – and leave no trace or track for them to follow by."

The child's heart beat high with hope and confidence.

At length the day began to glimmer, and the stars to grow pale and dim.

The child then took him by the hand, and they trod lightly and cautiously down the stairs, trembling whenever a board creaked, and often stopping to listen.

It was the beginning of a day in June; the deep blue sky unsullied by a cloud, and teeming with brilliant light.

The old man and the child passed on through the glad silence, elate with hope and pleasure.

## Good Fortune for Kit

Kit walked about, now with quick steps and now with slow; now lingering as some rider slackened his horse's pace and looked about him; and now darting at full speed up a bye-street as he caught a glimpse of some distant horseman going lazily up the shady side of the road, and promising to stop, at every door. But on they all went, one after another, and there was not a penny stirring.

He was quite tired out with pacing the streets, to say nothing of repeated disappointments, and was sitting down upon a step to rest, when there approached towards him a little clattering jingling four-wheeled chaise, drawn by a little obstinate-looking rough-coated pony, and driven by a little fat placid-faced old gentleman. Beside the little old gentleman sat a little old lady, plump and placid like himself, and the pony was coming along at his own pace and doing exactly as he pleased with the whole concern.

As they passed where he sat, Kit looked so wistfully at the little turn-out that the old gentleman looked at him, and, rising and putting his hand to his hat, intimated to the pony that he wished to stop.

"I beg your pardon, sir," said Kit. "I'm sorry you stopped, sir. I only meant did you want your horse minded."

"I'm going to get down in the next street," returned the old gentleman. "If you'd like to come on after us, you may have the job."

Kit thanked him, and joyfully obeyed.

The pony stopped no more until he came to a door whereon was a brass plate with the words "Witherden – Notary". Here the old gentleman got out and helped out the old lady, and then took from under the seat a nosegay resembling in shape and dimensions a full-sized warming-pan with the handle cut short off. This, the old lady carried into the house with a staid and stately air, and the old gentleman followed close upon her.

They went, as it was easy to tell from the sound of their voices, into the front parlour, which seemed to be a kind of office. The day being very warm and the street a quiet one, the windows were wide open, and it was easy to hear through the Venetian blinds all that passed inside.

At first there was a great shaking of hands and shuffling of feet, succeeded by the presentation of the nosegay, for a voice, supposed by the listener to be that of Mr Witherden the Notary, was heard to exclaim a great many times, "Oh, fragrant indeed!"

"I brought it in honour of the occasion, sir," said the old lady.

"Ah, an occasion indeed, Mrs Garland; an occasion which does honour to me, ma'am, honour to me," rejoined Mr Witherden the Notary. "I have had many a gentleman articled to me, ma'am, many a one, but there was never one among the number, ma'am, attached as I have been to many of them, of whom I augured such bright things as I do of your only son, Abel."

"Chuckster, bring in Mr Abel's articles. I am about to sign my name, you observe, at the foot of the articles which Mr Chuckster will witness. You see how easily these things are done!"

In about a quarter of an hour Mr Chuckster (with a pen behind his ear and his face inflamed with wine) appeared at the door, and informed Kit that the visitors were coming out.

Out they came forthwith; Mr Witherden, leading the old lady with extreme politeness, and the father and son following them, arm in arm.

The old gentleman, Mr Garland taking his seat and the reins, put his hand in his pocket to find a sixpence for Kit.

He had no sixpences, neither had the old lady, nor Mr Abel, nor the Notary, nor Mr Chuckster. The old gentleman thought a shilling too much, but there was no shop in the street to get change at, so he gave it to the boy.

"There," he said jokingly, "I'm coming here again next Monday at the same time, and mind you're here, my lad, to work it out."

"Thank you, sir," said Kit. "I'll be sure to be here."

At this Mr Witherden whispered behind the nosegay to the old gentleman that he believed the lad was as honest a lad as need be.

"Now," said Mr Garland, when they had made some further inquiries of him, "perhaps I may want to know something more about you, so tell me where you live and I'll put it down in my pocket-book."

Kit told him, and the old gentleman wrote down the address with his pencil.

The old gentleman took his place and they drove away, waving a farewell to the Notary and his clerk, and more than once turning to nod kindly to Kit as he watched them from the road.

Kit turned away, but when he came to the corner of the court in which he lived, lo and behold there was the pony again!

He lifted the latch of the door, and walking in, found them seated in the room in conversation with his mother, at which unexpected sight he pulled off his hat and made his best bow in some confusion.

"We are here before you, you see, Christopher," said Mr Garland, smiling.

"Yes, sir," said Kit; and as he said it he looked towards his mother for an explanation of the visit.

"The gentleman's been kind enough, my dear," said she, in reply to this mute interrogation, "to ask me whether you were in a good place, or in any place at all, and when I told him no, you were not in any, he was so good as to say that –"

"That we wanted a good lad in our house," said the old gentleman and the old lady both together.

Whereupon, Kit was formally hired at an annual income of six pounds, over and above his board and lodging, by Mr and Mrs Garland, of Abel Cottage, Finchley.

## The Travellers

It was not until they were quite exhausted that the old man and the child ventured to stop and sit down to rest upon the borders of a litte wood.

"We are quite safe now, and have nothing to fear, grandfather," Nell said.

When they rose up from the ground, and took the shady track which led them through the wood, she bounded on. The old man cast no longer fearful looks behind, but felt at ease and cheerful, for the further they passed into the deep green shade, the more they felt that the tranquil mind of God was there, and shed its peace on them.

At length the path, becoming clearer and less intricate, brought them to the end of the wood, and into a public road. A broken finger-post announced that this led to a village three miles off; and thither they resolved to bend their steps.

The miles appeared so long that they sometimes thought they must have missed their road. But at last, to their great joy, it led downward in a steep descent, with overhanging banks over which the footpaths led; and the clustered houses of the village peeped out from the woody hollow below.

It was a very small place. The men and boys were playing cricket on the green; and as the other folk were looking on, they wandered up and down, uncertain where to seek a humble lodging. There was but one old man in the little garden before his cottage, and him they were timid of approaching, for he was the schoolmaster, and had 'School' written up over his window in black letters on a white board.

"Speak to him, dear," the old man whispered.

Nell dropped a curtsey, and told him they were poor travellers.

"If you could direct us anywhere, sir," said the child, "we should take it very kindly."

"You're a young traveller, my child," he said, laying his hand gently on her head. "Your grandchild, friend?"

"Aye, sir," cried the old man, "and the stay and comfort of my life."

"Come in," said the schoolmaster.

Without further preface he conducted them into his little schoolroom, which was parlour and kitchen likewise. Before they had done thanking him, he spread a coarse white cloth upon the table, with knives and platters; and bringing out some bread and cold meat and a jug of beer, besought them to eat and drink.

By the time they were ready to depart, school had begun. The schoolmaster walked with them to the gate.

It was with a trembling and reluctant hand, that the child held out to him money, faltering in her thanks as she thought how small the sum was, and blushing as she offered it. But he bade her put it away, and stooping to kiss her cheek, turned back into the house.

They had not gone half-a-dozen paces when he was at the door again; the old man retraced his steps to shake hands, and the child did the same.

"Good fortune and happiness go with you!" said the schoolmaster. "I am quite a solitary man now. If ever you pass this way again, you'll not forget the little village school."

"We shall never forget it, sir," rejoined Nell; "nor ever forget to be grateful to you for your kindness to us."

They bade him farewell very many times, and turned away, walking slowly and often looking back, until they could see him no more.

Clear of town, they took a footpath which struck through some pleasant fields. It had been gradually getting overcast, and now the sky was dark and lowering. Large drops of rain soon began to fall and, as the storm clouds came sailing onward, others supplied the void they left behind and spread over all the sky. Then was heard the low rumbling of distant thunder, and lightning quivered.

Drenched with the pelting rain, confused by the deafening thunder, and bewildered by the glare of the forked lightning, they would have passed a solitary house without being aware of its vicinity, had not a man, who was standing at the door, called lustily to them to enter.

"What were you going past for, eh?" he added, as he closed the door and led the way along a passage to a room behind.

"We didn't see the house, sir, till we heard you calling," Nell replied.

"No wonder," said the man, "with this lightning in one's eyes. You had better stand by the fire here, and dry yourselves a bit. You can call for what you like if you want anything. If you don't want anything, you are not obliged to give an order. This is a public-house, that's all."

The night being warm, there was a large screen drawn across the room, for a barrier against the heat of the fire.

"Nell, they're – they're playing cards," whispered the old man, suddenly interested. "Don't you hear them?

"Do you hear, Nell, do you hear them?" whispered the old man again, with increased earnestness, as the money chinked upon the table.

"I haven't seen such a storm as this," said a sharp cracked voice of most disagreeable quality, when a tremendous peal of thunder had died away, "since the night when old Luke Withers won thirteen times running, upon the red. We all said he had the Devil's luck and his own, and as it was the kind of night for the Devil to be out and busy."

"Do you hear what he says?" whispered the old man. "Do you hear that, Nell?"

The child saw with astonishment and alarm that his whole appearance had undergone a complete change. His face was flushed and eager, his eyes were strained, his teeth set, his breath came short and thick, and the hand he laid upon her arm trembled so violently that she shook beneath its grasp.

"Bear witness," he muttered, looking upward, "that I always said it; that I knew it, dreamed of it, felt it was the truth, and that it must be so! What money have we, Nell? Come, I saw you with money yesterday. What money have we? Give it to me."

"No, no, let me keep it, grandfather," said the frightened child. "Let us go away from here. Do not mind the rain. Pray let us go."

"Give it to me, I say," returned the old man fiercely. "Hush, hush, don't cry, Nell. If I spoke sharply, dear, I didn't mean it. It's for thy good. I have wronged thee, Nell, but I will right thee yet, I will indeed. Where is the money?"

"Do not take it," said the child. "Pray do not take it, dear. For both our sakes let me keep it, or let me throw it away – better let me throw it away, than you take it now. Let us go; do let us go."

"Give me the money," returned the old man, "I must have it. There – there – that's my dear Nell. I'll right thee one day, child, I'll right thee, never fear!"

She took from her pocket a little purse. He seized it with the same rapid impatience which had characterised his speech, and hastily made his way to the other side of the screen. It was impossible to restrain him, and the trembling child followed close behind.

"Sit thee down, Nell," cried the old man, "sit thee down and look on. Be of good heart, it's all for thee – all – every penny. I don't tell them, no, no, or else they wouldn't play, dreading the chance that such a cause must give me. Look at them. See what they are and what thou art. Who doubts that we must win!"

As he spoke he drew a chair to the table; and the other three closing round it at the same time, the game commenced.

The child sat by, and watched its progress with a troubled mind. Regardless of the run of luck, and mindful only of the desperate passion which had its hold upon her grandfather, losses and gains were to her alike. Exulting in some brief triumph, or cast down by a defeat, there he sat so wild and restless, so feverishly and intensely anxious, so terribly eager, so ravenous for the paltry stakes, that she could have almost better borne to see him dead. And yet she was the innocent cause of all this torture, and he, gambling with such a savage thirst for gain as the most insatiable gambler never felt, had not one selfish thought!

At length the play came to an end, and Mr Isaac List rose the only winner.

"Do you know what the time is?" said Mr Groves, the

landlord, who was smoking with his friends. "Past twelve o'clock."

"It's very late," said Nell. "I wish we had gone before. What would it cost, sir, if we stopped here?"

"Two good beds, one and sixpence; supper and beer, one shilling; total, two shillings and sixpence," he replied.

She decided, after a great deal of hesitation, to remain. She took her grandfather aside, and telling him that she had still enough left to defray the cost of their lodging, proposed that they should stay there for the night.

"If I had had that money before – if I had only known of it a few minutes ago!" muttered the old man.

"We will decide to stop here if you please," said Nell, turning hastily to the landlord.

The old man took leave of the company, and they went upstairs together.

At last, sleep gradually stole upon her – a broken, fitful sleep, troubled by dreams of falling from high towers, and waking with a start and in great terror. A deeper slumber followed this – and then – what! That figure in the room!

A figure was there. Yes, she had drawn up the blind to admit the light when it should dawn, and there, between the foot of the bed and the dark casement, it crouched and slunk along, groping its way with noiseless hands, and stealing round the bed. She had no voice to cry for help, no power to move, but lay still, watching.

On it came – on, silently and stealthily, to the bed's head. The breath so near her pillow, that she shrunk back into it, lest those wandering hands should light upon her face. Back again it stole to the window – then turned its head towards her.

The dark form was a mere blot upon the lighter darkness of the room, but she saw the turning of the head, and felt and knew how the eyes looked and the ears listened. There it remained, motionless as she. At length, still

keeping the face towards her, it busied its hands in something, and she heard the chink of money.

Then, on it came again, silent and stealthy as before, and, replacing the garments it had taken from the bedside, dropped upon its hand and knees, and crawled away. How slowly it seemed to move, now that she could hear but not see it, creeping along the floor! It reached the door at last, and stood upon its feet. The steps creaked beneath its noiseless tread, and it was gone.

The first impulse of the child was to fly from the terror of being by herself in that room – to have somebody by – not to be alone – and then her power of speech would be restored. With no consciousness of having moved, she gained the door.

Once in her grandfather's room, she would be safe.

It crept along the passage until it came to the very door she longed so ardently to reach. The child, in the agony of being so near, had almost darted forward with the design of bursting into the room and closing it behind her, when the figure stopped again.

The idea flashed suddenly upon her – what if it entered there, and had a design upon the old man's life! She turned faint and sick. It did. It went in. There was a light inside. The figure was now within the chamber, and she, still dumb – quite dumb, and almost senseless – stood looking on.

The door was partly open. Not knowing what she meant to do, but meaning to preserve him or be killed herself, she staggered forward and looked in. What sight was that which met her view!

The bed had not been lain on, but was smooth and empty. And at a table sat the old man himself, the only living creature there, his white face pinched and sharpened by the greediness which made his eyes unnaturally bright, counting the money of which his hands had robbed her.

The first idea that flashed upon her mind was flight, instant flight; dragging him from that place, and rather dying of want upon the roadside than ever exposing him again to such terrible temptations.

Half undressed, and with her hair in wild disorder, she flew to the old man's bedside.

"What's this!" he cried, fixing his eyes upon her.

"I have had a dreadful dream," said the child, with an energy that nothing but such terrors could have inspired. "A dreadful, horrible dream. I have had it once before. It is a dream of grey-haired men like you, in darkened rooms by night, robbing the sleepers of their gold. Up, up!" The old man shook in every joint, and folded his hands like one who prays.

"Not to me," said the child, "not to me – to heaven, to save us from such deeds. This dream is too real. I cannot sleep, I cannot stay here, I cannot leave you alone under the roof where such dreams come. Up! We must fly."

"Tonight!" murmured the old man.

"Yes, tonight," replied the child. "Tomorrow night will be too late. The dream will have come again. Nothing but flight can save us. Up!"

The old man rose from his bed, his forehead bedewed with the cold sweat of fear and, bending before the child as if she had been an angel messenger sent to lead him where she would, made ready to follow her.

She took him by the hand as if she feared to lose him for an instant and then she led him forth. Up the steep hill they toiled with rapid steps, and not once looked behind.

## The Visitor

Besides becoming in a short time a perfect marvel in all stable matters, Kit soon made himself a very tolerable gardener, a handy fellow within doors, and an indispensable attendant on Mr Abel, who every day gave him some new proof of his confidence and approbation.

One morning Kit drove Mr Abel to the Notary's office as he sometimes did, and having set him down at the house, was about to drive off to a livery stable hard by, when Mr Chuckster emerged from the office-door, and cried, "Woa-a-a-a-a! You're wanted inside here."

Kit scraped his shoes very carefully, and tapped at the office-door, which was quickly opened by the Notary himself.

"Oh! come in, Christopher," said Mr Witherden.

"Is that the lad?" asked an elderly gentleman, but of a stout, bluff figure, who was in the room.

"That's the lad," said Mr Witherden. "He fell in with my client, Mr Garland, sir, at this very door. I have reason to think he is a good lad, sir, and that you may believe what he says. Let me introduce Mr Abel Garland, sir – his young master; my articled pupil, sir, and most particular friend."

"Your servant, sir," said the stranger.

"Yours, sir, I'm sure," replied Mr Abel mildly. "You were wishing to speak to Christopher, sir?"

"Yes, I was. Have I your permission?"

"By all means."

"My business is no secret; or I should rather say it need be no secret *here*," said the stranger, observing that Mr Abel and the Notary were preparing to retire. "It relates to a dealer in curiosities with whom he lived, and in whom I am earnestly and warmly interested. I have been making inquiries in the neighbourhood in which his old master lived, and I learnt that he had been served by this lad. I found out his mother's house, and was directed by her to this place as the nearest in which I should be likely to find him. That's the cause of my presenting myself here this morning."

He turned to Kit and said: "If you think, my lad, that I am

pursuing these inquiries with any other view than that of serving and reclaiming those I am in search of, you do me a very great wrong, and deceive yourself. Don't be deceived, I beg of you, but rely upon my assurance. The fact is, gentlemen," he added, turning again to the Notary and his pupil, "that I am in a very painful and wholly unexpected position. I came to this city with a darling object at my heart, expecting to find no obstacle or difficulty in the way of its attainment. I find myself suddenly checked and stopped short in the execution of my design by a mystery which I cannot penetrate. Every effort I have made to penetrate it has only served to render it darker and more obscure; and I am afraid to stir openly in the matter, lest those whom I anxiously pursue should fly still further from me. I assure you that if you could give me any assitance, you would not be sorry to do so, if you knew how greatly I stand in need of it, and what a load it would relieve me from."

Kit was then put under examination and closely questioned by the unknown gentleman about his old master and the child, their lonely way of life, their retired habits, and strict seclusion. The nightly absence of the old man, the solitary existence of the child at those times, his illness and recovery, Quilp's possession of the house, and their sudden disappearance, were all the subject of much questioning and answer. Finally, Kit informed the gentleman that the premises were now to let, and that a board upon the door referred all inquirers to Mr Sampson Brass, Solicitor, from whom he might perhaps learn some further particulars.

"Not by inquiry," said the gentleman, shaking his head. "I live there."

"Live at Brass's the attorney's!" cried Mr Witherden in some surprise, having professional knowledge of the gentleman in question.

"Aye," was the reply. "I entered upon his lodgings t' other day, chiefly because I had seen this very board. It matters little to me where I live, and I had a desperate hope that some intelligence might be cast in my way there, which would not reach me elsewhere. Yes, I live at Brass's – more shame for me, I suppose?"

"That's a mere matter of opinion," said the Notary, shrugging his shoulders. "He is looked upon as rather a doubtful character."

"Doubtful?" echoed the other. "I am glad to hear there's any doubt about it. I supposed that had been thoroughly settled, long ago. I'll not detain you any longer now," he said, putting a crown into Kit's hand, and looking towards the Notary. "You shall hear from me again. Not a word of this, you know, except to your master and mistress."

"Mother, sir, would be glad to know –" said Kit, faltering.

"Glad to know what?"

"Anything – so that it was no harm – about Miss Nell."

"Would she? Well then, you may tell her if she can keep a secret. But mind, not a word of this to anybody else. Don't forget that. Be particular."

"I'll take care, sir," said Kit. "Thankee, sir, and good morning."

## Quilp's Plans

In his secret heart, Daniel Quilp was both surprised and troubled by the flight which had been made. His uneasiness arose from a misgiving that the old man had some secret store of money which he had not suspected, and the idea of its escaping his clutches overwhelmed him with mortification and self-reproach.

Rumours had already got abroad that the little girl was the child of great people who had been stolen from her parents in infancy, and had only just been traced. Opinion

was divided whether she was the daughter of a prince, a duke, an earl, a viscount, or a baron, but all agreed upon the main fact, that the single gentleman who was asking questions all around was her father.

Mr Quilp soon made out that the single gentleman had been seen in communication with Kit, and had no difficulty in arriving at the conclusion that the intent and object of his correspondence with Kit was the recovery of his old client and the child.

"I am suspected and thrown aside, and Kit's the confidential agent, is he? I shall have to dispose of him, I fear. But for the lad and his mother, I could get this fiery gentleman comfortably into my net and chubby, rosy Nell. At the worst, it's a golden opportunity not to be lost. Let us find them first, and I'll find means of draining you of some of your superfluous cash, sir, while there are prison bars, and bolts, and locks, to keep your friend or kinsman safely. I hate virtuous people!" said the dwarf, throwing off a bumper of brandy, and smacking his lips, "ah! I hate 'em every one!"

This was not a mere empty boast, but a deliberate avowal of his real sentiments; for Mr Quilp, who loved nobody, had by little and little come to hate everybody nearly or remotely connected with his ruined client; the old man himself, because he had been able to deceive him and elude his vigilance – Kit most mortally, for the reasons already shown. Above and beyond that general feeling of opposition to them, which would have been inseparable from his ravenous desire to enrich himself by these altered circumstances, Daniel Quilp hated every one.

He travelled to the Wilderness, and ordered tea in the wooden summer-house that afternoon for three persons; an invitation to Miss Sally Brass and her brother to partake of that entertainment at that place having been the object of his journey.

It was not precisely the kind of weather in which people usually take tea in summer-houses, far less in summer-houses in an advanced state of decay, and overlooking the slimy banks of a great river at low water. Nevertheless, it was in this choice retreat that Mr Quilp ordered a cold collation to be prepared, and it was beneath its cracked and leaky roof that he in due course of time received Mr Sampson and his sister Sally.

"You're fond of the beauties of nature," said Quilp, with a grin. "Is this charming, Brass? Is it unusual, unsophisticated, primitive?"

"It's delightful indeed, sir," replied the lawyer.

"Cool?" said Quilp.

"N-not particularly so, I think, sir," rejoined Brass, with his teeth chattering in his head.

"Perhaps a little damp?" said Quilp.

"Just damp enough to be cheerful, sir," rejoined Brass. "Nothing more, sir, nothing more."

"And Sally?" said the delighted dwarf. "Does *she* like it?"

"She'll like it better," returned that strong-minded lady, "when she has tea; so let us have it."

"Sweet Sally!" cried Quilp, extending his arms as if about to embrace her. "A word," he said, "before we go further. Sally, hark'ee for a minute."

Miss Sally drew closer.

"Business," said the dwarf, glancing from brother to sister. "Very private business. Lay your heads together when you're by yourselves."

"Certainly, sir," returned Brass.

"There's a lad named Kit —"

Miss Sally nodded, implying that she knew of him.

"Kit!" said Mr Sampson. "Kit! Ha! I've heard the name before, but I don't exactly call to mind — I don't exactly —"

"You're as slow as a tortoise, and more thick-headed

than a rhinoceros," returned his obliging client with an impatient gesture.

"Don't let's have any wrangling," said Miss Sally, staying his hand. "I've showed you that I know him, and that's enough."

"She's always foremost!" said the dwarf, patting her on the back and looking contemptuously at Sampson. "I don't like Kit, Sally."

"Nor I," rejoined Miss Brass.

"Nor I," said Sampson.

"Why, that's right!" cried Quilp. "Half our work is done already. This Kit is one of your honest people, one of your fair characters; a prowling prying hound; a hypocrite; a double-faced, white-livered, sneaking spy; a crouching cur to those that feed and coax him, and a barking yelping dog to all besides."

"Fearfully eloquent!" cried Brass, with a sneeze. "Quite appalling!"

"Come to the point," said Miss Sally, "and don't talk so much."

"Right again!" exclaimed Quilp, with another contemptuous look at Sampson. "Always foremost! I say, Sally, he is a yelping, insolent dog to all besides, and most of all, to me. In short, I owe him a grudge."

"That's enough, sir," said Sampson.

"No, it's not enough, sir," sneered Quilp; "will you hear me out? Besides that I owe him a grudge on that account, he thwarts me at this minute, and stands between me and an end which might otherwise prove a golden one to us all. Apart from that, I repeat that he crosses my humour, and I hate him. Now, you know the lad, and can guess the rest. Devise your own means of putting him out of my way, and execute them. Shall it be done?"

"It shall, sir," said Sampson.

"Then give me your hand," retorted Quilp. "Sally, girl,

yours. I rely as much or more, on you than him."

## The Trick

"Mr Richard, sir, good morning. Here we are again, sir,
entering upon another day, with our bodies strengthened
by slumber and breakfast, and our spirits fresh and
flowing."

While he addressed his clerk in these words, Mr Brass
was somewhat ostentatiously engaged in minutely
examining and holding up against the light a five-pound
bank note, which he had brought in, in his hand.

He laid the bank-note upon the desk among some
papers, in an absent manner, and thrust his hands into his
pockets. Richard Swiveller pointed to it, and warned him
to take it up.

"No, Mr Richard, sir," rejoined Brass with emotion. "I
will not take it up. I will let it lie there, sir. To take it up, Mr
Richard, sir, would imply a doubt of you; and in you, sir, I
have unlimited confidence. We will let it lie there, sir, if you
please, and we will not take it up by any means." With that,
Mr Brass patted him twice or thrice upon the shoulder, in a
most friendly manner, and entreated him to believe that he
had as much faith in his honesty as he had in his own.

Just then some person knocked at the office-door; and
Kit looked in. "Is the gentleman upstairs, sir, if you please?"

"Yes, Kit," said Brass. "I am glad to see you, Kit, I am
rejoiced to see you. Look in again, as you come
downstairs, Kit."

When Kit, having discharged his errand, came
downstairs from the single gentleman's apartment after the
lapse of a quarter of an hour or so, Mr Sampson Brass was
alone in the office. He was not singing as usual, nor was he
seated at his desk. The open door showed him standing
before the fire with his back towards it, and looking so very

strange that Kit supposed he must have been suddenly taken ill.

"Is anything the matter, sir?" said Kit.

"Matter!" cried Brass. "No!"

"You are so very pale," said Kit, "that I should hardly have known you."

"Pooh, pooh! mere fancy," cried Brass.

"I have been thinking, Kit," said the lawyer, "that I could throw some employment your mother's way – you have a mother, I think? If I recollect right, you told me –"

"Oh yes, sir, yes, certainly."

"A widow, I think? An industrious widow?"

"A harder-working woman or a better mother never lived, sir."

"Ah!" cried Brass. "That's affecting, truly affecting. Put down your hat, Kit."

"Thank you, sir, I must be going directly."

"Put it down while you stay, at any rate," said Brass, taking it from him and making some confusion among the papers in finding a place for it on the desk. "I was thinking, Kit, that we have often houses to let for people we are concerned for, and matters of that sort. Now you know we're obliged to put people into those houses to take care of 'em – very often undeserving people that we can't depend upon. What's to prevent our having a person that we can depend upon, and enjoying the delight of doing a good action at the same time? I say, what's to prevent our employing this worthy woman, your mother? What with one job and another, there's lodging – and good lodging too – pretty well all the year round, rent free, and a weekly allowance beside, Kit. Now what do you think of that? Do you see any objection? My only desire is to serve you, Kit; therefore if you do, say so freely."

As Brass spoke, he moved the hat twice or thrice, and shuffled among the papers again, as if in search of

something.

"How can I see any objection to such a kind offer, sir?" replied Kit with his whole heart. "I don't know how to thank you, sir, I don't indeed."

"Why then," said Brass, suddenly turning upon him and thrusting his face close to Kit's with such a repulsive smile that the latter, even in the very height of his gratitude, drew back startled. "Why then, *it's done.*"

Kit looked at him in some confusion.

"Done, I say," added Sampson, rubbing his hands and veiling himself again in his usual oily manner. "Ha, ha! and so you shall find, Kit, so you shall find. But dear me, what a time Mr Richard is gone! A sad loiterer to be sure! Will you mind the office one minute while I run upstairs? Only one minute. I'll not detain you an instant longer, on any account, Kit."

Talking as he went, Mr Brass bustled out of the office, and in a very short time returned. Mr Swiveller came back almost at the same instant; and Kit left the room hastily to make up for lost time.

"He has minded the office," said Brass. "He has had my confidence, and he shall continue to have it; he – why, where's the –"

"What have you lost?" inquired Mr Swiveller.

"Dear me!" said Brass, slapping all his pockets one after another, and looking into his desk, and under it, and upon it, and wildly tossing the papers about. "The note, Mr Richard, sir, the five-pound note – what can have become of it? I laid it down here – God bless me!"

Mr Swiveller and Sampson Brass caught up their hats and rushed out into the street – daring along in the middle of the road, and dashing aside all obstructions as though they were running for their lives.

It happened that Kit had been running too, though not so fast, and having the start of them by some few minutes, was a good distance ahead. As they were pretty certain of the road he must have taken, however, and kept on at a great pace, they came up with him, at the very moment when he had taken breath, and was breaking into a run again.

"Stop!" cried Sampson, laying his hand on one shoulder, while Mr Swiveller pounced upon the other. "Not so fast, sir. You're in a hurry?"

"Yes, I am," said Kit, looking from one to the other in great surprise.

"I – I – can hardly believe it," panted Sampson, "but something of value is missing from the office. I hope you don't know what."

"Know what! good Heaven, Mr Brass!" cried Kit, trembling from head to foot; "you don't suppose –"

"No, no," rejoined Brass quickly, "I don't suppose anything. Don't say *I* said you did."

"Search me," said Kit, proudly, holding up his arms. "But mind, sir – I know you'll be sorry for this, to the last day of your life."

"It is certainly a very painful occurrence," said Brass with a sigh, as he dived into one of Kit's pockets, and fished up a miscellaneous collection of small articles; "very painful. Nothing here, Mr Richard, sir, all perfectly satisfactory. Nor here, sir. Nor in the waistcoat, Mr Richard, nor in the coat tails. So far, I am rejoiced, I am sure."

Richard Swiveller, holding Kit's hat in his hand, was watching the proceedings with great interest, and bore upon his face the slightest possible indication of a smile, as Brass, shutting one of his eyes, looked with the other up the inside of one of the poor fellow's sleeves as if it were a telescope, and bade him search the hat.

An exclamation, at once from Richard Swiveller and Kit himself, cut the lawyer short. He turned his head, and saw Dick standing with the bank-note in his hand.

271

"In the hat?" cried Brass, in a sort of shriek.

"Under the handkerchief, and tucked beneath the lining," said Dick, aghast at the discovery.

Mr Brass looked at Kit, who stood quite stupefied and motionless.

"And this," cried Sampson, clasping his hands, "this is the villain that I was going to benefit with all my little arts. A constable, sir, if you please!"

On arrival, the constable, holding Kit and pushing him on a little before him, so as to keep him at about three-quarters of an arm's length in advance, thrust him into a vehicle and followed himself. Sampson Brass got upon the box, and made the coachman drive on.

Still completely stunned by the sudden and terrible change which had taken place in his affairs, Kit sat gazing out of the coach window, almost hoping to see some monstrous phenomenon in the streets which might give him reason to believe he was in a dream.

Dream-like as the story was, it was true. He stood charged with robbery; the note had been found upon him, though he was innocent in thought and deed; and they were carrying him back, a prisoner.

All at once, as though it had been conjured up by magic, he became aware of the face of Quilp.

And what a leer there was upon the face! It was from the open window of a tavern that it looked out; and the dwarf had so spread himself over it, with his elbows on the window-sill and his head resting on both his hands, that what between this attitude and his being swollen with suppressed laughter, he looked puffed and bloated into twice his usual breadth. Mr Brass on recognising him immediately stopped the coach. As it came to a halt directly opposite to where he stood, the dwarf pulled off his hat, and saluted the party with a hideous and grotesque politeness.

272

"Aha!" he cried. "Where now, Brass? Where now? Dick? Pleasant Dick! And Kit? Honest Kit!"

"He's extremely cheerful!" said Brass to the coachman. "Very much so! Ah, sir – a sad business! Never believe in honesty any more, sir."

"Why not?" returned the dwarf. "Why not, you rogue of a lawyer, why not?"

"Bank-note lost in our office, sir," said Brass, shaking his head. "Found in his hat, sir – he previously left alone there – no mistake at all, sir – chain of evidence complete – not a link wanting."

"What!" cried the dwarf, leaning half his body out of window. "Kit a thief! Kit a thief! Ha, ha, ha! Why, he's an uglier-looking thief than can be seen anywhere for a penny. Eh, Kit – eh? Ha, ha, ha! Have you taken Kit into custody before he had time and opportunity to beat me! Eh, Kit, eh?"

With such good wishes and farewells, poured out in a rapid torrent until they were out of hearing, Quilp suffered them to depart; and when he could see the coach no longer, drew in his head, and rolled upon the ground in an ecstacy of enjoyment.

## An Old Friend

Day followed day and always morning came.

The child had not only to endure the accumulated hardships of their destitute condition, but to bear the reproaches of her grandfather, who began to murmur at having been led away from their late abode and demand that they be returned to it. Now penniless, Nell felt a hopelessness of their ever being extricated together from their miserable wanderings, a dull conviction that she was very ill, perhaps dying; but no fear or anxiety.

A loathing of food, that she was not conscious of until

they expended their last penny in the purchase of another loaf, prevented her partaking even of this poor meal. Her grandfather ate greedily, which she was glad to see.

Their way lay through the same scenes as yesterday, with no variety or improvement. There was the same thick air, difficult to breathe; the same blighted ground, the same hopeless prospect, the same misery and distress. Objects appeared more dim, the noise less, the path more rugged and uneven, for sometimes she stumbled, and became roused, as it were, in the effort to prevent herself from falling. Poor child! the cause was in her tottering feet.

Towards the afternoon, her grandfather complained bitterly of hunger.

With less and less of hope or strength, as they went on, but with an undiminished resolution not to betray by any word or sign her sinking state, so long as she had energy to move, the child throughout the remainder of that hard day compelled herself to proceed; not even stopping to rest as frequently as usual, to compensate in some measure for the tardy pace at which she was obliged to walk. Evening was drawing on, but had not closed in, when – still travelling among the same dismal objects – they came to a busy town.

Faint and spiritless as they were, its streets were insupportable. After humbly asking for relief at some few doors and being refused, they agreed to make their way out of it as speedily as they could, and see if the inmates of any lone house beyond would have more pity on their exhausted state.

They were dragging themselves along through the last street, and the child felt that the time was close at hand when her enfeebled powers would bear no more. There appeared before them, at this juncture, going in the same direction as themselves, a traveller on foot, who, with a case strapped to his back, leant upon a stout stick as he

walked, and read from a book which he held in his other hand.

It was not an easy matter to come up with him, and beseech his aid, for he walked fast, and was a little distance in advance. At length he stopped to look more attentively at some passage in his book. Animated with a ray of hope, the child shot on before her grandfather, and, going close to the stranger without rousing him by the sound of her footsteps, began in a few faint words to implore his help.

He turned his head, the child clapped her hands together, uttered a wild shriek, and fell senseless at his feet.

It was the schoolmaster. No other than the schoolmaster.

He threw down his stick and book, and dropping on one knee beside her, endeavoured by such simple means as occurred to him, to restore her to herself; while her grandfather, standing idly by, wrung his hands, and implored her with many endearing expressions to speak to him.

"She is quite exhausted," said the schoolmaster, glancing upward into his face. "You have taxed her powers too far, friend."

"She is perishing of want," rejoined the old man. "I never thought how weak and ill she was, till now."

Casting a look upon him, half-reproachful and half-compassionate, the schoolmaster took the child in his arms, and bidding the old man gather up her little basket and follow him directly, bore her away at his utmost speed.

There was a small inn within sight, to which it would seem he had been directing his steps when so unexpectedly overtaken. Towards this place he hurried with his unconscious burden, and rushing into the kitchen, and calling upon the company there assembled to make way for God's sake, deposited it on a chair before the fire.

# A Watery Grave

Mr Quilp remained shut up in his hermitage, undisturbed by any suspicion, and extremely well satisfied with the result of his scheming. Being engaged in the adjustment of some accounts, he had not strayed from his den for two whole days. The third day of his devotion to this pursuit found him still hard at work, and little disposed to stir abroad.

The day, in the highest and brightest quarters of the town, was damp, dark, cold, and gloomy. In that low and marshy spot, the fog filled every nook and corner with a thick dense cloud. Every object was obscured at one or two yards' distance.

"So! That little job being disposed of," said the dwarf, coolly, "I'll read my letter. Humph!" he muttered, looking at the direction. "I ought to know this writing. Beautiful Sally!"

Opening it, he read, in a fair, round, legal hand, as follows: "Sammy has been practised upon, and has broken confidence. It has all come out. You had better not be in the way, for strangers are going to call upon you. They have been very quiet as yet, because they mean to surprise you. Don't lose time. I didn't. I am not to be found anywhere. If I was you, I wouldn't be, either. S. B."

To describe the changes that passed over Quilp's face as he read this letter half-a-dozen times would require some new language. For a long time he did not utter one word; but after a considerable interval, he contrived to gasp out, "If I had him here. If I only had him here – I should drown him! Too easy a death, too short, too quick – but the river runs close at hand. Oh! If I had him here! Just to take him to the brink, coaxingly and pleasantly – holding him by the button-hole – joking with him – and with a sudden push, to send him splashing down! Drowning men come to the surface three time, they say. Ah! To see him those three times, and mock him as his face came bobbing up – oh, what a rich treat that would be!

"And this, like every other trouble and anxiety I have had of late times, springs from that old imbecile and his darling child – two wretched feeble wanderers. I'll be their evil genius yet. And you, sweet Kit, honest Kit, virtuous, innocent Kit, look to yourself. Where I hate, I bite. I hate you, my darling fellow, with good cause, and proud as you are tonight, I'll have my turn. What's that!"

A knocking at the gate. A loud and violent knocking. Then a pause; as if those who knocked had stopped to listen. Then the noise again, more clamorous and importunate than before.

"So soon!" said the dwarf. "And so eager! I am afraid I shall disappoint you. It's well I'm quite prepared. Sally, I thank you!"

The noise at the gate still continuing, he felt his way to the door, and stepped into the open air.

It was about eight o'clock; but the dead of the darkest night would have been as noon-day, in comparison with the thick cloud which then rested upon the earth, and shrouded everything from view. He darted forward for a few paces, as if into the mouth of some dim yawning cavern; then, thinking he had gone wrong, changed the direction of his steps; then stood still, not knowing where to turn.

"If I could find a wall or fence," said the dwarf, stretching out his arms, and walking slowly on, "I should know which way to turn. A good, black, devil's night this, to have my dear friend here. If I had but that wish, it might, for anything I cared, never be day again."

As the word passed his lips, he staggered and fell; and

next moment was fighting with the cold, dark water.

It was of no avail. The strong tide filled his throat, and bore him on, upon its rapid current. Another mortal struggle, and he was up again, beating the water with his hands. One loud cry now – but the resistless water bore him down before he could give it utterance, and, driving him under it, carried away a corpse.

## Good News for Kit

By degrees they let Kit know that doubts have arisen, that inquiries are to be made, and perhaps he may be pardoned after all. At last, the evening being come, they bring him to a room where some gentlemen are assembled. Foremost among them is his good old master, who comes and takes him by the hand. He hears that his innocence is established, and that he is pardoned. He cannot see the speaker, but he turns towards the voice, and in trying to answer, falls down insensible.

Mr Garland, taking him into a room where they could be alone, told him that he had something yet to say, which would surprise him greatly. Kit looked so anxious and turned so pale on hearing this, that the old gentleman hastened to add that he would be agreeably surprised; and asked him if he would be ready next morning for a journey.

"For a journey, sir!" cried Kit.

"In company with me and my friend in the next room. Can you guess its purpose?"

Kit turned paler yet, and shook his head.

"Oh yes. I think you do already," said his master. "Try."

Kit murmured something rather rambling and unintelligible, but he plainly pronounced the words, "Miss Nell," three or four times – shaking his head while he did so, as if he would add there was no hope of that.

"The place of their retreat is indeed discovered," he said.

"And that is our journey's end."

Kit faltered out such questions as where was it, and how had it been found, and how long since, and was she well, and happy?

"I trust she will be soon. She has been weak and ailing. In the meantime," said the old gentleman, rising and laying his hand on Kit's shoulder, "you have great need of rest, for such a day as this would wear out the strongest man. Good night, and may our journey have a prosperous ending!"

Kit was no sluggard next morning, but springing from his bed some time before day, began to prepare for his welcome expedition.

Nor was he alone excited and eager. Before he had been up a quarter of an hour the whole house were astir and busy.

Now the single gentleman and Mr Garland were in the carriage, and the postboy was in the saddle, and Kit, well wrapped and muffled up, was in the rumble behind.

It was a bitter day. A keen wind was blowing, and rushed against them fiercely; bleaching the hard ground, shaking the white frost from the trees and hedges, and whirling it away like dust. But little cared Kit for weather.

The two gentlemen inside, who were little disposed to sleep, beguiled the time with conversation.

The single gentleman turned to his companion and said, "Are you a good listener?"

"Like most other men, I suppose," returned Mr Garland, smiling. "Why do you ask?"

"I have a short narrative on my lips," rejoined his friend, "and will try you with it. It is very brief."

Pausing for no reply, he proceeded thus: "There were once two brothers, who loved each other dearly. There was a disparity in their ages – some twelve years. Wide as the interval between them was, however, they became rivals too soon. The deepest and strongest affection of

280

both their hearts settled upon one woman.

"The youngest was the first to find this out. I will not tell you what misery he underwent, what agony of soul he knew, how great his mental struggle was, but when the time of trial came, he left his brother to be happy. The truth never passed his lips, and he quitted the country.

"The elder brother married her. She was in Heaven before long, and left him with an infant daughter.

"In this daughter, the mother lived again. She grew to

womanhood, and gave her heart to one who could not know its worth.

"Through all the misery which followed this union; through all the cold neglect and through all the poverty he brought upon her, she never bewailed her fate. Patient to the last, she died a widow of some three weeks' date, leaving to her father's care two orphans; one a son of ten or twelve years old; the other a girl – an infant child.

"The elder brother, grandfather to these two children, was now a broken man; crushed and borne down by the heavy hand of sorrow. With the wreck of his possessions, he began to trade – in pictures first, and then in curious ancient things.

"The boy soon spurned the shelter of his roof, and sought associates more congenial to his taste. The old man and the girl dwelt alone together.

"The younger brother had made his pilgrimage through life alone. His voluntary banishment had been misconstrued, and communication between him and the elder often failed.

"Then, dreams of their young, happy life visited his pillow yet oftener than before. He settled his affairs and, with honourable wealth enough for both, arrived one evening at his brother's door!"

The narrator, whose voice had faltered lately, stopped. "The rest," said Mr Garland, pressing his hand, "I know."

## Sad Reunion

"This is the place, gentlemen," said the driver, dismounting from his horse, and knocking at the door of a little inn. "Hallo! Past twelve o'clock is the dead of night here."

The dull, red glow of a wood fire showed them a figure, seated on the hearth with its back towards them, bending over the fitful light.

The form was that of an old man, his white head akin in colour to the mouldering embers upon which he gazed. And the failing light and dying fire, the time-worn room, the solitude, and wasted life, and gloom, were all in fellowship. Ashes, and dust, and ruin!

Kit tried to speak, and did pronounce some words, though what they were he scarcely knew. Still the same terrible low cry went on – still the same rocking in the chair – the same stricken figure was there, unchanged and heedless of his presence.

He had his hand upon the latch, when something in the form – distinctly seen as one log broke and fell, and, as it fell, blazed up – arrested it. He returned to where he had stood before – advanced a pace – another – another still. Another, and he saw the face. Yes! Changed as it was, he knew it well.

"Master!" he cried, stooping on one knee and catching at his hand. "Dear master. Speak to me!"

The old man turned slowly towards him; and muttered, in a hollow voice, "This is another! How many of these spirits there have been tonight!"

"No spirit, master. No one but your old servant. You know me now, I am sure? Miss Nell – where is she – where is she?"

"They all say that!" cried the old man. "They all ask the same question. A spirit!"

"Where is she?" demanded Kit. "Oh tell me but that – but that, dear master."

"She is asleep – yonder – in there."

They watched him as he rose and stole on tiptoe to the other chamber where the lamp had been replaced. They listened as he spoke again within its silent walls.

He came back, whispering that she was still asleep, but that he thought she had moved. It was her hand, he said – a little – a very, very little – but he was pretty sure she had moved it – perhaps in seeking his. He had known her do that before now, though in the deepest sleep the while. And when he had said this, he dropped into his chair again, and clasping his hands above his head, uttered a cry never to be forgotten.

For she was dead. There, upon her little bed, she lay at rest. The solemn stillness was no marvel now.

She was dead. No sleep so beautiful and calm, so free from trace of pain, so fair to look upon. She seemed a creature fresh from the hand of God, and waiting for the breath of life; not one who had lived and suffered death.

Her couch was dressed with here and there some winter berries and green leaves, gathered in a spot she had been used to favour. "When I die, put near me something that has loved the light, and had the sky above it always." Those were her words.

She was dead. Dear, gentle, patient, noble Nell, was dead.

Where were the traces of her early cares, her sufferings, and fatigues? All gone. Sorrow was dead indeed in her, but peace and perfect happiness were born; imaged in her tranquil beauty and profound repose.

When morning came, they heard how her life had closed.

She had been dead two days. She died soon after daybreak.

She would like to see poor Kit, she had often said of late. She wished there was somebody to take her love to Kit.

For the rest, she had never murmured or complained; but, with a quiet mind, and manner quite unaltered – faded like the light upon a summer's evening.

Along the path they bore her, and the old church received her in its quiet shade.

They carried her to one old nook, and laid their burden softly on the pavement. The light streamed on it through the coloured window – a window, where the boughs of trees were ever rustling in the summer, and where the birds sang sweetly all day long. With every breath of air that stirred among those branches in the sunshine, some trembling, changing light would fall upon her grave.

Earth to earth, ashes to ashes, dust to dust. Many a young hand dropped in its little wreath, many a stifled sob was heard. Some – and they were not a few – knelt down. All were sincere and truthful in their sorrow.

For many days, the old man pined and moped away the time, and had no comfort. Whatever power of thought or memory he retained, was all bound up in her. He never understood, or seemed to care to understand, about his brother.

Dead! He could not hear or bear the word. The slightest hint of it would throw him into a paroxysm, like that he had had when it was first spoken. In what hope he lived, no man could tell; but that he had some hope of finding her again – some faint and shadowy hope, deferred from day to day, and making him from day to day more sick and sore at heart – was plain to all.

And thenceforth, every day, and all day long, he waited at her grave for her. When it grew quite dark, he rose and returned home, and went to bed, murmuring to himself, "She will come tomorrow!"

He would sit at night, pondering with a secret satisfaction, upon the flight that he and she would take before night came again; and would whisper in his prayers, "Oh! Let her come tomorrow!"

The last time was on a genial day in spring. He did not return at the usual hour. He was found lying dead upon the stone

They laid him by the side of her whom he had loved so well; and, in the church, the child and the old man slept together.